THE GREAT

ANIMAL

ESCAPADE

Jane Kerr

Chicken House

KT-376-370

2 PALMER STREET, FROME, SOMERSET BA11 1DS
WWW.CHICKENHOUSEBOOKS.COM

Text © Jane Kerr 2019

First published in Great Britain in 2019
Chicken House
2 Palmer Street
Frome, Somerset BA11 1DS
United Kingdom
www.chickenhousebooks.com
Jane Kerr has asserted her right under the Copyright, Designs and
Patents Act 1988 to be identified as the author of this work.

Cover design and interior design by Steve Wells
Illustration © Alexis Snell
Typeset by Dorchester Typesetting Group Ltd
Printed and bound in Great Britain by CPI Group (UK) Ltd, Croydon, CR0 4YY

The paper used in this Chicken House book is made
from wood grown in sustainable forests.

1 3 5 7 9 10 8 6 4 2

British Library Cataloguing in Publication data available.

ISBN 978-1-911490-34-0
eISBN 978-1-911490-96-8

To Mum and Mark,
and to Dad and Brenda,
with love.

Also by Jane Kerr

The Elephant Thief

Chapter One

'Ladies and gentlemen! Boys and girls! Welcome to Belle Vue . . . the most magical, marvellous and mesmerizing zoological gardens on this great earth!'

The bellow rolled across the heads of the waiting crowd with the force of summer thunder – and Danny grinned. He couldn't help it. Even though he'd heard the speech too often to count, he never tired of it.

'Come and flock to our flamingos. Peer at our penguins. Gape at the gazelles. Marvel at the monkeys. Coo at the camels. And admire the finest specimens of lion and lioness in the entire country.'

Danny waited for the pause – the hitch of breath that meant Mr Cogwell was preparing for the final roar. 'But please, we beg of you, leave time for our star attraction:

Her Majesty's personal favourite. An elephant without equal . . . the biggest, brightest, most bewitching beast at Belle Vue . . . Maharajah the Magnificent!'

Loud applause followed the gatekeeper's grand announcement. It was Danny's cue to move. He took a breath, whistled sharply and raised an arm. Beneath him, Maharajah swayed heavily then stomped forward. The crowd turned towards the noise – and everyone's mouths dropped open.

Danny was wrapped in a cape of purple silk; on his feet were a pair of embroidered slippers; and coiled around his head sat a bright green turban topped with peacock's feathers. But far more incredible than that – Danny was sitting on an elephant.

Maharajah the Magnificent. Larger than a mountain. Wider, higher and just as indestructible. With ears like tablecloths, and tusks as tough and hard as bone.

'Will you look at that!'

'Biggest animal I've ever seen!'

'Aye. I reckon there's countries smaller.'

Gently, Danny eased Maharajah to a stop in front of the visitors, then leant forward to stroke a hand across the solid dome of Maharajah's skull. A happy rumble vibrated through his palm and Danny's nerves eased.

He looked down. A cluster of faces stared back at him. Despite the early hour, Belle Vue Zoological Gardens had already attracted a crowd and, from this height, Danny could see even more people lining up at the ticket office. It was going to be another busy day.

Hastily, he whistled again and Maharajah dropped to his knees. Danny slid down but as soon as his feet touched the ground, he felt a tug on his cape. A small girl, eyes as wide as copper pennies, had pushed through the spectators.

'Can I touch him, mister? Please? Can I?'

Smiling, Danny nodded. And the girl lifted up on to her toes, tracing her fingers over Maharajah's rough, wrinkled skin; across the deep ridges that criss-crossed his trunk and then through the tufts of hair on his forehead and chin. Soon, other children were pressing forward to do the same. But if the attention bothered Maharajah, Danny could see no sign. He simply knelt patiently, and eventually it was Danny who made the signal to Mr Cogwell.

The gatekeeper nodded back. 'That's enough, ladies and gentlemen! Boys and girls! Maharajah needs his rest but if you make your way to the elephant enclosure later today, you'll see him again.' He waved a fan of folded paper above his head. 'Now, can I recommend one of our illustrated maps? Yours for only a halfpenny – the 1872 guide to all the great wonders of the park . . . the cobras, the camels, the cockatoos. And of course, our new Nile crocodile, Cleopatra . . .'

Mr Cogwell's voice faded into the distance as Danny led Maharajah down the tree-lined avenue that cut across Belle Vue. Past the lions and tigers pacing in their cages; past the monkeys chattering in the ape house; and past the brick-walled pit, where the great Siberian bear reared up on his huge hind legs to glare at them.

At the end of the avenue, a stone archway led into the Italian gardens. Danny ducked inside, guiding Maharajah into the shade of a giant palm. Immediately the elephant lifted his trunk to pull down a branch and chew through the leaves.

Dropping the harness, Danny glanced around. Good. The gardens were empty. Hurriedly, he untied the purple cloak then tugged off the feathered turban. The slippers would have to stay, but he stuffed the rest of the clothes into a bag slung across Maharajah's back. It felt ridiculously good to get rid of the costume.

'Oi, you! Boy!'

Danny turned and all his good humour vanished. Tom Dalton was striding down the path towards him, shoulders wide, every step a swagger. Tom was the grandson of one of Mr Jameson's most trusted workers. He was also the only person who'd never welcomed Danny to Belle Vue.

'I've a message from Mr Jameson. He needs to speak to you. Says it's important.'

'Where . . .' Danny's chest tightened and he had to stop to take a breath. For most of his life, he'd been mute – unable to talk – and even though his voice had returned, speech still didn't come easily. 'Where . . . where is he? Mr Jameson. Where is he now?'

Danny hated that his words stumbled into each other, and he hated it even more when Tom's lips curled into a sneer. They might be a similar age, but they had little in common. While Danny was slight and scrawny, a brown-skinned boy still growing into his bones, Tom [...] broad with a shock of fair hair and all the co[...] height and muscle.

'Calm down! No need to get so excited.' Tom's sneer deepened. 'He's over by the lake. On the shore opposite Firework Island. But you'd better get a move on. He said you're to be quick.'

Danny heard Mr Jameson before he saw him. His voice boomed out from among a group of finely dressed gentlemen. They stood, poised like penguins, on a platform jutting into the boating lake.

'. . . and let me say again, my dear sirs, you won't regret puttin' your money into Belle Vue. This is goin' to be the biggest show you've ever seen. "Prince Dandip and the Fight for Flamenca." A rip-roarin' re-enactment of one of the greatest battles of our time. Told in twenty minutes, and all for only two shillin's.' A pause. 'Or a half-crown, after four o'clock.'

As Danny walked nearer, the group parted. A stout, solid man in a bright red waistcoat stood in the centre, gesturing furiously. James Fredrick Henry Jameson, owner of the Belle Vue Zoological Gardens – and, as usual, he was weaving a plan.

'Now, take a look over there.' Mr Jameson stabbed a finger across the lake, and the men swivelled to follow his direction. 'You see that island? We're stagin' the whole show right there. It'll be set in Spain. Near a village. The

...itish army against the French. The fireworks will blast away as the battle begins. Rockets. Firecrackers. Sparklers. All fallin' like raindrops across Belle Vue.' He waggled his stubby fingers in the air.

'Everythin' will look hopeless but then Prince Dandip and Maharajah will appear on the top of the hill. The hero of the hour – and his elephant – ridin' down to stop the fightin'. Just exactly as it happened in the village of Flamenca.'

Standing at the edge of the jetty, Danny only just managed to stop a snort. Not one word of the story was true. Flamenca didn't exist – and neither did Prince Dandip. Every part of the battle was a figment of Mr Jameson's imagination. Over the last few weeks, he'd mapped it all out, scene by scene, on the huge, battered desk in his study.

'And of course, there'll be explosions. And in between, an orchestra playin' music. And right at the very end, Her Majesty's face will appear, lit up against the horizon. Big as a house. My man, George Dalton, has it all worked out, and there's nothin' he doesn't know about fireworks.'

Danny stepped on to the platform, letting his boots thud loudly on the wooden boards. Immediately Mr Jameson turned towards the noise.

'There you are, lad. At last! I've some people I want you to meet.' He motioned Danny closer. 'These are the gentlemen from Thirsby and Snade. The bank that's puttin' money into Belle Vue.' Clapping a hand around one shoulder, Mr Jameson pulled Danny to face the group. 'And this is the boy I've been telling you about. Danny . . . Prince Dandip of Delhi, himself.'

The silence that followed was deeper than a winter forest. The gentlemen looked at Danny, and Danny looked at the gentlemen. And then the man at the front of the group broke the silence. '*This* is the boy?'

Mr Jameson nodded. 'Yes.'

'*He's* the star of the show? The boy on all the posters? The prince?'

'Yes, Mr Snade. This is him.'

The banker's mouth thinned. 'Well, I can't say I'm not disappointed, Jameson. I'd imagined he'd be bigger. More regal. Less . . . less . . .' His eyebrows rose, almost to the line of dark curls across his forehead. 'Less foreign-looking.'

Mr Jameson's grip tightened, and Danny knew it was both an instinctive reaction and a warning. So, he stayed silent – even though his chest churned angrily.

'I don't know why you'd think that. Danny's done this before. He rode Maharajah more than two hundred miles – from Edinburgh to Manchester – dressed as an Indian prince. You might remember it. The story was in all the newspapers. People loved him. The *Queen* loved him!'

'Yes, that may well be true.' Mr Snade's lips curled. 'But I'm only concerned about the here and now. You've borrowed a great deal of money to fund this show of yours and there's no room for mistakes! Because let me make it clear, I expect to at least double the bank's investment.'

'You will, sir. Don't you worry about that.'

'Let's hope so.' With a scowl, Mr Snade snapped his attention away from Danny. 'But I suppose the main draw will be the elephant. I'm assuming we are able to see him, Jameson? The bank must check on *every* detail.'

Slowly, Mr Jameson released his grasp on Danny's shoulder then jerked his chin. 'Go on, lad. You'd better fetch Maharajah.'

As Danny walked back along the jetty, he could still feel the anger churning in his chest, and he hoped that for once, Maharajah had ignored his instructions to stay nearby. Mr Snade and the other bankers wouldn't wait for long, and if Danny took his time, they'd be gone soon enough.

But when he searched along the shore, Maharajah was exactly where he should have been – under the shadows of the stone archway. And Danny knew there would be no sneaking away unnoticed.

Slowly, he reached for the long, wooden cane tucked into his belt. His ankus – with this he could command elephants. It had taken practice and patience, but eventually he'd mastered the complicated combination of movements and whistles. And, so far, Maharajah had never failed to understand.

Raising the cane, Danny blew out a sharp signal, and Maharajah's head lifted, ears flapping. He lumbered out from his hiding place and down towards the lake. On the jetty, Danny heard shouted exclamations from the bankers.

'Good Lord!'

'What a creature!'

'Extraordinary!'

Grinning, Mr Jameson marched along the platform towards Danny. 'You haven't seen the best of him yet, gentlemen,' he shouted. 'Go on, lad. You show 'em!'

Danny paused for a heartbeat before lifting the ankus into the air once again. Obediently, Maharajah strode into the water, dipping beneath the surface until his silver skin turned dark. Ripples billowed across the lake. Standing suddenly, Maharajah raised his trunk and a stream of water arched upwards then cascaded down into a graceful fountain. There were more gasps from the bankers.

Only Mr Snade looked unimpressed. Pulling back his jacket, he pushed his thumbs into the pockets of his waistcoat. 'Yes, not bad, I suppose. Although, it's hardly earth-shattering entertainment. Surely the animal is capable of something a little more dramatic? I was led to believe elephants are intelligent creatures . . .' He sniffed. 'But apparently not.'

Danny tightened his grip on the ankus. A knot had formed in the back of his throat, closing up his chest. He could ignore insults directed at him, but no one was allowed to insult Maharajah. *No one.*

With a quick flick of his wrist, Danny twisted the cane in the air. Gold eyes met his, and there was only the slightest hesitation before Maharajah skimmed his trunk across the surface of the lake.

The water lifted in a giant wave, rising up above the jetty

and over the heads of the bankers. A moment later, the wave came plunging down, soaking everyone beneath. Water dripped off faces. And suits. And hats. Trickling over shoes, and in between collars and shirt cuffs.

'What on earth . . . ?'

'Good grief!'

But Maharajah hadn't finished. With a sharp blast he lifted his trunk again and emptied the remaining water over the platform. It was Mr Snade who took most of the impact. His hat tumbled off. Unfortunately, so did all of his hair. The luxuriant cap of dark curls was a wig. And without it, Mr Snade's head was pink, shiny and completely bald.

'What the devil, Jameson . . . ? This is outrageous!'

Spluttering, Mr Snade snatched his hairpiece from the ground and shoved it back on to his head. A trickle of dirty water ran down one cheek. Along the lakeside, laughter and jeers came from a handful of visitors who'd gathered to watch.

'Sir! Mr Snade, sir!' Mr Jameson scurried forward. 'I do apologize. I can't imagine what happened. Maharajah is usually as good as gold. Obedient as a child. Butter wouldn't melt. The best-trained animal in the park.'

'Then I suggest he needs *more* training. And *more* discipline.' Mr Snade's eyes spat fire. 'And so does that boy of yours! You fix it, Jameson! You fix it now!'

'I'll certainly do my best, sir, I can promise you that. Now come along and let's get you dried off. Perhaps a little drop of whisky might take the edge off . . . ?'

Hurriedly, Mr Jameson ushered Mr Snade and the other bankers off the jetty but before following, he turned to Danny. Disappointment darkened his face. 'What on earth were you thinkin'? You know what's at stake. There's a fortune ridin' on this show . . . and these men have put a lot of money into Belle Vue.'

'But he said . . . Maharajah was . . . was . . . and I . . . I . . .' Danny swallowed. He couldn't get the words out. The band of muscle across his chest had grown tighter.

'No! I don't want to hear excuses! You've let me down. These are important men. And we need to be impressin' them, not embarrassin' them.' Mr Jameson jabbed a finger at Danny. 'So you get Maharajah out of my sight. And yourself with him. Now!'

Chapter Two

Danny plunged a cloth into the bucket and swiped at the mud on Maharajah's back. The dirt melted away. He did the same again – and again – until he was sure no trace of Belle Vue's lake remained.

The hum sounding from the back of his throat faded and he patted the tough skin. A trunk wrapped around his neck, pulling him close. They stood locked together just long enough for Danny to feel the warmth, then Maharajah spotted some sugar cane and let go. The loud munching almost made him smile.

'I thought you'd be here.'

Danny jerked. Hetty Saddleworth stood in the open doorway of the elephant house, her yellow curls piled into a haphazard crown on her head. A torn hem hung from the folds of her dress. Hetty was the daughter of Belle Vue's animal doctor, Mr William Saddleworth – but more importantly, she was his first real friend.

'This is where you always come when you're . . .' She broke off as if struggling for the right word. 'Well, you know when!'

Picking up her skirts, she marched inside, and sank down on one of the hay bales that lined the walls. Silently, Danny packed away the cleaning cloths and waited. It didn't take long. It was nearly impossible for Hetty to stay quiet.

'So, I heard what happened at the lake. Everyone's talking about it. The story's right across Belle Vue.' Her expression battled between delight and regret. 'Oh, I wish I'd been there! Please tell me you told Maharajah to do it . . . to knock Snade's wig right off! Tell me it wasn't an accident!'

The corner of Danny's mouth lifted and he dipped his head slightly. Hetty's grin widened. 'I knew it. How marvellous! Snade is a fool . . . and now everyone knows he's a bald fool!'

Danny let out a laugh but then his smile faded. He slumped down into the space next to Hetty and, almost without thinking, rubbed one finger along the tangle of scars on his wrist.

'Mr Jameson wasn't happy. He said . . .' Danny stopped. Over the last few weeks, he'd discovered that talking was always more difficult when he was upset or angry. Instead, it was better to break his speech into small, slow pieces. 'He said . . . he said I'd let him down.'

'No, that's not true!' Furiously, Hetty twisted towards him. 'You mustn't think that, Danny! And I don't imagine Mr Jameson really believes it either. The whole episode will blow over soon enough, you'll see. And then he'll see the funny side!'

'I just wish the Jamesons didn't . . . didn't have to ask those men for money. I could have helped . . . if things had worked out differently.'

The thought had been plaguing Danny for weeks. Just two months ago, he'd found a small fortune hidden away by Maharajah's previous owner – and for a brief, glorious moment, the possibilities had been endless. But much of the money had gone to pay off old debts, and now a courtroom of lawyers were arguing over who should have the rest.

'Listen, Danny. Mr Jameson knows what he's doing. The show is certain to be a success. Why wouldn't it be? There are fights. And fireworks. And explosions. Everything you could wish for! People will be desperate to come to see it and then Mr Jameson will be able to pay back all that he owes.'

Hetty looked away and plucked at the folds of her dress. 'Anyway, there's something else I wanted to tell you . . .' She lifted her chin. 'I've decided I'm going to be in it. The show, I mean. I want to take part. To be a performer. Just like you. And Maharajah.'

The snort of disbelief emerged before Danny could stop it. And Hetty scowled. 'What is it? Don't you think I can do it?'

'Yes. I think you could do anything you want.' Danny's answer was instinctive, mostly because it was true. In the short time he'd known her, Hetty had never once turned down a chance for adventure. But what did surprise him is that her father had agreed. William Saddleworth was more than a little protective of his only child.

'Have . . . have you asked your father?'

'Of course! I spoke to him last night after supper. He said yes. Why wouldn't he?'

Danny raised his eyebrows. There was something she wasn't telling him. For a moment, Hetty hesitated then she sighed.

'Well, if you must know, Papa wasn't happy. You know how careful he can be. He says I'm the only family he has left . . . since Mama died. And he's made me promise to stay away from the fireworks. And I'm to keep in the background. And if there's a problem, I won't be allowed to carry on.'

Danny felt a tug of sympathy at Hetty's obvious frustration.

'I know Papa worries about me, I just wish he wouldn't. There's really no need. Besides, I'm sure everything will be fine.' A sudden smile lit her face. 'Rehearsals start this week. And Mr Jameson says that he's expecting twenty thousand visitors on show night. Twenty thousand, Danny! Just imagine it!'

Danny pulled a loose straw from the hay bale and tried to ignore the sudden swoop of his stomach. Twenty thousand people. He remembered what Mr Snade had said. There could be no room for mistakes. Nothing could go wrong. There was simply too much money at stake. His throat dried.

Perhaps Hetty sensed his mood because she stood abruptly and shook out her skirts. 'So, are you finished in here? Papa said he was going to examine the new crocodile today. And I thought we could go and watch.' She tilted her head. 'Well? Do you want to come?'

Danny twisted the straw between his fingers then threw it away. After this morning's disaster, maybe he'd best stay out of Mr Jameson's way for a while. He looked up and nodded.

Hetty grinned. 'Then let's go!'

'. . . so yesterday, Papa said Cleopatra attacked one of the keepers. Nearly bit his hand clean off! And then she tried to eat a baby lizard. But the poor thing managed to escape before she could do any harm.'

Hetty paused for breath, just long enough for Danny to close the door of the elephant house, and click it shut. Cleopatra was the new Nile crocodile, and rumours about her were already circulating the park. Said to be longer than a man, she had teeth that could rip through wood, and a wide whip of a tail. For the last few days, Danny had been itching to see her for himself.

'So now all the keepers are terrified. No one wants to get too close. And they're having to feed her with fish on the end of a long pole. But Papa is going to try to get near enough to examine her. He wants to make sure she's not been hurt during the journey to Manchester.'

Together, Danny and Hetty walked around the curve of Belle Vue Lake and across the smooth, clipped lawns of the Italian gardens, and then alongside the bandstand with its ornate domed roof and metal arches.

'And if there's time, Papa said he'll take a look at the snakes. Did you know some of them could kill you? He told me the name of one of them. It has a sort of hood, a bit of skin . . . around its neck, I think. But I can't quite remember—'

'The king cobra,' Danny interrupted. He wasn't sure where the name had come from, only that a vivid picture had appeared in his head. 'It flares out its hood before attacking.' He swallowed. 'There's enough poison in one bite to kill twenty people.'

Hetty's eyes widened. 'Yes, that's right! I remember now! And Papa said they have to be kept in cages, behind glass . . . just in case.'

They'd reached the last grotto where they turned to zigzag through the aviary. Squawks greeted them as they passed the parrots, cockatoos and macaws. Alongside was a long, low shed that housed the birds of prey. Through the mesh window, Danny could just see one of the white-tailed eagles spread its wide wings then settle back to sleep. Moving on, they emerged on to a track next to the ostrich and emu enclosures.

Hetty was still talking. 'But can you imagine if one of the cobras did get free? Think of the panic! Why, it could very well . . .'

Abruptly, Danny stopped. Turned. And went back. One of the pens was wide open, its gate bent and buckled, and the padlock hanging loosely from its hook. Inside, the small square plot looked empty.

'Danny? What on earth are you doing? We're going to be late.' Hetty bounced impatiently on her heels. 'Papa will have finished. He wanted to do all the examinations before lunch. And it's nearly twelve o'clock now.'

'Just wait. One moment!'

Carefully, Danny slipped through the broken gate, and stood in the centre of the pen. He pivoted on his toes, then paced his way around the grass just to make sure. But there was no mistake. Whatever creature had been here before, was now long gone.

'What is it?' Hetty had moved to stand near the fence. Curiosity had replaced her impatience. But Danny scanned the enclosure again before he answered.

'I think . . .' He drew in a breath. 'I think one of the animals has escaped.'

Chapter Three

They found Mr Saddleworth in the reptile house, inspecting a glass cabinet stuffed with brown-and-gold snakes. Their glossy skins matched the colours of the large python that hung around Mr Saddleworth's neck. As they got closer, the python lifted its head and hissed sulkily. Lightly, Hetty's father pushed it back down.

'You're late! I'm afraid I've already finished the examinations for this morning. You should have been here half an hour ago. I did tell you, Hetty!'

'I'm sorry, Papa, but there was a reason.' Hetty glared at Danny and jerked her chin. Hesitantly, Danny stepped forward. For some reason he felt nervous. As though discovering the empty cage had somehow made him responsible for the animal's escape.

'Sir . . .' His throat clogged, and he had to stop to clear

it. 'Sir, one of the large birds is missing. The bird in the far pen.'

'The last enclosure? Are you certain?' Mr Saddleworth frowned. Fine lines fanned out from around eyes that were the same keen, clear blue as his daughter's. He'd never been a man who was easy to fool. 'Perhaps one of the keepers has her?'

Danny shook his head. 'I don't think so, sir. The gate's broken. Looks like . . .' He swallowed. 'Looks like it's been forced. And the pen's empty.'

Mr Saddleworth's scowl deepened. Carefully, he unwound the snake from around his neck and lowered it into the cabinet. The python slithered across the tangle of brown-and-gold skins before curling into a corner. 'Come on. Show me.'

When Danny, Hetty and Mr Saddleworth arrived at the pen, the damaged gate was swinging, backwards and forwards, against the fence. Mr Saddleworth pushed it to one side and repeated the search that Danny had already carried out. The result was no different.

'You're right. She seems to have battered her way out.'

'She?' Hetty asked.

'Emerald. The Tasmanian emu.'

Emerald. Something about the name tugged at Danny's memory. Something important. 'Isn't . . . isn't she the only one left?'

'Yes.' Mr Saddleworth rubbed the back of his neck. 'She's thought to be the last of her kind alive in captivity. Possibly the last one in the entire world – thanks to trophy hunters and poachers.' The muscles in his jaw tightened. 'And now it looks like we've managed to lose her.'

Danny stared at the empty enclosure. He tried to think of something reassuring to say. 'At least she can't fly.'

'What do you mean? Of course she can fly.' Hetty gestured towards the neighbouring cages. 'She's a bird, isn't she? Like the others?'

'Hetty, sometimes I wish you would listen more. And talk a little less.' Mr Saddleworth's tone was gentler than his words. He crouched to inspect the ground around the broken gate. 'Not all birds are able to fly. You explain, Danny. You've worked in the aviary. Let's see what you remember.'

For a moment, Danny's mind went blank. Compared to Mr Saddleworth, he knew nothing. And unlike Hetty, he'd never been to school. Until two months ago, he'd been a thief, pickpocketing on the streets of Edinburgh. He wasn't educated. He could barely even read. The only lesson he'd ever learnt was how to steal. The idea that he could teach anyone anything was ridiculous.

Then fragments began to filter through; pieces of knowledge that he didn't even know he had, just like his memory of the king cobra.

'Emus *do* have wings . . .' Danny began slowly. 'But underneath all those feathers they're small. As small as crows' wings, I think. So, they're no good for flying. But their legs are powerful . . . and long. And their feet are strong.'

Danny could feel his confidence growing. Kneeling beside Mr Saddleworth, he pointed at the dry earth. It was littered with footprints – animal and human – but the most obvious was a line of three-toed tracks. Emerald's footmarks. Over his shoulder, Hetty peered closer.

'Look. All her toes point forward. That helps her to build up speed. It means an emu can run as fast as a horse. Faster sometimes, I reckon. So even though Emerald can't fly, she can run. And she's quick. Very quick.'

It was the most Danny had said in days. Maybe it was the most he'd ever said. He just hoped he'd remembered everything correctly.

'Well done, Danny. You're quite right.' Mr Saddleworth pushed to his feet and brushed the dirt from his knees. 'Unfortunately, that's bad news for us. Judging by these tracks, Emerald was moving fast. And, if she's managed to get out of Belle Vue, she could be anywhere in Manchester.'

'I'll have to organize a search party. This has all the makings of a catastrophe.' Mr Saddleworth was striding ahead so quickly that Danny and Hetty had to run to catch up. They'd already passed the maze and the bear pit and he'd still not slowed down.

'But it's not your fault, Papa! The lock was broken. She must have forced her way out.'

'All the animals at Belle Vue are my responsibility, Hetty.' Mr Saddleworth stopped abruptly, his expression fierce. 'There are too many people in this world willing to hunt down and harm creatures like Emerald, and I won't fail any one of them. Which means we have to find her before she gets hurt.'

He set off again. Danny and Hetty followed, veering around the edge of the lake where the penguins were already lined up in neat black-and-white rows. One by one, they shuffled into place before diving head first into the water. The gathering crowd cheered loudly, but today Danny didn't stop to admire the show. 'Sir? Last night . . . did anyone check on Emerald?'

'I imagine someone must have. She's a touchy creature, likes to sneak off whenever your back is turned. But none of the keepers reported any problems.' Mr Saddleworth sighed. 'Anyway, how she got out is not the issue. What I need to know is – where is she now?'

It was an impossible question to answer. They'd already followed Emerald's footprints out of the pen and through the aviary. But, once they'd reached the cinder paths criss-crossing Belle Vue, there had been too many other tracks to separate one group from another. The sharp outline of Emerald's prints had softened and blurred before disappearing altogether.

'Don't worry, Papa.' Hetty hooked her hand into Mr Saddleworth's arm. 'We'll find her. I know we will.'

Belle Vue's keepers were based in a hut on the south side of the park, close to the giraffe house. Danny and Hetty waited impatiently while Mr Saddleworth gathered the men together and snapped out orders.

'. . . I want the entire site searched. All one hundred acres. Divide into groups and check each area separately. Look inside pens. Open outhouses. Crawl into cages. Make sure every corner's covered. And spread the word among the rest of the staff.' He paused. 'But be discreet. Mr Jameson's had the men from the bank here this morning. And I don't want to cause a panic.'

The men left, filtering out through Belle Vue, until only one worker remained. Nelson Crimple, the head keeper. He was a great bear of a man, with a hard face and big fists. Danny had first met him in Edinburgh. Distrust still lingered on both sides.

'Crimple, just the person!' Mr Saddleworth beckoned him over. 'Might I have a word?'

'Gov?'

'You've got your ear to the ground. Has anything odd been reported this morning? Anything from outside the park? Something that might be connected to Emerald?'

Crimple shook his head. 'Just the usual, Gov. Reverend Threlfall's been complainin' about the noise again. Says it's gettin' worse. And the landlord of the Frog and Bucket reckons he saw a panther in his yard. Turned out to be a cat.' His brow wrinkled.

'. . . and one of the omnibus drivers spotted somethin' at Gorton Reservoir. Right over on the far bank. But when I asked him, he thought it was probably just shadows.' A shrug. 'That's about it.'

Mr Saddleworth frowned. 'I suppose the reservoir might

be worth a look. But it's a good mile away, and we need to search Belle Vue first. That'll take every man I've got.'

'We could go, Papa. Couldn't we?' Hetty's elbow dug into Danny's side.

'Yes, sir. We could.' Danny released a breath. Maybe this was his chance to win back Mr Jameson's trust. Finding Emerald would surely make up for humiliating Mr Snade and the other bankers. Without allowing himself more time to think, he spoke quickly. 'And we can take the horse and cart. Mr Jameson says I can drive it.' It was a lie. Danny was only allowed to hold the reins if Mr Jameson was sitting right beside him. But if he was going to risk another lecture, he might as well make it worthwhile.

'Very well.' Mr Saddleworth nodded. 'It's probably nothing. But if you do see Emerald, send word back here immediately. Don't try to catch her on your own!'

Chapter Four

Even travelling by horse and cart, it took Danny and Hetty almost an hour to reach the narrow lane that led to the reservoir. They pulled to a stop on a ridge overlooking the water. Trees fringed the edges, casting shadows that danced across the surface. It was a pretty place, quiet and peaceful. And there was absolutely no sign of an emu.

'She's not here,' Hetty announced. She'd clambered on to the box seat of the cart to get a better view.

Disappointed, Danny tugged her back down, and grabbed the reins again. 'We've come this far. Let's look by the shore.' With more luck than skill, he steered the horse and cart along the narrow track. They stopped at the water's edge then scrambled out. The reservoir lay in front of them, still and silent.

'Look!' Hetty pointed suddenly. 'Over there. What's that?'

A shadow flickered between the leaves of a heavy willow. Danny walked a little nearer until he could see through the branches. He stifled a laugh. It was – quite unmistakably – Emerald.

No one would ever have described her as beautiful. A ragged curtain of dark feathers covered most of her body. But her head and neck were bare as though any suggestion of plumage had been rubbed away. Her long legs were muscular, with huge, gnarled knees and three-toed feet. And every so often a deep grunting noise emerged from her throat.

But to Danny, the biggest surprise of all was that she appeared to be dancing. Although, it was nothing like the graceful twists and turns he'd seen in the grand ballroom at Belle Vue. Instead, Emerald's dance was a curious mishmash of moves.

At first, she skipped from side to side. Then with sudden bravery, she leapt into the water before making a swoop downwards and finally, a fast scuttle away like a fallen leaf buffeted by the wind.

Fascinated, Danny watched while she did it again. And again. He stepped nearer. Now he could see what was holding her spellbound. A few feet away, a child's red ball bobbed up and down in the shallows. Emerald was trying to catch it, but every time she got close, the water swept it back, just out of reach. It was a game she was never likely to win.

Hetty peered over his shoulder. 'So now that we've found her,' she whispered softly. 'What are we going to do with her?'

Danny stared at the solid mass of feathers, sharp beak and powerful legs. He didn't have the slightest idea.

By mutual agreement, Danny and Hetty decided to ignore Mr Saddleworth's instruction to send word back to Belle Vue. A quick search of the cart had uncovered a net and some rope. It was enough to make them feel confident.

'I'm sure it can't be that hard to catch an emu,' Hetty declared. She'd rolled up her sleeves and tightened the messy crown of hair on top of her head. 'Besides, by the time we get back to Belle Vue, she might have disappeared again. I think we should have a go first.'

Danny nodded. Now that they were this close, Emerald didn't look that big. Or that fierce. But she did look fast.

'So, what's our plan?' Hetty asked.

Danny had thought through various possibilities but the simplest method seemed best. 'You chase her towards me. I'll grab her. Then you throw the net over the top.'

'And what happens if you miss?'

'Wave her back. And I'll try again.'

Hetty didn't look entirely convinced but she nodded anyway. 'Very well,' she said.

At first it seemed as though the plan would work. Hetty circled behind Emerald, the net grasped in one hand. A little distance away, Danny stood, legs apart, braced like a captain on a ship. 'Go!' he shouted.

Flapping her arms with the energy of a startled chicken, Hetty ran towards Emerald. Almost immediately, the emu lurched into a sprint. She ran far more gracefully than she danced. Her feathered body stayed steady while underneath her long legs pistoned rapidly. Up and down. Down and up.

Danny stretched his arms wide. Then wider still. Emerald kept coming. She was getting closer. Now they were eye to eye. Suddenly, Emerald verged to the left as if some primeval instinct had warned her of danger.

Desperately, Danny reached for her . . . and missed. Emerald shot past. Danny swivelled, lost his balance and fell face first into the muddy bank. The ugly squelch was sticky in his ears.

He lifted his head. Mud dripped down his face and into his eyes. He wiped it away. Hetty was bent over at the waist, cheeks wet with tears. She couldn't speak for laughter. Raising a hand, Danny flicked a fistful of dirt, and was quietly pleased when most of it landed on Hetty, clinging to her collar and chin. She stopped laughing.

Danny staggered upright. 'This isn't going to work.'

'Really?' Hetty's voice was tart. 'I never would have guessed.'

Another trickle of mud slid down Danny's face, and Hetty started laughing again. He scowled at her. 'Let's try something else.'

The sun had begun to drop in the sky as they stood

together at the side of the reservoir. Further along the bank, Emerald watched them, her head bobbing back and forth nervously. And for a moment, Danny was struck with a wave of compassion. *He* knew they were trying to help her; to keep her safe. But she didn't. All she understood was the fear of pursuit – and he knew exactly how that felt.

Then Danny spotted the red ball. It was caught near the water's edge, trapped between reeds and rocks. He bent to swoop it up. 'I have an idea,' he said.

The plan was simple. Skewer the ball on the end of a long branch and use it as bait – much like the Belle Vue keepers had done to feed Cleopatra. Danny only hoped that Emerald remained as curious now as she had been earlier. Because if she did, they could lure her close enough to catch.

It took a long time and a great deal of patience. But step by step, Emerald crept nearer. And nearer. Until finally, Danny pounced and this time, he didn't miss. Hooking one arm around Emerald's neck, he wrapped the other across her back, pinning her small wings against her sides. She wriggled and bucked but he clung on, the feathers soft and slippery beneath his fingers. Hetty edged towards them.

'Now,' he shouted.

With one quick movement, Hetty threw the net – right across Emerald.

'Get the rope! We need to tie her legs as well. She's strong.'

Emerald fought hard against the ropes; she didn't like being gift-wrapped. And Danny couldn't blame her. But once she realized there was no escape, her resistance seemed to drain away.

As the cart trundled down Hyde Road, curious stares followed. This time Hetty held the reins while Danny sat alongside, with Emerald lodged between them, her head poking out from a gap in the net. Danny was certain she stayed still only because of his vice-like grip around her neck.

Once they reached Belle Vue, news of their success must have spread because a small crowd gathered near the aviary. Emerald seemed glad to be home. She barely waited to be untied before leaping into her pen. Danny propped himself against the fence to watch – Hetty beside him – but Emerald didn't look back. They'd been forgotten as quickly and easily as last Sunday's supper.

At least she was safe, Danny thought. The only Tasmanian emu in captivity – very possibly the only one left in the entire world – had been found thanks to Hetty's eagle eyes and a great quantity of luck.

'There you are! Thank heavens.' Danny turned. Mr Saddleworth stood behind them, his expression battling between relief and exasperation. 'I heard you found her.'

'Yes, Papa. At the reservoir. She must have slipped out of the park overnight and run straight down Hyde Road. That's why no one saw her.' Hetty lifted her chin, and the lines across Mr Saddleworth's forehead deepened.

'You're probably right, but what did I tell you about sending word back? You were supposed to let me know.

Immediately! Not try to catch her on your own.'

'But Papa, we couldn't leave her there! Anything could have happened. Besides it was easy enough. Hardly any bother at all.'

'Really?' Raising an eyebrow, Mr Saddleworth looked at their mud-splattered clothes and dirty faces. Danny had to resist the urge to fidget.

'Fine!' Hetty said at last. 'Maybe there were one or two small difficulties. But it was worth it, Papa. She's back now. And safe. That has to be the most important thing.'

'Yes, I suppose so. But next time . . .' Mr Saddleworth rubbed the back of his neck. 'Well, hopefully there won't be a next time. The blacksmith's fixed the gate and replaced the lock. But from now on, we all need to take a great deal more care.'

Danny wasn't sure how that was possible. Like all Belle Vue's staff, he locked each enclosure after entering and leaving. It had become as much of a habit as washing his face every morning. But perhaps there was another explanation. The padlock on the emu pen had probably been old – or damaged.

'Now Hetty, let's get you home so you can clean up.' Mr Saddleworth slipped an arm around his daughter's shoulders. 'And on the way, perhaps you can tell me the real story of how you came to be so grubby.'

'Yes, Papa.'

Hetty slid Danny a small smile then allowed her father to lead her away. It was only after they'd gone that Danny realized how he must look. The mud had dried into a crust on his skin, and his clothes were caked in dirt. A trough of water stood by Emerald's gate; it seemed clean enough. Wetting his hands, Danny scrubbed at his face and neck. The muddy water trickled down his arms and dripped from his elbows.

He leant back against the fence, hoping the sun would dry off the worst of the damp. Idly, he glanced down at the gate. The new padlock looked sharp and shiny on the hook but a few yards away, abandoned on the ground, was a lump of rusted metal. It must be the old lock from Emerald's enclosure.

Curious, Danny picked it up. Despite the rust, the case seemed solid enough. Carefully, he rolled it between his fingers then frowned. On the left side, close to where the lock normally snapped together, his thumb slipped into a shallow groove. He looked closer. The dent was circular – larger than a farthing, but smaller than a penny – almost as though it had been caused by one sharp hammer blow.

Tightening his grip, Danny worked through the possibilities. If he was right, the lock hadn't been faulty or crumbling with age. Nor had the emu enclosure been left unlocked by accident. No. This neat, tidy dent could only mean one thing.

The padlock had been deliberately broken. Someone had helped Emerald to escape.

Chapter Five

'I'm asking you again, Mr Jameson. Close Belle Vue down.'

'And I'm tellin' you again, Reverend. I will not!'

Danny had barely stepped inside the Jamesons' front door when he heard the loud voices. They leaked from the study and bounced down the hallway. Belle Vue House stood in the middle of the park, and Danny was used to visitors calling at all times of the day. But he'd never heard anyone this loud. Or this angry.

'Sir, you're being unreasonable!'

'I've never been unreasonable in me life.' Mr Jameson's voice rose another notch. 'I'm the very model of reason. Ask anyone!'

Danny clamped his teeth together – hard – and let the broken padlock slip back into his trouser pocket. He crept closer to the study. To his great good fortune, the door stood slightly ajar. And through the gap, he could just see Mr Jameson sitting opposite another man. The sight made Danny's fists curl.

Reverend Eustace Threlfall was Belle Vue's worst critic. Every day, he found something to complain about – the customers were too rowdy; the noise too loud; and the animals too fierce. He was the sort of man who fired out his opinions like buckshot. Unfortunately, his opinions were as narrow and restricting as his shirt collars.

'Sir! You must appreciate that Sunday is the Lord's Day. It's a day for spiritual reflection. Not jollification and revelry. And on Sundays, Belle Vue should not open.'

'Sunday is our busiest day of the week. And I've no intention of shuttin' up shop just because you think people should be sittin' in church, listenin' to you pontificatin'.'

'That's exactly my point, Mr Jameson. My congregation can barely hear my sermon thanks to the unruly hordes heading to your pleasure park.' Reverend Threlfall must have realized his voice had turned shrill because his next words were quieter. 'The noise is simply unbearable. Omnibuses arc up and down the road every few minutes. Every corner is littered with rubbish. And I strongly suspect families have been picnicking in my churchyard!'

There was a short, tense silence and Danny watched Mr Jameson pull himself upright in his chair. 'Those people are good, solid, workin' folk whose only wish is to forget their worries for one day of the week and enjoy themselves. And

I'm makin' sure they do just that. Besides, Belle Vue employs most of the men in this area. Without us, there'd be no work.'

It was a powerful argument. Even in the short time he'd been here, Danny could see that Belle Vue was at the heart of everything. As well as the menagerie, there were three new refreshment rooms, one brewery, a bakery, two dance halls and a bandstand. In the winter, there was ice skating and bonfire parties. And in the summer, cricket matches and archery contests. Every bucket and barrel was made by the park's own cooper, and every pot and pan came from its braziers. Even the nearby streets were lit by gas supplied by Belle Vue.

'Daniel Jameson, what do you think you're doing?'

Danny jerked back from the door. Mrs Jameson was standing in the hallway, her hands braced on bony hips; hair pulled back so tightly that one more twist might just snap it off.

'Listening, ma'am.' Danny was too startled to think of a lie. But fortunately, he knew that Ethel May Jameson was more forgiving than she looked. She had to be, she'd been married to Mr Jameson for fifteen years.

'Humph. Well, I suppose I was daft enough to ask.' Her eyes flickered across his muddy clothes. 'And what happened to you? You look like—'

A sudden thud from the study surprised them both. It was followed by a scraping noise as if furniture was being dragged along the floor, and then the argument began again. This time Danny didn't have to strain to listen.

'I find your attitude extremely difficult, sir. It's quite obvious that you're not a God-fearing man.'

'I'm as God-fearin' as you, Reverend, but I don't believe I have to go to church every week to prove it. Any road, my wife says enough prayers for me. So I won't be needin' your help to get me into heaven.'

In the hallway, Mrs Jameson muttered something under her breath. Danny didn't think it was complimentary.

'Sir! Have you no decency? No respect?' Once again, the vicar's voice was shrill enough to cause headaches.

'I've plenty of respect for those who earn it. As for you, you pompous windbag—'

Danny didn't hear any more because Mrs Jameson had already flung open the door. Like a fighter stepping into the ring, she straightened her shoulders and marched inside. Danny followed.

The two men stood at either side of the fireplace, their chairs pushed back to the far corners of the room. Mr Jameson's face was an ugly, angry red. The vicar looked like he'd swallowed something unpleasant and the taste had not quite disappeared.

'For goodness, sake, gentlemen! The whole of Belle Vue can hear you. What in heaven's name is going on?' Mrs Jameson tapped a foot. 'Well?'

Reverend Threlfall recovered first. He bowed briefly. 'My apologies, Mrs Jameson. I was trying to persuade your husband to close Belle Vue on Sundays, but I'm afraid our discussion became a little overheated.'

'So I heard.' Mrs Jameson strode across the room and hooked a hand around her husband's arm. Danny couldn't tell if she was supporting him – or holding him back. Maybe it was both. 'What I don't understand is why now? Why all this fuss? Belle Vue has been here for years, and we've always been good neighbours. I can't see that anything's changed.'

Reverend Threlfall smoothed a hand down his jacket. Everything about him looked tightly held together as though he'd been pushed and prodded and poked into his clothes. 'I'm afraid this has been a problem for some time, Mrs Jameson. But the final straw came today. I'm told an emu escaped from your zoological gardens and is running loose around Manchester!'

Danny looked at Mr Jameson and waited for another explosion. But the menagerist seemed calmer now that his wife stood beside him. He even managed a tight smile. 'Fuss and nonsense over nothin'. My head keeper says the emu's already back in her pen. Found at the Gorton Reservoir, with no damage done to anyone. I can't see there's anythin' to complain about.'

'Of course, *you* would think that.' Reverend Threlfall's lips curled back from his teeth. 'But this time, the escaped animal was an overgrown bird. Next time, the creature could be far more dangerous. People in my parish are nervous. Some are terrified. Closing on a Sunday is the very least you can do.'

Danny was sure he saw Mr Jameson twitch. Or maybe it was because Mrs Jameson had tightened her grip on his arm. 'I'm sorry you feel like that, Reverend,' he said finally. 'But you needn't concern yourself about any escaped animals. It won't happen again. I can promise you.'

'I'm afraid that's not—'

'Reverend, perhaps we can continue this another time.' To Danny's relief, it was Mrs Jameson who interrupted. She gestured towards the clock above the fireplace. 'Don't you have an evening service at eight?'

Scowling, the vicar glanced up. 'Yes. It's later than I'd realized. But don't imagine this subject is closed, Mrs Jameson. We simply cannot continue as we are.' He made a beckoning motion towards the corner of the room. 'Come along, Constance.'

And for the first time, Danny noticed a woman perched awkwardly on the chair near Mr Jameson's desk. She was looking down – staring at her boots as though there was nothing more appealing than the line of stitching across the toes.

'Constance!' the vicar said again.

The woman jerked upright. Her face was plain – soft and round as a moon, with eyes that had almost no colour at all. And while Reverend Threlfall appeared to have been sewn into his suit, her clothes flapped loosely around her long body.

'Oh, Miss Threlfall, I do beg your pardon.' Mrs Jameson seemed almost as surprised as Danny. 'With all the commotion, I didn't see you there.'

'That's quite all right, ma'am.' Clumsily, Miss Threlfall slid to her feet. Her smile was shy and sweet. 'My brother said I had to be quiet. And I was, wasn't I, Eustace?'

'Yes, Constance. So, you were. Well done. But now do hurry up! We've no time for idle chit-chat.'

Hastily, Reverend Threlfall waved his sister towards the door. She scurried out obediently but before following, the reverend turned to Mr Jameson. 'Be warned, sir. You haven't heard the last of this. I shall be speaking to the Manchester Corporation at the first opportunity – and they have the power to close you down!'

The door slammed shut behind him. Immediately, Mr Jameson pulled a cigar from his jacket. 'Who does that man think he is? How dare he come in here and tell me how to run my business!'

'*Our* business, Jamie.'

'Of course, that's what I said, me dove. Our business.' He lit the cigar and blew out a stream of smoke.

Mrs Jameson sighed. 'Well, perhaps we should reduce our hours. Just on Sundays. It might help to keep the peace.'

'No, Ethel May. I said no, and I meant it. And there's not a thing Threlfall can do to make me. Any road, the Manchester Corporation won't listen to a windbag like him. They know we're good for business. And for this city.'

Striding to the hearth, Mr Jameson flicked cigar ash into the fireplace. Danny glanced at the door. He wondered if he'd been forgotten, and whether he could sneak away. But just as the thought entered his head, Mr Jameson turned towards him.

'As for you, lad. I told you to keep out of trouble. But away you go, ridin' off in the horse and cart when you know fine well you're not allowed. What if somethin' had gone wrong? Haven't I made it clear? I can't afford for anythin' to happen to you! You're the star of the show. People are payin' to see you and Maharajah.'

Danny felt anger bubble up in his throat but it was Mrs Jameson who came to his rescue.

'Jamie, calm down! You're being ridiculous. You should be thanking Danny for finding Emerald, not scolding him.'

'Someone else could have found that bleedin' bird, Ethel May. He didn't have to go. The truth is the boy disobeyed me. And just look at him! Grubbier than a coalman's apron. And not even wearin' his costume! Haven't I enough to worry about? I've already had to make everythin' right with Snade. And now I've Threlfall breathin' down my neck as well.'

Mr Jameson took a quick puff of his cigar and glared at Danny. 'Tomorrow evenin' I'm holdin' the first costume fittin' for the show . . . and I expect you to be there, all cleaned up and dressed as Prince Dandip. No excuses!'

Danny felt for the broken lock, buried inside his pocket. His thumb smoothed over the dent in the metal. But he said nothing, because Mr Jameson's words were running in a loop around his head.

' . . . *You know what's at stake. There's a fortune ridin' on this show . . . and your name's everywhere . . .'*

' . . . I can't afford for anythin' to happen to you . . .'

' . . . You're the star of the show. People are payin' to see you and Maharajah . . .'

A hollow feeling twisted in his stomach. Because over the last few days, Mr Jameson hadn't sounded like a father worried about his adopted son – the mute, brown-skinned boy he'd saved from poverty in Edinburgh, dressed up as an Indian prince and brought home to Manchester.

No.

Mr Jameson sounded like a man worried about his business. About the money he would lose if anything went wrong.

Chapter Six

'Surrender. Or I'll shoot!'

'You daft halfwit, you couldn't hit a barn door if you were sat next to it!'

'I could as well!' As he spoke, the soldier lifted his rifle and hoisted it on to his shoulder. And if he hadn't tripped over his own bootlace, Danny was almost sure that blood would have been spilt.

But thank goodness, this wasn't a real war – and these weren't real soldiers. It was the first costume fitting for 'Prince Dandip and the Fight for Flamenca'.

The men were among eighty volunteers recruited from Gorton on the promise of a shilling a day and as much food as they could eat. On arrival, they'd been divided into groups, taken to the Italian gardens and given uniforms. On the left side were the British, wearing scarlet coats and polished helmets. While on the right, the French dazzled in blue jackets trimmed with gold braid.

Danny had marvelled at the sheer brightness of the costumes. Not that his outfit was any less colourful. As ordered, he'd arrived dressed in his Prince Dandip clothes. And as usual he felt ridiculous. Alongside the purple cloak and embroidered slippers, Mrs Jameson had made him a new emerald-green waistcoat and a matching pair of baggy trousers. Three large feathers bobbed from his turban, and Danny had to push them away to be able to see.

'Danny! Over here!'

He turned and immediately his mouth dropped loose. It was Hetty – but Hetty like he'd never seen her before. She wore a white peasant's blouse, tied at the waist with a yellow silk sash. Her butter-coloured skirt fell in tiers to her ankle boots, and a red shawl, complete with tassels, covered her shoulders.

'Isn't it marvellous?' Hetty held up the sides of the skirt and twirled in a circle. Her hair had tumbled down, spiralling into curls around her face. 'I'm to be one of the Spanish villagers, caught up in the fight for Flamenca.'

'Oh,' Danny said. 'Wonderful.' He couldn't stop staring. She looked so completely different from her everyday self. As if some extraordinary, glowing creature had burst out of an ordinary brown shell. He wished he felt half so comfortable. But he'd never enjoyed pretending to be a prince. The problem was that Mr Jameson seemed to expect it. And now most mornings, Danny dressed up in his Prince

Dandip costume to welcome visitors at the gate. Only riding Maharajah made it bearable.

Sliding a hand into his pocket, Danny pulled out the padlock. He'd been carrying it around since yesterday, torn between telling Mr Jameson, regardless of the consequences – and trying to solve the mystery by himself. 'I found this. Outside the emu pen. It's the old lock.'

He held out his palm so that Hetty could see, but to his disappointment, she barely glanced at it. 'That rusty old thing? No wonder Emerald was able to break out of the aviary. Maybe the lock snapped open when she battered down the gate.'

'No.' Danny shook his head. Every instinct told him that someone had helped Emerald to disappear. He turned the metal case so the shallow, circular dent was visible. 'I think someone hammered it. To force it open.'

'Really? Let me take another look.' But before Hetty could peer closer, they were interrupted.

'Miss Henrietta! Good evenin' to you!' Tom Dalton was marching towards them, dressed in a scarlet soldier's jacket and carrying a rifle. Hastily, Danny closed his fingers over the padlock and stuffed it back into his trouser pocket.

'Tom! I didn't know you were going to be here.' Hetty pushed a stray curl behind one ear and smiled brightly.

'Yes. I thought I should volunteer for duty.' He braced the rifle against one shoulder, clicked his heels and saluted. Danny wanted to roll his eyes but Tom was already turning towards him.

'So you're here as well, Prince Dandip. Interesting hat.' He flicked a finger at one of the peacock feathers, and Danny curled his hands into fists. The urge to throw a punch was almost overwhelming.

Quickly, Hetty moved to stand between them. 'Well, you certainly look the part, Tom. Being in uniform suits you.'

'Thank you, Miss Henrietta.' Tom's chest puffed out. And for a moment, he reminded Danny of one of the howler monkeys from the ape house, just before it let out an ugly screech. 'Of course, soldiering's not for me. I'm going to be a pyrotechnist. One day I'll take over from my grandpa at the firework factory. He's teaching me everything he knows.'

'How wonderful!' Hetty's smile brightened. 'I saw some of the test rockets a couple of nights ago from my bedroom window. They were incredible, the most beautiful thing I've ever seen.'

'Yes, we've been working on them for weeks. Grandpa even let me make one myself. The Red Fire Peony, it's called. Grandpa reckons I've a gift for pyrotechnics. He says together, we could be famous. Everyone in the country will know our names.'

Danny let out a snort before he could think to stop it. And Tom's eyes swivelled towards him. For a long moment, they glared at each other, neither willing to look away. Then finally, Tom curled his lip and switched his attention back to Hetty. 'So, what were you looking at?'

'Nothing particularly interesting. Just an old lock. Danny found it by Emerald's cage. He thinks someone took a hammer to it.' Hetty nudged Danny's side. 'Why don't you show him?'

Reluctantly, Danny pulled out the padlock from his pocket. Tom snatched it from his hand and turned it over. 'I don't know what you're making such a fuss about,' he sniffed. 'This is just old. Tools and cages get broken all the time. If you'd been at Belle Vue as long as I have, you'd know that.'

Danny scowled. 'No. I think—'

'I reckon you're better off throwing it away. In fact, why don't I do it for you?'

Tom had already drawn back his arm before Danny could protest. With a quick flick of his wrist, he tossed the lock into the air. It arched across the rows of flower beds before falling straight into the ornamental pond. The resulting splash was deep and final. Danny was so angry he couldn't move. Once again, words were stuck in his throat, as hard and uncomfortable as pebbles.

'Attention everyone! I want all the soldiers over here now. The French and the British.' Mr Jameson had appeared on the far lawn, bellowing like a tinpot general. 'Come along! Line up for inspection. We haven't got all night.'

Tom glanced over his shoulder. 'I'm afraid I have to go. The army's callin'. But I hope to see you soon, Miss Henrietta.'

Nodding a goodbye to Hetty, Tom strode off down the path, swinging his rifle with a swagger. Danny watched, hoping the gun would trip him up. Instead, Tom was forced to avoid another figure who was cutting through the blue and red armies.

'It's Papa! What's he doing here?' Hetty scowled, pulling her shawl more tightly around her shoulders. 'Oh, I hope he's not changed his mind about the show. He promised me!'

Danny was still struggling to conjure up some words of reassurance when Mr Saddleworth spotted them. He marched across the lawn.

'There you are! Good. I have some news. And, I thought Hetty ought to know straight away...' He took a breath and rubbed the back of his neck. '... your Aunt Augusta is coming to Belle Vue.'

Hetty's hand loosened on the shawl. Her face lost what little colour it had. 'Aunt Augusta? Coming here? But why?'

'I have to travel to France in a few days. Mr Jameson wants me to look at some zebras that are coming up for auction in Paris. I'll be gone about a week. Maybe a fortnight if I can arrange to bring the animals back with me. So, I've asked your aunt to take care of you while I'm gone.'

Danny could almost feel Hetty's desperation. 'But Papa, I can look after myself. There's no need to invite Aunt Augusta. I'll be perfectly fine.'

'No, Hetty. I'm not leaving you on your own.' Mr

Saddleworth's voice flattened. 'And there's no one else I can ask. Your aunt may be a little strict but she's a good woman.'

'What about the Jamesons? I could stay at their house. I'd be no trouble.'

'Mr and Mrs Jameson are busy enough without adding to their workload. And your aunt says she's happy to come.'

'You asked her . . . without speaking to me first?' Frown lines had appeared between Hetty's eyes. A muscle twitched in her cheek.

'Yes. I'm sorry but this trip was unexpected. I had to make the arrangements quickly.'

'But what about the show? You said I could be in it. That you'd come and see me and—'

Mr Saddleworth put up a hand, palm flat. 'I'm sorry, Hetty, but I'm unlikely to be back in time for the performance. You'll have to discuss the show with your aunt. It'll be her decision.' He dropped his arm. 'Now, no more arguments. Aunt Augusta arrives tomorrow and that's the end of it. I'll see you at home.'

He turned to push his way back through the line of volunteer soldiers. But Hetty didn't watch him leave. Instead, she sank on to the grass until her skirts pooled around her in yellow waves. 'That's that then. It's over. I won't be able to be in the show. I might as well give up now.'

Danny frowned. He'd never known Hetty to back down so easily. 'Maybe your aunt won't mind.'

Hetty released a laugh but there was little humour in it. 'You haven't met Aunt Augusta. She'd never let me be part of anything like this. I can hear her now: '*A show in public! How outrageous! Someone might see your ankles!*' I only just managed to persuade Papa. But once Aunt Augusta's here, she'll never let me out of her sight. It'll be dreadful. I'll have to act like a proper lady. And I won't be able to do anything fun. Or interesting. Or . . .'

Having a conversation with Hetty was sometimes like playing with a skipping rope. Danny had to choose exactly the right moment to leap in. 'Listen,' he said, and then when that didn't work, he said it again. 'Listen! Listen to me!'

Abruptly Hetty broke off, mid-flow.

'You can't give up now.' For some reason that Danny couldn't quite explain, it seemed important that Hetty be allowed to do this. As though her battle for freedom had become his own.

Besides, he owed her more than he could ever repay. Hetty had been the first friend he'd ever had. It hadn't mattered to her that he wasn't a real prince. That he was only a street thief who Mr Jameson had found pickpocketing in Edinburgh. It hadn't mattered that he hadn't been able to speak or that he had no money and very little education.

It hadn't mattered because she'd wanted to be his friend – just at the time when he'd needed one the most.

'Why shouldn't I give up?' Hetty looked at him, suspiciously. 'No one believes I can do this . . . Even you laughed when I first told you!'

'Well, if I did, I was wrong.' Danny swallowed.

'Whatever your aunt says, I'll help you . . . I'll help you be in the show.'

'Truly?' Hetty's smile took his breath away.

'Yes,' he said. 'After all, your aunt can't be that terrible.'

Chapter Seven

Danny didn't go straight home after the costume fitting. Instead, he spent an hour with Hetty dreaming up schemes to win over Aunt Augusta. And then another hour, on his own, trying to find the padlock in the pond where Tom had thrown it.

Neither effort yielded any success.

But it did mean that he was still wandering through the park when the first explosion blasted across Belle Vue. Heart drumming, Danny looked up. A shower of sparks shimmered overhead, illuminating every corner of the night before falling like silver tears.

His pulse slowed. It was only a firework. George Dalton and his team of pyrotechnists must be testing some more of the new rockets for the show.

But he hadn't been the only one startled. From the

menagerie, a babble of screeches and snarls filled the air. Danny frowned. He hated hearing the animals' fear. But Mr Jameson had insisted on the firework testing and there had been no persuading him otherwise.

'Look, it has to be done,' he'd said. 'We have to practise everythin'. Work out all the timings until they're spot on. This is goin' to be the most fantastical show Belle Vue has ever seen. And we can't afford for anythin' to go wrong. Besides, it'll be over in a few days.'

Another blast sounded – a little louder than the first – and a streak of scarlet arched across the sky before crumbling into hundreds of petals. A heartbeat later, each petal burst into hundreds more. Danny felt his jaw loosen. The night had blossomed into flowers.

'Will you look at that!'

Further down the path, a handful of Mr Jameson's volunteer soldiers stood, gazing upwards. One of the men pushed back the peak of his helmet. 'Aye,' he said. 'I reckon next time George Dalton's goin' to fire a rocket so high he'll hit the moon.'

Laughter mingled with the heavy stomp of boots as the soldiers continued down the path and disappeared. Moments later, another firework soared into the sky. And then another. And another. Until finally, there was silence.

Danny relaxed. And around him, Belle Vue settled down to sleep. He turned, quickening his pace a little. He was abruptly conscious of his own solitude. He'd lingered too long in the park and now the last of the visitors had gone. Belle Vue was virtually empty.

Suddenly, a sharp blast cracked the darkness.

He looked up. But even as he searched the sky, Danny knew it hadn't been a firework. The sound was too quick. Too piercing. More like a bang than a boom. No, it hadn't been one of Dalton's rockets.

The noise had been a gunshot.

Hastily, Danny pivoted on his heels, looking for any sign of life among the shadows. Almost immediately another shot rang out. This one was near enough to make his pulse pick up.

But he'd no reason to worry. It was probably one of the show soldiers showing off with his rifle. Or perhaps a night keeper warning away an animal that had got too close.

A third shot.

Unease tightened Danny's stomach. Quickly, he spun round. The ornamental maze was only a short distance away. Its high hedges might provide some protection. He darted inside and let the walls close around him. For a brief moment, he felt safe.

Then the shooting began again, splintering the branches above him. And Danny knew he couldn't pretend any longer. He was being followed. Someone was shadowing his path, with all of the cunning of a lion hunting its prey.

He started to run – straight down the narrow strip of grass between the tall hedges. Around one corner, and then the next. And the next. He didn't think he would ever stop.

But now there were choices; the maze split into three directions. He took the left fork, flinging himself along the path like a moth seeking light.

It was a dead end.

Frantically, Danny turned back, sprinting down the opposite passageway. His heart was drumming, pounding hard against his ribs. He'd only just realized the full stupidity of his actions. There may be countless paths and hiding places inside the maze. But there was only one way in – and one way out. The gunman need only sit outside and wait.

He was trapped.

Panic knifed through him, sharp and unwelcome. And then he turned another corner and the fear stabbed even deeper. Because he was back exactly where he'd started – at the entrance to the maze.

Desperately, Danny spun on his heels, sucking air in deep hungry gulps. He started running again, the terror close to blinding. And perhaps that was why he didn't see the shadowed figure until it was far too late. The collision was ugly and painful. Nose and forehead crunching against chest and collarbone.

He toppled backwards, sprawled across the ground like a rag doll, but when he tried to get up, hands pressed him down. He tried to twist away. Lashing out with every bone and muscle and sinew in his body.

There was only one man he knew who wanted to hurt him. One man who would like to see him hurt. Frank

Scatcherd. The man who Danny had sent to jail.

Panic threatened to cut off his breath.

'Stop! STOP!'

Confused, Danny lifted his head and stared. It wasn't Scatcherd's voice – or his face. This man's speech was polished and perfect, and his features were slim and fine-boned. Nothing like Scatcherd's rough accent or his solid bulk of muscle.

'Just listen to me! I'm not going to hurt you. I want to help.'

Danny struggled again but this time his movements were weaker – less certain – and the man's grip only tightened. He was surprisingly strong for someone so slight.

But in the end, it was another gunshot which made the decision. It split the ground behind them, spraying up dirt and soil into the air. And Danny knew he had no choice. He dropped his legs and stopped kicking.

'Good.' Loosening his hold, the stranger eased upright. 'Stay there. And keep quiet! Let me deal with this.'

The man dug a hand into the folds of his jacket and when he pulled back, Danny flinched. He was holding a gun. Neat, practical and obviously well used. Instinctively, Danny dug his heels into the soil and pushed backwards. But the stranger didn't seem to notice. Instead, he lifted his arm, and fired straight into the air. He waited a heartbeat then did it again. And again. It was probably a full minute before he dropped his hand. The silence around them seemed to vibrate.

'There! Whoever it was, I reckon I've frightened him off.'

The man tucked the pistol back inside his jacket; Danny watched carefully just to make sure. He wasn't stupid. Guardian angels didn't exist, and this stranger had arrived – most conveniently – at exactly the right time. And in exactly the right place.

'It looks like someone wanted to give you a scare. Any idea who?'

Danny's mind whirled – it was too big a question to answer. Scatcherd? Tom Dalton? Mr Snade? So instead of speaking, he shrugged and let his head slump on to his chest. In the past, he'd found it useful to pretend to be stupid as well as mute. It nearly always made people wary.

But instead of stepping back, the stranger's gaze only sharpened. 'Well, maybe it was one of those fancy-dressed soldiers I saw wandering around earlier. There were enough of them waving rifles about – and it only needs one idiot to show off with a gun.'

Maybe, Danny thought. Or maybe there was another explanation. It was the second strange event in only two days. And every instinct told him that neither one had been an accident.

But he didn't have the time to think about it now. He had another, far more pressing problem: how to get away.

Slowly, Danny climbed to his feet, making his movements deliberately clumsy. This time, the stranger moved back. And over his shoulder, Danny could just see the opening to the maze. It was near enough to make escape seem possible.

Carefully, he tilted on to his toes, tipping his weight forward. He waited a heartbeat – until he was certain his balance was just right – and then he pushed off.

Behind him, he heard a shout but he didn't stop. Instead, he ran and ran. Faster and faster.

And he didn't look back.

Chapter Eight

Danny didn't stop to knock before bursting into the Jamesons' parlour. Maybe if he had, he might have wondered why the gas lamps were still blazing at such a late hour. And why an unfamiliar voice had joined the muttered conversation.

But he didn't stop. Because he wanted to pour out the story while the panic was still fresh and the memory was still vivid. He flung open the door and the words died in his throat.

The Jamesons sat together on the sofa near the fire. Mr Jameson looked grim; the cigar in his hand was already burnt to a stub. Beside him, his wife had knotted her fingers so tightly together that the knuckles were bone-white. And sitting on the chair opposite them was a policeman.

'Good heavens, Danny! What d'you think you're doin'?

Clatterin' in like that?' Mr Jameson scowled. 'Can't you see we've company?'

'Sorry, sir.' Danny dipped his head and slid a glance towards the visitor. No. There was no mistake. The constable's high-collared tunic and heavy boots gave him away. And for a brief moment, Danny wondered whether he'd come about the shooting in the maze.

Almost immediately, he dismissed the idea. There certainly hadn't been enough time for word to spread, especially not to the ears of the Manchester City Police.

'I do apologize, Constable Oversby.' Mr Jameson leant forward. The movement strained the seams of his scarlet waistcoat. 'You were sayin' . . . ?'

'To be honest, sir, I think I've told you everything I know. Except to say, it'll do no harm for you to keep a watch out. It's better to be safe than sorry.'

'Couldn't agree more! I'll make sure we do just that.' Mr Jameson glanced at his wife. If possible, she twisted her hands together even more tightly.

'Yes. It was good of you to come and tell us in person, Constable. We're very grateful.'

'That's quite all right, ma'am.' The officer stood and settled his helmet back on to his head. 'Now, if you'll excuse me, I'll see myself out. Goodnight.'

He gave a brief nod before marching from the room. Silence. Uneasily, Danny shifted from foot to foot, and wondered what he'd done wrong this time. Abruptly Mr Jameson stood, crossed to the fireplace and threw his cigar stub into the flames.

'We've somethin' to tell you,' he said. For a moment, his reflection caught in the mirror above the hearth. Unease clouded his eyes but when he turned back, all traces had been wiped clear. Danny waited, heart drumming.

'Frank Scatcherd's escaped.'

The sentence seemed to hang in the air, like a bird gliding on the breeze. Then the words swooped down and hit home. Danny's stomach pitched. Fear clawed at his insides. It must be a mistake. It had to be. He sifted through the words but the meaning stayed the same.

Frank Scatcherd was free.

'I'm sorry, Danny. There's no mistake. Constable Oversby said they've had word from the city police in Edinburgh. It happened a day ago. He broke out of his prison cell and disappeared. They've been searchin' ever since.'

'Yes, the constable says . . .' Mrs Jameson's voice faded a little then recovered. 'He says we should be on our guard. Just in case.'

The panic flared again. Danny could feel it, whirling through every nerve. For a moment, the only sound was the ticking of the parlour clock and the effort of his breathing.

Mr Jameson tucked his thumbs into his waistcoat pockets.

'Now I don't want you to worry, lad. Scatcherd won't have had time to get far. Besides, you're as safe as houses at Belle Vue. We've more than two hundred staff, and every one of them will keep a watch out. And by tomorrow

Scatcherd's picture will be at all the entrances to Belle Vue. There's no way he could slip in without us knowin'. Isn't that right, me dove?'

'Of course it is.' Mrs Jameson had pinned on a smile. It wobbled only slightly. 'Nothing to worry about at all.'

'There, you see? But just to be sure, you stay inside Belle Vue. No going outside these walls, not without me or Mrs Jameson. Or Crimple. You're to stay here where it's safe.'

Danny's mouth dried. 'But—'

'No arguments, Danny. I can't take the risk. The posters for the show have already gone up. And the public are payin' to see you and Maharajah. I told you: there's too much at stake. So you stay where it's safe. Understood?'

For a moment, the pressure to tell them about the shooting in the maze was overwhelming. But the impulse faded as quickly as it had come. Because Danny knew what would happen if he did.

Once Mr Jameson found out, his freedom would be taken away altogether. Not only would he be forbidden to leave Belle Vue, he'd not even be allowed outside the house. After all, Prince Dandip was the star of the show. And Mr Jameson couldn't risk anything happening to his prize investment.

So, he nodded – and said nothing.

Besides, he was probably imagining danger when there wasn't any. Scatcherd may have escaped but he was still hundreds of miles away. Tonight's shooting was surely no more than an unfortunate coincidence. The stranger had almost certainly been right – it was simply one of the show soldiers showing off with his gun.

'Good. Now off you go.' Mr Jameson jerked his chin towards the door. 'Get some rest. We've a busy few days ahead of us.'

Slowly, Danny crossed the floor; but he knew sleep was unlikely. The man who'd haunted his nightmares was some-where out there. Loose, vengeful and as dangerous as a ticking time bomb. Behind him, the parlour door swung closed, but not quite quickly enough.

'Perhaps we shouldn't have told him.'

'Nonsense, Ethel May. We had to. It'll be all over the newspapers tomorrow.' Danny heard a clink of glass and knew Mr Jameson must have reached for the whisky decanter that sat above the fireplace. 'Besides, when the man who wants to kill you escapes from jail, I reckon you've a right to know.'

The nightmare woke Danny sometime in the early hours of the morning. He wasn't exactly sure when, only that fingers of light were slipping through the gaps in the curtains.

It had been the usual dream. Frank Scatcherd had had the starring role, silhouetted in moonlight and playing with the knife in his hand. This time, the blade had been long and jagged. Last time, it was small and sharp-edged. It didn't really matter. The rest of the nightmare always stayed the same.

Scatcherd held the knife to Danny's wrist, slicing

through the skin. A trickle of blood ran from the cut. And Danny's white shirt turned red. The stain spread – much like the pain did – slowly then more and more rapidly. Until finally, his entire body seemed to throb and burn. And then came the familiar threat.

'Remember. I warned you. The next time will be your last.'

And that was when Danny woke.

Heart thumping, he swung his legs from under the sheet, and sat at the edge of the bed. Carefully, he pushed up the sleeve of his nightshirt. The scars were still there. Just as he had known they would be. Letters carved into his skin by the man who for so long had ruled his life.

FS – for Frank Scatcherd. They were a mark of ownership. A permanent reminder of who he'd belonged to. And a punishment for failing to carry out orders.

With sudden energy, Danny pushed off the mattress, and strode to the washstand. He dipped his hands into the bowl and splashed water on to his face. The cold plunged him back into the real world.

How could the King of Cowgate have escaped from a prison cell more tightly guarded than the Queen's palace? The news had been so unexpected, he'd forgotten to ask how it had actually happened. It should have been impossible.

But of course, nothing was beyond Scatcherd. For years, he'd controlled a complex criminal empire virtually single-handed. And even when he was being led away to prison, he'd been defiant. Two months later, Danny could still remember every word.

'Don't think you're rid of me, Boy,' he'd spat. 'The next time we meet, your friends won't be around to help. And I'll finish you. *For good.*'

At the time, the threat had seemed more than a little ridiculous. Scatcherd had been handcuffed between two burly policemen. Barely an hour earlier, he'd been lying unconscious on the floor – cornered and caught because of his own greed. And Danny had been certain that his troubles were over.

But not now. Not any more.

Now every part of his new life seemed fractured and unsettled.

In the last few days, he'd found – and caught – a missing emu; uncovered evidence of deliberate sabotage; and humiliated Belle Vue's chief investor. He'd been shot at, wrestled to the ground and rescued by a stranger. He'd argued with Mr Jameson, upset Mrs Jameson and made an enemy of Tom Dalton.

And now Frank Scatcherd had escaped. The man who wanted to kill him.

Danny walked to the window and pushed back the curtain. The early-morning sun was only just beginning to rise above Belle Vue. He'd have to wait a little longer to speak to the one person who would understand.

Hetty.

Chapter Nine

The path to Hetty's house was more familiar to Danny than any other route through Belle Vue. From the Jamesons', he headed towards the bear pit, past the new tea rooms, then a sharp right at the giraffe enclosure and finally, up the steps of Kirkmanshulme Cottage.

Danny rapped hard on the door and waited, nervously. He'd not been able to sneak away until late morning – largely because Mrs Jameson had kept him busy with jobs around the house – and now the park was teeming with visitors. Normally, he loved mixing with the crowds, watching the excited faces as they came through the gates.

But after last night, he felt uneasy. Unsettled.

Suddenly, footsteps hurried down the hallway and the door flew open. It was Hetty, but looking very different from when he'd last seen her. The bright curls had been scraped back and she was wearing her best Sunday dress – dark green with lace around the collar and a line of pearl buttons down the front. Not an inch of skin showed from her chin to her toes.

He opened his mouth but didn't get the chance to speak.

'Danny! Oh, I'm so glad it's you. Have you heard the news?' Grabbing his sleeve, Hetty pulled him through the hall and into the front parlour. 'I didn't believe it at first. I thought Papa must have made a mistake. But it's all over *The Times*. Look.'

She thrust a crumpled newspaper under his nose. Here and there, were letters he recognized from the reading lessons Hetty had given him. But none of the words helped. Scowling, he pushed her hand away. 'I can't! You know that.'

'Fine. Then I'll read it.' With a huff of breath, Hetty smoothed out the front page, and plumped herself down on the sofa. He hesitated then sank down next to her.

'*Criminal Mastermind Escapes Jail.*' Excitement leaked into Hetty's voice. '*Police are hunting one of the country's most dangerous criminals following a daring and murderous prison escape in Edinburgh. Mr Frank Scatcherd – otherwise known as the King of Cowgate – disappeared from Calton Jail this Thursday, 20th June, 1872. His current whereabouts remain unknown.*'

Hetty paused and glanced up. Impatiently, Danny gestured for her to continue. Now that she'd started, he was anxious to hear every detail.

'Many of our readers will recognize Mr Scatcherd as the leader of the Leith Brotherhood, a notorious gang responsible for numerous murders, robberies and frauds in Scotland and beyond. He was being held at Calton Jail while awaiting trial for his many crimes.

'But two nights ago, by some foul means, he broke out of his cell and killed the officer on guard. He escaped into the prison yard, where it's claimed he simply vanished. No trace of him has been found since.

'Inspector Clarence Quick of the Edinburgh City Police is leading the search once again. He has assured this newspaper that the prisoner will be found but he added a stark warning. "Members of the public should not approach Mr Scatcherd. He's a dangerous man, and I cannot predict what he might do. There is no doubt that he is capable of great evil."'

When Hetty lowered the newspaper, her blue eyes seemed too large for her face. 'Good Lord! There really isn't any mistake.'

'No.'

'And now, he's out there somewhere. On the loose.'

'Yes.' Danny rubbed the scars on his wrist then stopped when he realized what he was doing. Hastily, he tugged at his sleeve so the ugly marks were covered. Hetty was staring at him, her expression soft.

'Don't worry. You're safe here. The Jamesons would never let anything happen to you. Besides, Scatcherd's in Scotland. Miles away. There's no need to be scared.'

'I'm not scared!' And to Danny's surprise, it was true. Mostly. The first wave of panic had ebbed away and in its place was a mixture of frustration and fury. Just when he thought he'd built a new life, his past had returned to shake the foundations. Why had he ever believed it could be any different?

'Well, even if you were, there's no need to be. Papa says Scatcherd won't be on the loose for long. He reckons the police are so desperate to get him back, every constable in the country will be on the lookout. By the end of next week, he'll be in jail again. You'll see.'

Danny remembered last night's shooting. His terror as he fled from the unknown gunman. And the relief of stumbling across a stranger willing to help. Now every feeling was beginning to muddle together.

'There's something I want to tell—' He stopped. Outside, carriage wheels were rattling loudly across the courtyard. The sound was followed by Mr Saddleworth's shouted summons.

'Henrietta? Henrietta! Where are you? I need you here. Now.'

Hetty's face paled. 'Oh, I can't believe I forgot the time! Aunt Augusta was due to arrive at Longsight Station this morning. Crimple went to fetch her from the train.' She walked to the window and pulled back the lace curtain. And it seemed to Danny that her whole body slumped. 'That's her,' she said.

*

Mr Saddleworth was already standing in the courtyard when Danny and Hetty went outside. Together, they watched the carriage pull to a standstill. Crimple climbed down from the driver's seat and turned to lift a large trunk from the roof. He staggered under its weight.

Immediately, the carriage door cracked open, and a woman emerged at the top of the steps. Augusta Carkettle didn't have to shout for her voice to carry.

'My good man, that luggage was handcrafted from calf-skin before you were even born. It has survived two wars, one rail accident and an ill-advised holiday in St Andrews. I have every hope that it will return unscathed from Manchester.' She paused. 'And if doesn't, I will have questions. Do you understand me?'

'Yes, ma'am.' Crimple nodded. The strain of holding the trunk was beginning to show. Danny was sure sweat was beading his brow.

'Good. Now lower the trunk carefully. Then come and help me down. Quickly, if you please!'

Crimple did as he was told, and Danny had his first good look at Hetty's Aunt Augusta. In reality, she wasn't a big woman; although neither was she particularly small. And it was just possible that, a long time ago, she might have been pretty because Danny could see traces of Hetty in her face. But now all that was left were clipped lines and sharp curls.

'Augusta.' Mr Saddleworth stepped towards her, arms outstretched. They fell back to his sides when Miss Carkettle's gloved hands remained folded. 'I hope you had a pleasant journey.'

'I suppose some people might complain, but I don't care to. I shall simply show my displeasure by never travelling with that train company again.' Miss Carkettle sniffed. 'Now where's my great-niece?'

Hetty had been standing in the front doorway, half hidden behind Danny. Reluctantly, she stepped forward then sank into a deep curtsy. 'Aunt Augusta. H–how wonderful of you to come.' And Danny almost turned around to check who was speaking because it didn't sound like Hetty.

'You've a crease in your skirt, child. And your hair needs a good brushing. But at least you haven't forgotten how to curtsy. Girls should always know how to curtsy. One never knows whom one might meet. The royal family get everywhere.'

Miss Carkettle bent slightly so that her cheek was only an inch or two from Hetty's face. Obediently, Hetty leant forward and kissed the pale, powdered skin.

'Yes, aunt. Thank you.'

Abruptly, Miss Carkettle straightened and stared at Danny. Her expression held all the warmth of a rain cloud. 'And who, may I ask, is *this*?'

'This is Danny . . . Daniel Jameson. He's my–my friend.'

Miss Carkettle's lips tightened; the black centres of her eyes shrank to narrow points. And it seemed to Danny that in that moment, she took note of every one of his differences – his brown skin, slow speech and lack of education. 'I see,' she said. And his heart sank.

Now he understood why Hetty was so upset. Miss Carkettle was not someone who would be easily charmed – or tricked. And he wondered how he could possibly keep his promise to Hetty.

'Well, young man, I've no doubt you are . . .' For a moment, Miss Carkettle seemed to struggle for the right word. '. . . *interesting* company. But I haven't seen my great-niece for several months so I'm sure you'll understand that this is a time for family. And *just* for family. Maybe you can arrange to see Henrietta in a few days?' A pause. 'Or better still, next week?'

It wasn't really a question. And Danny didn't argue. There would be no point. Instead, he waited until Miss Carkettle turned away before tugging Hetty's sleeve. 'I need to speak to you,' he hissed. 'On your own. It's important.'

Hetty darted a glance towards her aunt. Fortunately, she was now supervising Crimple and the removal of her remaining luggage from the carriage.

'I don't think there'll be a chance today.' Her teeth bit into her bottom lip. 'But maybe tomorrow? Aunt Augusta always goes to church on a Sunday. We could talk after the service. There'll be so many people around, she probably won't even notice . . . And Danny?'

The desperation in her voice would have persuaded Danny to agree to anything. He nodded to show he was listening.

'Please help me. I don't think I can bear two weeks on my own with Aunt Augusta.'

Chapter Ten

Danny lifted the bucket lid and the smell of raw chicken hit the back of his throat with a kick. It was Sunday, and for once he was not expected at the main gate to welcome visitors. Instead, he'd been given the job of feeding the big cats. The lions, tigers and leopards were kept in neighbouring pens a little distance from the other animals, and the fence around them was higher than the rest.

Raising the bucket, Danny stepped up to the railings and leant over. Below him, the lions were already gathering, strolling backwards and forwards with every expectation of being fed. He searched for his favourite, and within minutes, she'd padded into view.

Victoria was a beautiful creature – and she knew it. Thick fur rippled across her back like molten gold, before fading to white around her chest and stomach. Her dark eyes glittered under kohl-coloured lashes, and she moved the way water slipped around rocks, fluid and graceful with every sweep of her tail.

Danny grabbed a piece of chicken and threw it into her pen. 'Here!'

He watched as Victoria caught the meat between strong white teeth. And in two neat bites, it had disappeared. She swiped a long pink tongue around her jaws and waited for more.

Danny grinned. It was true that no one would ever be able to take Maharajah's place. Whatever happened, Maharajah would always come first in his affections. But over the last few weeks, he'd realized there were many other incredible creatures at Belle Vue.

Like Victoria.

And Emerald.

And Cleopatra.

And even Captain, the blue-faced mandrill who tumbled around the ape house like a clown. Danny had once spent an entire afternoon studying the monkey's bright features – the long red nose and yellow beard – marvelling that such a strange-looking animal could possibly be real. Then he'd slipped next door to see the camels, who were almost as peculiar but much less conceited.

He threw another piece of chicken into Victoria's pen then tipped the rest of the meat into the other cages. Almost immediately, growls rose up. The lions were competing for food. Usually Danny stayed until the last mouthful was gone but today he needed to get back.

He didn't want to miss the chance of speaking to Hetty. There were too many mysteries to solve. Too many questions without answers. Grabbing the empty bucket, he pulled the gate firmly shut.

At home, Danny changed quickly, peeling off his grubby work shirt and trousers, and tugging on his Sunday suit. Staring in the mirror, he pushed a cow's lick curl away from his forehead and knotted his tie. He looked very different from the street thief who'd first met Mr Jameson in Edinburgh. Now, there were some days when he didn't recognize himself at all.

In the hall, Mrs Jameson was fixing her bonnet in place with a long hat pin. She smiled when she saw him. 'I must say, Danny, I am pleased you want to go to church this morning. We need to show Reverend Threlfall we can be good neighbours. I'm sure he'll be less upset when he sees we want to be part of the parish.'

'Yes, ma'am.' Danny scuffed his boots against the hall floor. He doubted the vicar would ever change his mind, but just now he had other concerns. He needed to find a way to talk to Hetty alone. The direct approach seemed best.

'I saw Hetty yesterday. Her aunt had just arrived from Edinburgh. I wondered...' He hesitated. Asking for favours still felt uncomfortable, even after two months of living with the Jamesons. 'I wondered if we could invite them here . . . to tea? After the service?'

Mrs Jameson's eyes widened. 'Yes, well. That's very thoughtful of you, Danny. As a matter of fact, I've already sent a note asking them to call. I have to admit I'm curious to meet Hetty's aunt.'

She picked up her gloves from the hall table and pulled them on, fastening the buttons with quick, practised movements. 'Now, have you seen Mr Jameson? I told him to be here ten minutes ago. He knows we're to go to church.'

Danny shook his head, and Mrs Jameson frowned. 'Good heavens! I might have known. Well, we can't afford to wait any longer. Come along.' She swept through the front door in a bustle of skirts, and Danny followed.

St Mark's Church stood less than a stone's throw away from Belle Vue, just outside the main gate on Hyde Road. It was almost full when they arrived – and everyone turned to stare. Danny felt the glares heat the back of his neck as they marched down the aisle, but Mrs Jameson didn't seem to notice.

Halfway along, she settled into one of the hard wooden pews. Danny slid in next to her. He was relieved to see Hetty, just a few rows in front, sitting with her father and Miss Carkettle. Beyond them, in the choir stalls, Constance Threlfall caught his eye and smiled shyly.

'Welcome!' Reverend Threlfall's voice suddenly thundered through the church. He was standing in the high-raised pulpit, looking down on his congregation like a hawk eyeing a field of mice.

'Welcome, all of you, to the house of the Lord. And may I give a special welcome to the Lord Mayor of Manchester, Mr Harold Goadsby.' He nodded to a sharp-featured man in one of the side pews, a glittering chain of office hung around his neck. 'Sir, I'm delighted you accepted my invitation to attend today.'

Solemnly, Mr Goadsby nodded back, and the vicar's gaze continued around the congregation. 'But remember this . . . whoever you are, however high or low, you are all *sinners . . .*'

Danny shifted uncomfortably in his seat. He rarely went to church, and he hated sitting still. But if nothing else, perhaps the morning service might distract from the swirl of questions racing around his head.

Just where was Frank Scatcherd?

Still roaming free in Edinburgh? Or on his way to Manchester?

And could he have had anything to do with the shooting in the maze?

The idea carved a hole in Danny's stomach. Desperately, he tried to focus on something else but Reverend Threlfall's sermon was even duller than usual. So, he counted the panes of coloured glass on each of the altar windows. Forty-two. Then he traced the fall of a feather from the high beamed ceiling, all the way to the floor. For a little while, he even examined the back of Hetty's neck, willing her to turn around just so he could roll his eyes. But she kept staring straight ahead.

So, perhaps it was his need for a distraction that kick-started his imagination. Because halfway through the service, Danny was sure he heard a familiar sound coming from outside. A curious mixture of a rumble and a cackle, like someone trying to hold in laughter – and failing.

And then the noise came again. This time it was louder, far more difficult to ignore, and he wasn't the only one who heard it. In the pews, people were turning their heads and whispering. Only Reverend Threlfall appeared unaware. He was still shouting.

'*Behold, the Lord said you shall listen only unto me . . .*'

The rumble started for a third time, and now there could be no doubt. Danny knew that sound. He knew it very well indeed.

'I'll go.' He slipped from the pew before Mrs Jameson could stop him. Heads turned again, and curious stares followed his progress down the aisle.

And still Reverend Threlfall kept on talking. '*And to the wicked and unbelieving, let me give you this warning: you will be cast out, never to return . . .*'

Carefully, Danny prised open the back door and slid through the gap. Immediately, his mouth dropped loose. He'd been right. Standing just outside the porch was a twelve-foot elephant. Maharajah the Magnificent had come to church.

'Danny, there you are! Excellent!'

Mr Jameson's voice jarred Danny out of his daze. The menagerist was standing next to Maharajah; Crimple on his other side, holding the elephant harness as though the three of them attended Sunday service every week.

'I thought I'd bring Maharajah along to show him off. Let Threlfall and his flock get a taste of Belle Vue. Meet our star attraction.' Mr Jameson patted the top pocket of his waistcoat. 'And I've a treat for all the congregation. Free tickets for the show. I don't know why I didn't think of it sooner. Everyone loves fireworks. This will sort everythin'. Get things back to normal.'

'But—' Danny stopped. Behind him, the church doors had swung open, and parishioners began pouring out – a colourful tide of flowery hats, Sunday frocks and smart suits. Even Hetty had managed to tug her aunt outside. And right at the back, Danny was certain he could see the Lord Mayor, his gold chain glinting in the sun.

His heart sank. The service must have finished early. It had been too much to hope that Maharajah's presence would go unnoticed – and that he could persuade Mr Jameson to return home before trouble began.

But if Danny was worried, Maharajah seemed delighted with the new arrivals. He stomped forward, flapping his ears in welcome, a low rumble vibrating from his trunk. And for a moment, the flow of people paused. Then the woman wearing the largest hat began to scream. And scream. And scream. Only willpower stopped Danny from covering his ears.

'Can someone tell me what in the good Lord's name is happening here?' Reverend Threlfall was cutting through the crowd. His white vicar's robes made him easy to spot among the bright colours.

'Threlfall!' Beaming, Mr Jameson spread his arms wide. Most people would have thought he was greeting an old and dear friend. Only Danny knew differently.

'I'm here to deliver a personal invitation to you and your congregation. Come to Belle Vue and put all your worries to rest. And to prove it, let me introduce you to the biggest, most powerful animal in our menagerie. Maharajah the Magnificent!' Lightly, he patted Maharajah's side. 'He may look frightening but he's a gentle giant. Isn't that right, Danny?'

Danny had no time to reply. Before he could open his mouth, Maharajah reached across the heads of the crowd towards the screaming woman. Coiling his trunk, he grabbed her hat and began chewing through the brim. Danny winced as the screams grew louder. And the cries began to spread. On the other side of the churchyard, he could see Hetty trying not to laugh. Miss Carkettle looked shocked. While the Lord Mayor's face held no expression at all.

'Good heavens, Jameson! This is outrageous.' The vicar's voice had risen yet again but even he was struggling to make himself heard above the noise. 'How could you possibly think this was acceptable? Bringing an elephant to church? To the house of God? You're a madman!'

From the back of the crowd, Mrs Jameson hurried forward. She brushed past her husband – and Maharajah – and went straight to the vicar. 'I do apologize, Reverend Threlfall. I really don't know what to say. I'm sure my husband didn't mean to cause offence.'

'Oh no. I'm afraid it's far too late for apologies, Mrs Jameson.' A sudden breeze lifted the white robes away from the vicar's body like the wings of an avenging angel. 'This is no longer a dispute among neighbours. This is a war.'

Chapter Eleven

'What on earth were you playing at, James Jameson? I've never been so mortified in all my days. These people are our neighbours. And after the argument the other day! What were you thinking? You've made everything worse.'

'I thought it would help, me dove. Everyone loves Maharajah.'

They were returning home on foot; Danny, Mr Jameson and Crimple trailing in Mrs Jameson's wake down Belle Vue's main avenue. At their side, Maharajah swayed nonchalantly, but Danny recognized the mischief in his eyes. Gently, he stroked a palm across the deep grooves on his trunk.

'Everyone loves Maharajah? Are you quite sure of that, Jamie?' Mrs Jameson's voice had risen to a peak. 'What about Mr Snade and the other bankers? I don't imagine they're particularly fond of him. Not after being half drowned in the lake.'

Mr Jameson cleared his throat. 'Well, maybe not everyone. But Ethel May, you know as well as I do, it's the customers that matter. And every week, hundreds of 'em come here just to see Maharajah. So as long as the money keeps rollin' in, I reckon Snade will be happy. Profits – that's all he cares about.'

'Hmmph!' Mrs Jameson snorted. 'Well, after this morning, I don't imagine Reverend Threlfall or his parishioners will want to set foot inside Belle Vue, and to be frank, I shan't blame them.' Her mouth twitched. 'Maharajah's an elephant, Jamie. And you took him to church! He ate Mrs Smalley's hat. In front of the Lord Mayor!'

'The silly thing had flowers on it, Ethel May. Maharajah thought it was his dinner. Anyway, it was an ugly hat. And I reckon Mayor Goadsby thought so too.'

Danny sniggered. He turned it into a cough when Mrs Jameson glared at him. They walked a few steps further then she stopped, twisted on her heel and jabbed a finger at her husband. 'I don't know what I'm to do with you, Jamie. You promised me. No tomfoolery. No tricks; not this time. Just good honest hard work, you said.'

'And that's exactly what I'm doing, me pet. Workin' hard. Keepin' the investors happy. And tryin' to get that puffed-up vicar off our backs.'

Mrs Jameson opened her mouth but no sound came out.

Turning, she stalked off down the avenue at even greater speed. Danny and the others followed far more slowly.

They caught up with her a short distance from home. An open carriage was pulling to a standstill in the courtyard at the front of Belle Vue House. Mr Saddleworth climbed out then helped Hetty and Miss Carkettle down from their seats.

'Oh! They've arrived.' Mrs Jameson patted the coil of hair at the back of her neck, then fixed the tilt of her bonnet. 'And we would have been home to welcome them if we hadn't had to apologize to half the parish. This is your fault, Jamie.'

Mr Jameson looked at the carriage and scowled. 'Why did you invite them anyway, Ethel May? We're busy enough without havin' to entertain callers.'

'You know why. The Saddleworths are our friends and this is Miss Carkettle's first visit to Belle Vue. It's important to make a good impression – especially after the disaster this morning.' Mrs Jameson's face tightened. 'So, you behave yourself, Jamie. No mention of any grand plans or ridiculous notions. And get Crimple to take Maharajah back to the elephant house! He's caused enough trouble for today.'

She paused long enough to shake out her skirts then glided across the courtyard to greet the guests. 'Welcome! We're so pleased you were able to come. Do let's go inside, and I'll arrange for tea in the front parlour.'

*

Danny should have known the visit would not go well. All the signs were there. Right from the start, Mrs Jameson and Miss Carkettle settled at opposite ends of the parlour, stiff and straight-backed, like two carved wooden bookends.

'I'm delighted to finally meet you, Miss Carkettle. I'm sorry that we didn't manage to speak after the service this morning. I'm afraid we were a little . . . busy.'

'Yes.' Miss Carkettle's mouth was pursed so tightly that her lips barely moved. 'So I saw.'

The room fell into an awkward silence, and Danny almost wished he'd left with Mr Jameson and Mr Saddleworth while he'd had the chance. The two men had disappeared into the study – apparently to discuss the forthcoming trip to Paris, although Danny suspected it was simply an excuse to get away.

But Danny had stayed in the parlour. The entire aim of this visit was to get the chance to speak to Hetty alone. He just needed to find the right moment.

The tension eased a little when the maid came in, carrying a tray of the best china – a rose pattern with swirls of gold leaf on the handles. Mrs Jameson poured the tea before offering a cup to Aunt Augusta, and then taking one for herself. Neither one of them added sugar.

'And what do you think of life at Belle Vue, Miss Carkettle?'

'I must say I'm extremely glad to be here.'

Smiling, Mrs Jameson relaxed her shoulders slightly and took a sip of tea. 'I'm very happy to hear it.'

'Yes, indeed,' Miss Carkettle continued. 'I can't imagine the extent of the damage had I arrived any later. Henrietta is already half-wild. Why, I believe she spends most of her days wandering around the park with that boy you've taken in.' Danny stiffened. 'A little longer and there's no telling what might have happened. As it is, I will have my work cut out.'

'Aunt! Danny and I are not causing any trouble! We're only—'

'Henrietta, was I addressing you? No, I was not. And that's because this is a conversation between adults, not children. So, please do not interrupt.' Delicately, Miss Carkettle sipped her tea. 'As you see, there is much to be done.'

Mrs Jameson's spine had snapped straight. 'Let me make sure I understand you correctly – are you suggesting that Belle Vue is an improper home for your niece?'

'I'm not suggesting it, Mrs Jameson. I'm telling you. I was always against William bringing Henrietta to Manchester. And so far, I've seen nothing to change my mind.' Another sip. 'A zoological pleasure park is hardly the right environment in which to raise a young girl.'

Danny could see the muscles in Mrs Jameson's face tighten. Her cup and saucer met with a clatter; and drops of tea splashed on to the rug. 'I couldn't disagree more, Miss Carkettle. My parents began Belle Vue when it was no more than a vegetable garden. My brothers and I were raised here, and our childhood was extremely happy. This is a wonderful place to live.'

Carefully, Miss Carkettle lowered her teacup. The china didn't so much as rattle. 'Then I suppose we'll have to agree to disagree, Mrs Jameson.'

If possible, the silence that followed was even more awkward than it had been before. Hetty sat in the corner, biting her lip. Danny had never seen her look so frustrated. He wished he could help, but he didn't know how to.

Perhaps Mrs Jameson had also noticed because, after taking a deep breath, she tried again. 'You may not approve of zoological animals, Miss Carkettle, but you must have heard of our summer production? 'Prince Dandip and the Fight for Flamenca'? Everyone is so excited. Most of the staff are involved, as well as many local people and their families. It's certain to be a wonderful show.'

'So I'm told. And while I can't stop it from happening, I shall not be attending. No one should have fun on a Sunday. I'm just glad no member of my own family will be taking part.'

Hetty made an inarticulate sound but fortunately her aunt didn't hear. Someone was knocking on the Jamesons' front door, pounding so hard that the sound seemed to bounce along the hall.

Danny jumped to his feet. He didn't care who it was – this was the excuse he'd been waiting for. Staring at Hetty, he tilted his head towards the door, hoping she'd understand. Fortunately, it didn't take long. She slid from her chair.

'Aunt Augusta, why don't Danny and I see who's calling, while you get to know Mrs Jameson a little better. I'm sure you'll be much happier without us in the way. Then there'll be no risk of interruption.'

They were both out of the room before either woman could protest. In the hallway, Hetty grabbed Danny's arm. 'What did I tell you? She's even worse than she was before. You have to help me.'

'Of course, I will . . .' Danny paused. The knocking still hadn't stopped, and there was no sign of the Jamesons' maid. He sighed. 'Wait here. It's probably not important.'

But when he wrenched open the door, Tom Dalton was standing on the top step, twitching with impatience. 'About time! I need to speak to Mr Jameson. Is he in?'

'He's busy. If you've a message, give it to me.' Danny didn't care that he was being rude. He needed to talk to Hetty. Alone.

'Fine. Then you can be the one to tell him.' A sly expression crossed Tom's face. 'Tell him . . . tell him the lioness has disappeared.'

Danny's fingers tightened around the door frame. 'What do you mean?'

'Just what I said. The lioness – Victoria – has escaped. She's been gone at least two hours. Probably more. And from what I've heard, her cage door was left wide open.'

Chapter Twelve

'Danny, I want an honest answer. Did you leave that cage unlocked?' Mr Jameson sat behind his desk and stared across at Danny. The distance between them seemed far wider than usual.

'No, sir.'

'Are you certain?'

'Yes, sir.'

Silence. Mr Jameson leant forward and rested his fists on the desk. They were clenched tight. 'I'm goin' to give you one more chance to change your answer. Did you leave the lion enclosure open?'

The injustice of it blocked Danny's throat. It was true that he had finished his jobs quickly, rushing to be on time to see Hetty at church. But that didn't mean he'd been careless. He knew he hadn't left Victoria's cage unlocked. He *knew* it.

'NO!' It was almost a shout.

'Fine! I hear you.'

Abruptly, Mr Jameson pushed back his chair and walked to the window. A knock on the door broke the silence. It was Hetty's father.

'William! Any news?'

Mr Saddleworth shook his head. 'Nothing yet. I've got as many staff as I can spare out searching for her. And the message has gone out across Belle Vue. But if we're not careful, we'll have a panic on our hands. Losing a lioness is a far more serious problem than losing an emu.'

'Yes. You don't have to tell me.' Mr Jameson scowled, and shot a narrowed glance at Danny. 'I've been tryin' to find out how it happened.'

Mr Saddleworth rubbed the back of his neck. 'Does it matter, James? Surely, the important job is to find the lioness. Let's leave who was to blame until after we get her back.'

'Maybe you're right. But this is the second animal in only a few days that's managed to escape.' This time, Mr Jameson's gaze moved to Danny and stayed there. 'I have to know if it was an accident or if someone's makin' mischief for Belle Vue. Do you understand what I'm sayin', lad? Cos I'd rather have the truth now, than later.'

'I told you . . . it wasn't me!' Danny didn't know how many times he'd have to say it before he was believed. But like an annoying fly, his conscience buzzed at him. 'But . . .'

'But what? Come on, lad. If you have somethin' to say, just say it!'

He took a breath. 'But . . . I don't think Emerald's escape was an accident.'

'Why not?'

'I found the old lock from her cage. I think someone hammered it. That's why she was able to get out.'

Frowning, Mr Jameson walked around from behind the desk. 'And why didn't you tell me this before?'

'I meant to, but I didn't . . . I thought . . .' Danny trailed off. How could he explain that he'd been so full of anger and resentment that he'd deliberately said nothing? Now the reasons sounded stupid and petty.

'So where is this lock now?'

Danny swallowed. Already he could feel his throat closing up. 'At the bottom of the pond. In the Italian gardens . . . sir.'

Mr Jameson let out a snort. 'Well, that's no good to me. Without proof, I've only your word for it. And let me tell you, at the moment your word's not worth a great deal.' He stared at Danny. 'So, is there anythin' else you're hidin' from me?'

Briefly, Danny thought about last night's shooting, and about the stranger who had come to his rescue. 'No, sir,' he said. 'Nothing.'

'Go on then. Get out and make yourself useful. But remember you're not to leave the park on your own. Not without someone with you. Not with Frank Scatcherd roamin' loose. And this time you make sure to do as I say. Understood?'

'Yes, sir.'

Danny slipped from the room but he didn't leave the house. Instead, he rested his head against the wall outside the study and waited. It didn't take long.

'You heard him. He says he didn't do it.' Despite the muffled effect of the closed door, the frustration in Mr Jameson's voice was obvious.

'And you believe him?'

Danny held his breath.

A sigh. 'I don't know. The head keeper swears Danny was the last person in that enclosure. It was his turn to feed the big cats. No one else went in there afterwards, he says. And there's no sign that the gate was forced.' A pause. 'So, who else could it be?'

Footsteps moved across the floor. Now Mr Saddleworth sounded closer. 'Look James, even if Danny did leave the cage unlocked, I can't believe he did it on purpose. He's a good lad. You know that.'

'A week ago, I'd have said the same. I thought he was settlin' into Belle Vue. Makin' his home here with Ethel May and me. But in the last few days, somethin's been off. And I'm sure he's hidin' things from us. Of course, this news about Frank Scatcherd doesn't help. Ethel May's worryin' herself sick.'

Mr Saddleworth's exclamation was loud enough to be heard on the other side of the house. 'There you are, then!

Danny's not hiding anything from you. He's just worried about Scatcherd escaping. Lord knows, he's got every reason.' A floorboard creaked as though he'd taken a sudden step forward.

'Listen, James. Being a father isn't easy. I struggle with it myself. Hetty thinks I'm too protective, and Augusta doesn't think I'm protective enough. You can never get it right all the time. The important point is to keep trying.'

This time Mr Jameson's sigh was much deeper. 'Maybe, William. You've a lot more experience at parentin' than me. But to be honest, I'm wonderin' if me and Ethel May . . . well, maybe we made a mistake. Bringing him here, I mean . . .'

Danny felt the words like a punch. They seemed to land somewhere in the centre of his chest, forcing the air from his lungs. Blindly, he pushed himself away from the wall and stumbled out of the house. He didn't know where he was going, only that he needed to get away.

How had this happened? How – in just a handful of days – had his safe, comfortable life at Belle Vue fallen apart?

Danny was at the gate of the elephant enclosure before he realized how far he'd travelled. Shocked, he looked around. He didn't remember choosing this path. Or walking this far.

He opened the gate and stared across the paddock. Maharajah's outline was clearly visible on the far side. Danny began to run, stumbling in his haste. Suddenly,

Maharajah raised his head, flapped his great ears and lumbered forward.

They met somewhere in the middle. And Danny laid his hand against the warm, rough skin, then rested his cheek in the spot next to it. He took a deep breath. And another.

His mind was whirring like the innards of a clock, every cog and wheel spinning in different directions. But here, like this, with Maharajah's warmth around him, the chaotic whirling seemed to slow. And stop. Gradually, he eased back. Above him, gold eyes glittered, bright as candle flames. They stood watching each other for a moment. Then Maharajah turned and ambled towards the pond.

Danny watched him go.

He slid down on to the grass, lay on the ground and stared into the sky. It seemed to him that in the last few days, nothing had gone right. From the moment he'd humiliated Mr Snade and the other investors at the lakeside, he'd been in trouble. Later that same day, Emerald had escaped – very probably helped by someone who'd hammered through the lock on her pen.

Then two nights ago, he'd narrowly missed being shot at in the maze, and just when he was about to blurt out the full story, Constable Oversby had brought news of Scatcherd's escape. But if those weren't disastrous enough, Victoria the lioness had vanished from her cage – and Danny was the last person to have seen her.

Someone was causing trouble at Belle Vue, pulling strings with the expertise of a puppetmaster. But even worse, whoever was responsible had left Danny in the centre of the storm.

The thought carved a hollow in his stomach.

'Hello? Hello there!'

Danny lifted his head, shading his eyes against the brightness. A man stood looking down at him, the sunlight cast his face in shadow. But even though his features weren't clear, there was something about him that was oddly familiar.

'I thought it was you.' The man hesitated. And then, in just a handful of words, Danny's life changed for ever. 'I want to introduce myself . . . I'm your father.'

Chapter Thirteen

Danny sat up. His head felt dizzy. The blood pounded through his temples. He pressed his palms against his eyes until the lids prickled. Then he opened them again.

The man was still there.

Danny scrambled away, crawling backwards along the grass like an upturned crab, arms and legs splayed out in all directions. The stranger didn't move. Danny stopped. Across the short distance, they watched each other warily.

'I'm sorry. I should have realized it would be a shock. It was foolish of me to blurt it out like that. But after seeing you a few nights ago, I just . . . I just couldn't wait.'

And then Danny realized something – he knew this man. It was the stranger who'd helped him in the maze. Although, it wasn't his face that Danny recognized; it was his voice. So polished. So perfect. And so precise.

'You see, I've been looking for you for some time. And I meant to do this carefully. But then there were those gunshots, and I had to do something. Because otherwise . . .' He let the thought trail off, before swallowing visibly. 'Well? Won't you say something? Anything at all?'

Danny lifted his chin but he stayed silent.

Because he knew this was a trick. A lie. A joke.

It had to be.

He looked nothing like this man. They didn't share a single feature in common. While Danny's skin was bronze-brown – just a few shades lighter than his dark hair – the stranger was pale, lightly freckled and pink-cheeked, the perfect complement to his sandy curls and hazel eyes.

No. Danny was certain. This stranger could not possibly be his father. He would have laughed if he hadn't been so angry. Instead, he bit down on his lip until he tasted blood.

'I know it's hard to believe. But it's true. I'm only sorry it's taken so long to find you.' The man stepped forward, almost as though he couldn't restrain himself. Quickly, Danny scrambled back, and the man stopped. 'Maybe I should have waited. For a better moment.'

Distractedly, the stranger lifted his hat and combed a hand through his hair. A sandy curl flopped down on to his forehead. He pushed it away but the curl refused to stay. And suddenly, the safe, solid ground underneath Danny disappeared.

Because he recognized that gesture. Every morning, in

front of the mirror in his room, he did exactly the same. And every morning, a cow's lick curl fell stubbornly back into the centre of his forehead.

He trembled. And he remembered the first time he'd climbed up on to Maharajah's back – the dip of his stomach as he'd risen upwards and the giddy, rocking motion that had followed. This felt exactly the same.

'Look. I'll go now and give you time to think. But all I ask is that you do the same for me. Give me some time . . . to get to know you. And for you to get to know me.'

The stranger paused but if he was expecting a response he was disappointed. Because a thousand thoughts were beating in Danny's brain and not one of them made enough sense to voice aloud.

'I'm staying at the Longsight Hotel on Redgate Lane. When you're ready to talk, come to me there. Ask for Larkin. Charles Larkin. I'll wait for you. It doesn't matter how long it takes, I'll wait.'

Chapter Fourteen

Two days later there was still no sign of the lioness; Frank Scatcherd had still not been recaptured; and Danny had still not visited the Longsight Hotel.

For the past forty-eight hours, it was as though he'd been living in a fog. A fog that dulled everything except for the constant questions in his head.

Conversations had gone on around him, and yet he hadn't heard any of them. People had talked to him and he'd answered back, but he didn't remember what they'd said. Decisions were made, but he couldn't have explained what they were.

He was distantly aware that the hunt for Victoria had moved away from Belle Vue, and on to the neighbouring streets. There had been no news, despite a five-shilling reward offered by Mr Jameson. And the newspaper headlines were growing increasingly excited.

KILLER LION ON THE LOOSE! ANOTHER BEAST ESCAPES BELLE VUE MANCHESTER'S MENAGERIE: THE MOST DANGEROUS ZOO IN ENGLAND!

Once, any type of publicity would have delighted Mr Jameson – good or bad. He'd always said that being talked about was better than not being talked about at all. But not this time. These news stories only seemed to make him angrier, and even Mrs Jameson hadn't been able to lift his spirits. Eventually, after her husband had lashed out once too often, she'd taken Danny to one side. It was one of the few conversations he did remember.

'Don't let it worry you, Danny. He'll be fine in a few days, I promise. It's just that . . .' She'd hesitated. 'Well . . . Mr Snade and the other men who've put money into Belle Vue are a little worried . . . about all the stories. But once Victoria's back home, everything will be back to normal. You'll see.'

Danny had nodded to show he'd understood but, compared to what the stranger had told him, nothing else had seemed important.

I'm your father . . . he'd said. *I'm your father . . .*

Was it true?

Danny didn't know.

But he kept remembering how Larkin had pushed back the cow's lick curl. And he couldn't help wondering – what if it was true? What if by some curious twist of fortune, Charles Larkin had met Danny's mother years ago in Edinburgh. What if they'd had a child together? A boy? And what if that boy was him?

'Danny? DANNY!'

His head snapped up. He was supposed to be sweeping the courtyard at the front of Belle Vue House, but he'd not got very far along the path. And now Mr Jameson was scowling down at him from the front step.

'What's the matter with you, lad? Weren't you listenin'? I asked you to take a message. Go to the firework factory. Tell George Dalton the final load of gunpowder he wanted has arrived. The order's ready to be picked up.'

'Yes, sir.' Danny hesitated. Finally, this was his chance to tell Mr Jameson about Charles Larkin. But before he could open his mouth, Mr Jameson's scowl deepened.

'And before you ask, this doesn't mean I want you messin' around at the factory and gettin' into trouble. It's too dangerous. I've just got no one left to send. So, you give Dalton that message and then you come straight back here. Understood?'

Danny took a deep breath and nodded. 'Yes, sir.'

The firework factory was nothing more than a long shed that over the years had expanded with no particular system or method. Danny had only been inside once before, during his first week at Belle Vue when Mr Jameson had given him a tour of the entire park.

He didn't remember much about it. The factory had simply been one fascinating place among many. Everything had seemed so incredible then; from the steam-driven paddle boats on the lake, to the glass hothouses filled with lemon trees. And that was even before he'd seen the menagerie.

No one answered when Danny knocked on the factory door. So he turned the handle and gave it a slight push. The hinges creaked but the door swung open easily enough.

'Hello!' he shouted. Silence.

Curiously, he stepped inside. Shelves lined the main room, each stuffed with supplies. Jars of coloured powders and coils of string jostled for space alongside trays of cardboard casings and wooden pegs used for staking out the fireworks. And piled floor to ceiling, against the long wall at the far end, were barrels and barrels of what Danny knew must be gunpowder. He didn't go any nearer.

Instead, he examined the long workbench standing in the centre. Several small brass bowls littered the surface, and a pair of leather gloves lay abandoned on a high stool. And most curiously of all, leaning at the back, was an outline of Queen Victoria's face pinned on to a large wooden board.

Suddenly, he heard the rattle of a curtain being pulled back, and George Dalton emerged from one of the alcoves, his brows drawn into an angry line. Instinctively, Danny took a step backwards. Dalton was head of the firework factory but he was also Tom's grandfather, and Danny had never been quite sure whether he was a friend or an enemy.

'What you doin' here, lad? No one's allowed in the factory without my permission.' Dalton's brows lowered into an angry line.

'I–I've a message, sir. From Mr Jameson. He says the rest of the gunpowder's arrived. It's ready to be picked up.'

'Oh . . . well, good. That'll be the last of the barrels for the show. You can tell him I'll get it sorted. Soon as I can.'

Mr Dalton's words were obviously meant as a dismissal, but Danny didn't move. Instead, he flicked another glance around the room. And with sudden vivid clarity, he remembered the explosions. The whizz and hum and whistle of the rockets. The streaks of colour. It seemed extraordinary that all that beauty could be created in this small, dark space.

'You interested in fireworks, boy?' Mr Dalton was studying him carefully, no longer looking quite so annoyed.

'Maybe.' Danny shrugged. But the truth was he was interested in anything that would distract him from thinking about Charles Larkin. Or from making a decision about going to the Longsight Hotel. He hadn't been able to shake either thought from his head, however much he tried.

'Well, if I remember rightly Mr Jameson weren't too keen on you learnin' about pyrotechnics. Told me he reckoned it's too dangerous.'

'But if I learn then it won't be dangerous, will it?'

Unexpectedly, Mr Dalton let out a bark of laughter. 'You've got a point there, lad.' He rubbed a gloved hand down the grey curls of his beard and narrowed his eyes.

'Well, I suppose I could teach you a few things. But it'd have to be just between you and me.'

Reaching up, he lifted one of the boxes from the highest shelf and opened the lid. Inside were rows of fireworks wrapped in scarlet paper. And Danny wondered if these were the new Red Fire Peony rockets that Tom had boasted about.

'So here's the most important lesson of all: you can't be brave with fireworks. And you can't be stupid. What you need is the right amount of fear.'

Danny frowned. He didn't have any idea what Dalton meant. He might as well have spoken in Chinese for all the sense he made. But the pyrotechnist only smiled at his confusion.

'Imagine being on a window ledge, high above the ground. One wrong step – one foolish move – and you'd go plummetin' right the way down. But if you're careful and if you're clever, you could climb further up. Right up to the rooftop so all you see are stars.' He held Danny's gaze. 'Well, that's pyrotechnics.'

It was an oddly poetic choice of words, Danny thought, particularly coming from a man who dealt in the practicalities of science every day. But it was obvious that, if nothing else, George Dalton was passionate about his work.

'So this is how it happens. And don't imagine I'll be repeatin' this again. You listen and you listen well.' Delicately, he picked one of the red rockets from the firework box and cradled it with the same care as a mother would hold her baby.

'We light a fuse. The fuse ignites the gunpowder. The gunpowder sends the firework shell shootin' in the air. The fuse keeps on burnin' as the shell goes up.' He lifted the rocket higher and trailed his fingers down the string. 'The longer the fuse, the higher the firework goes. Then the shell explodes and the stars inside burn, makin' all those pretty sparks that everyone loves so much.'

In his head, Danny saw the beauty of the night sky above Belle Vue once again – the glittering rainbow of flickers and flashes and flares. 'What about the colours?' he said.

'That's all to do with the mix of powders.' Dalton pointed to the shelves. Glass bottles stood in rows, as smart as soldiers, each marked with a neat label. 'Blue stars come from copper. Red from lithium or strontium. And sodium makes anythin' from yellow to gold.'

'Are they dangerous? The powders?'

'Not if you're careful. And you know what you're doin'. But it's not them you should be worried about when you're dealin' with fireworks. It's gunpowder.'

He pulled off one of the leather gloves and held up his hand. Danny sucked in a breath. Scars pitted the pyrotechnist's skin and his smallest finger was missing, right down to the second knuckle. It was difficult to look away. 'Too much gunpowder and not enough care. That's how I found myself like this. And there's not a day goes by when I don't regret it.'

'Grandpa!'

They both turned. Tom was standing in the doorway, jaw set like stone.

'Tommy! I've been wonderin' where you'd got to.' Carefully, Mr Dalton returned the firework to its box then closed the lid. 'Have they caught that lioness yet? Victoria – wasn't it?'

'No. There's still no sign.' Scowling, Tom jerked his chin in Danny's direction. 'What's he doing here?'

'Learnin'.' Dalton pushed the box back on to the shelf and placed the leather gloves in the space next to it. 'The show's only a few days away. And we've a lot to do. It might help to have another pair of hands.'

'No. Not him. Not in here.' Tom shook his head violently. 'There's enough gunpowder in here to blow up the whole island! If he messes up, he could cause big trouble. And he's already done enough damage.'

'That's not fair! I haven't—'

In his frustration, Danny flung his arms wide. Almost immediately, there was a loud clatter. He turned. Queen Victoria's sihouette lay in pieces on the floor. The regal profile that had been so carefully pinned on to the wooden board, was now twisted and broken.

'What in heaven's name do you think you doin', boy?' Dalton stared down at the splintered frame. 'That was for the finale of the show. Her Majesty's face lit up against the sky in coloured rockets. Mr Jameson ordered it specially.'

'There. Didn't I tell you?' Tom was almost spitting with

rage. 'He's a clumsy halfwit. He can't be trusted around fire-works. Around gunpowder! Around anything!'

'It—it was an accident! I don't know how it happened. I . . . I didn't touch it.'

But Danny's stuttered protest was ignored.

'Maybe Tom's right.' Dalton leant forward and rested his hands on the workbench. The burnt skin puckered around his fingers. 'Maybe this isn't the place for you. It's too dangerous – just like Mr Jameson said. I reckon you're better off stayin' at home. Forget everythin' you saw here.'

Chapter Fifteen

'I think we've found her, Gov.'

Crimple stood in the hallway. Rain had been falling for the last hour, and in his excitement, he'd forgotten to shake the damp from his clothes. Water dripped steadily on to the floor. 'Victoria, I mean. I reckon it's her.'

'Thank the good Lord. Where is she?' Mr Jameson was already pulling on an overcoat. Hastily, Danny grabbed a lantern from a hook by the door and slipped into his boots.

'In the Frog and Bucket, Gov. Down on Cornwall Street.'

'She's in a public house!'

'Yes, Gov. In the cellar . . . so the landlord reckons.'

Mr Jameson frowned. 'How on earth did she get in there? And why in the blue blazes didn't we find her sooner?'

Crimple looked uncomfortable. He opened his mouth and closed it again. Another raindrop fell from his nose. When he finally spoke, his words crawled out reluctantly. 'Smarsden . . . the landlord . . . he's always complainin' about animals gettin' on to his property. Normally, there's nothin' to it. But it looks as if he might be right this time. A couple of his customers reckon they saw her too.'

Mr Jameson scooped up his hat. He looked about as pleased as a wet cat. 'Danny, go and fetch Mr Saddleworth. Tell him we're off to the pub, but there won't be any drinkin' tonight. We have to catch ourselves a lioness.'

Danny dipped his head and turned to leave, then he stopped. He had a feeling that if he didn't ask, the invitation was unlikely to be offered. And he didn't want to stay in his room, stewing in his own thoughts.

He was still angry about being thrown out of the fire-work factory – but far more importantly, he didn't know what to do about Larkin. Should he forget they'd even met? Or find out more? The indecision was giving him a headache. He needed a distraction, and catching a lioness seemed as good as any.

'Can I come too, sir? I'd like to help.'

For several moments, Mr Jameson stared at him. But at last, he nodded curtly. 'Very well. But you're to do exactly as you're told. And stay close!'

Alf Smarsden was a narrow, mean-shaped man who looked like he didn't enjoy food. Or drink. Or much of anything else. He was as far away from Danny's idea of a pub landlord as a laundry woman was from the Queen.

He greeted them at the door with a scowl before leading them through the pub's smoky taproom. 'I told you, the animal was round here. But no one listened. I might as well have been talkin' to myself.'

'Well, we've had to be careful, Mr Smarsden. People's imaginations appear to have been running wild these last few days. There's been sightings of Victoria all over the place. And I believe a week ago, you complained about an escaped panther.' Deliberately, Mr Saddleworth paused, eyes narrowed. 'Didn't she turn out to be a cat?'

Smarsden flushed. 'Yes . . . well, I'm not apologizin' for that. It's an easy mistake to make in the dark. But let me tell you, there's no doubt about it tonight. Two of my regulars saw your animal get in through the back door. Headed right down the cellar stairs, quick as a wink, they said. They're still shaking now. I've had to give them a free pint, just to stop their bellyachin'.'

His gaze flicked towards Mr Jameson and lingered on his silk waistcoat and gold buttons. 'So, I'll be expectin' payment for that. And for anything else your animal damages while she's here. I'm not going to be out of pocket because of your carelessness. And I reckon that five-shilling reward is mine.'

'Don't worry. I'll pay you everythin' you're owed,' Mr Jameson snapped. 'Now tell us how to get to your cellar.'

'Through the kitchen – there's a door on the far wall

that opens on to the stairs.' Smarsden gestured towards the back of the pub. 'But don't expect any more help from me. I'm busy enough tonight as it is, and now my pot boy's disappeared. Dirty glasses all over the place and no one here to wash 'em.' He stomped off towards the taproom without another word.

In the kitchen, Mr Saddleworth pushed open the cellar door but it moved less than a finger's length before stopping. The gap was just big enough to release a pocket of damp air, along with a low rumbling growl. The noise sent prickles sparking along Danny's spine.

'That certainly sounds like Victoria.' Mr Saddleworth shoved at the door again with his shoulder. 'But I can't open this any wider. Something seems to have fallen against the other side.'

'Here, let me have a go.'

But even after several attempts, Mr Jameson could do no better. He drew back. And abruptly, a choked noise rose up from the depths of the cellar; more like a human whimper than an animal sound. 'What on earth was that?' Kneeling, he put his ear to the floorboards. Another muffled sob leaked from below. 'Good Lord, I reckon someone's down there with her!'

Mr Saddleworth nodded, his expression grim. 'I think you're right, James. In fact, my guess is we've just found Smarsden's missing pot boy. Let's hope for all our sakes the child's unharmed.'

Danny's mouth dried and he offered up a silent prayer.

Victoria might be sleek and beautiful but she was also clever and unpredictable. Even her keepers dared not get too close.

'So how in the blue blazes are we goin' to get her out?' Mr Jameson had found a cigar in his jacket and was puffing on it furiously.

'Well, we can't break open the door. There's no telling how Victoria might react to all that noise. And I don't want to risk her panicking – not if the boy's down there. We'll have to think of another way.'

A spark of an idea flickered into Danny's head, and he wondered if for once, his past might prove useful, rather than an embarrassment. Stumbling over the words, he spoke quickly. 'There must be a coal hole . . . going into the cellar. If we found it . . . we . . . we'd be able to see inside. See what's happening.'

For a moment, there was silence, then Mr Saddleworth's eyes narrowed thoughtfully

'Good plan, Danny. It's worth a look. And we've certainly no better ideas. Let's go.'

They found the coal hole in the alley running alongside the Frog and Bucket. It was hidden by a row of beer barrels, and covered by a round, metal lid. Set into the floor, the hole was just wide enough for a coalman to tip his sack directly into the cellar. It meant tradesmen didn't have to tread dust and dirt through the public house when making deliveries.

Carefully, Danny slid his fingers into the grooves around

the lid and heaved. The cover came off with an ease that suggested it was well used. Immediately, Mr Saddleworth gestured for silence.

'Listen! Can you hear that?' The soft sobbing sounded louder now that the coal hole was open. 'It has to be Smarsden's boy.'

'Well, I can't see him.' Mr Jameson had crouched on the ground and was peering into the cellar. 'The openin's too small. But there's a light comin' from somewhere. Maybe Smarsden left a lantern burnin".'

'I could look.' Danny swallowed. 'I can get through the hole . . . see—see what's happening.'

'Are you sure? It looks narrow, even for you.'

'No, I can do it.' He hesitated. 'I've done it before.'

It had been back when Danny was living in Edinburgh with Mr and Mrs Dilworth. He'd been much smaller then – maybe only five or six – with no memory of how he came to be in their care. One day, they'd sneaked him into the garden of a grand house. He'd been told to squeeze down the coal hole, creep through the cellar and unlock the kitchen door. The plan must have worked. Because Danny remembered how there'd been enough food and drink to live comfortably for weeks.

Above Danny's head, the two men exchanged glances. 'I see,' Mr Saddleworth said at last. 'Very well, you have a go. But be careful. Don't drop down. Just slide inside as far as you can get, and then tell us exactly what you see. We'll hold you up.'

Cautiously, Danny knelt on the ground directly in front of the coal hole then he rolled his shoulders inwards until his arms curled into his chest. The width of his body almost halved. He eased his head through the opening and wriggled so the upper half of his body slipped inside. It was uncomfortable but not painful.

Slowly, his eyes adjusted to the dim light. From this position, he had a bird's-eye view of the entire cellar. And now it was just possible to see Victoria's sleek shape prowling below him. A continuous snarl rumbled from her chest but the soft pads of her paws made no sound on the floor. If she had heard Danny, she didn't bother raising her head. She was too busy examining the small figure standing frozen in the corner.

The boy was young, probably a few years younger than Danny. Pale and terrified, he was breathing in short, chattering bursts. And mixed with the damp of the cellar was a sour, acidic scent. Danny recognized it immediately.

It was the smell of fear.

Carefully, Danny slithered backwards, keeping his shoulders hunched. Even so, it seemed more difficult to ease out than it had been to wriggle in. Suddenly, he felt hands pulling from behind, and a forceful tug on his belt finally jerked him free. Sitting at the edge of the hole, he took in a gulp of air.

'Well?' Mr Jameson looked anxious.

Danny tried to order his thoughts. 'The cellar is big. And square. The steps from the kitchen go down into the far corner. And Victoria is at the bottom. Opposite her are a stack of beer barrels.' He swallowed. His tongue felt as if he'd used it to clean a grate. 'The boy's in that corner. Facing Victoria. He looks . . . he looks scared. But he's not hurt.'

Mr Jameson released a breath. 'Thank the good Lord!' 'Anything else?'

'There's a length of wood leaning against the door. Maybe a handle from a broom. Or a spade. I'm not sure. But that's what's blocking the way.'

Mr Saddleworth looked thoughtful. He opened his medicine bag and began sorting through the bottles of potions and tonics, lifting up each one to examine the label.

'We need a distraction. Something that'll draw Victoria's attention away from the boy. Meat would be best . . . and I've laudanum somewhere. A drop or two in the food will send her to sleep. It won't be quick but once she's unconscious, we've a chance of getting them both out safely.'

Mr Jameson waved his cigar at Danny. 'Go and ask Smarsden for some meat, lad. Tell him we need something tasty enough to tempt a lioness.' He breathed out another cloud of smoke. 'And tell him I'll pay!'

In the kitchen, Smarsden handed over a side of beef. Reluctantly. Even after Danny told him why it was needed. He seemed less worried about his pot boy, and far more concerned about being out of pocket.

'Make no mistake – I'll be addin' this to your bill.' He tied a piece of old newspaper around the meat before handing it over. 'And if there's anythin left, I want it back. Food's not cheap.'

It took Mr Saddleworth only a few seconds to drug the meat. The drops soaked into the beef quickly, and Danny wrapped the paper back round, before re-tying the string.

'Drop it as near as you can to her. She should take the bait. And then all we can do is wait.'

Danny squeezed through the coal hole in the same way he'd done before, with Mr Saddleworth holding on to his legs for support. Only this time, with the package clutched to his chest, it was a great deal more awkward. He managed by pushing his shoulders even tighter together and wriggling a little harder. Once his head and arms were inside, he let the meat drop to the floor.

It landed just behind Victoria's back paws but she didn't even turn to look. Her eyes remained firmly fixed on the boy. A sleek, clever cat toying with a timid mouse, Danny thought.

Suddenly, a soft sob bounced around the cellar. The boy had begun crying again but he was trying to do it quietly. And just as quickly a memory flickered into Danny's head. A memory from a time when he'd been small and trapped and alone; a time when no one had come for him. Not even the Dilworths.

Without giving himself a chance to change his mind, Danny twisted sharply. The sudden movement jerked his legs from Mr Saddleworth's grip. Unfortunately, now there was nothing to support him but air. And Danny had only just enough time to tuck his head into his chest, before he fell forward. He landed on his back with a thud, and a cloud of coal dust puffed up from the floor.

'What in the bloomin' heck are you doing, lad? You come back here! You come back here right now!'

Mr Jameson's angry shout echoed around the cellar, but Danny scrambled to his feet and ignored it. Abruptly, Victoria turned. Her cold, clear gaze was very different from the warm welcome of Maharajah's eyes. And in the dim light of the lantern, she looked to be made from faded gilt. Danny wondered if she recognized him. And whether if she did, it would make any difference at all.

Moving carefully, he curled the toe of one boot under the beef and gave a firm kick. The parcel skidded across the floor and stopped, right next to Victoria's front paws. Slowly, she bent her neck and sniffed. Then, with a speed that showed her hunger, she sank her teeth into the meat until the paper turned pink.

'Run!' Danny shouted. 'RUN!'

But the boy didn't move. He stood frozen, more ice than flesh and blood. And in two quick steps Danny was at his side.

'Come on!' Blankly, the boy turned his head and blinked, his eyes red-rimmed from crying. Danny grabbed his sleeve and tugged. Hard. 'You have to follow me. Now!'

The boy blinked again but this time, he jerked into motion. They ran to the stairs. At the top, Danny pushed away the wooden pole, and yanked the door open. He dived through the gap and pulled the boy after him. Beneath them, Victoria let out a roar.

Chapter Sixteen

'What in the blue blazes did you think you were doin', lad?' Mr Jameson's fury was painted across his face. Danny didn't think there was an inch of his skin that wasn't purple. 'That was the most stupid ... the most foolhardy ... the most reckless thing, I've seen in my entire life. You could have broken your neck!'

Danny bristled. They were standing outside the Frog and Bucket waiting for Mr Saddleworth to finish examining Victoria. A cart stood ready to take her back to Belle Vue. But despite the success of the rescue, it hadn't taken long for Mr Jameson to start shouting.

'Did you even know what you were doin'? Well, did you? Cos it sure didn't look like it!' He puffed frantically on his cigar. And Danny's chest tightened. It seemed everything he did was wrong. Even though for weeks, he'd tried to be exactly what Mr Jameson wanted. Polite. Hard-working. Trustworthy. Now he wondered why he'd bothered trying. Because in the last few days, he'd heard nothing but criticism and disapproval. Maybe he would be better off trying to find Larkin at the Longsight Hotel. Maybe he'd be welcome there. Anything had to be better than this.

'. . . and don't you remember what I told you? You're to keep safe. Not go about, puttin' yourself in stupid—'

'James!' Mr Saddleworth had returned from examining Victoria. Now he moved to stand between them. 'Remember that without Danny, everything could have turned out very differently. Victoria is fine – a little thin perhaps, but there's no sign of any injury. And, more importantly, Smarsden's boy is unharmed. His mother couldn't have been more grateful. She thinks Danny's a hero.'

It was embarrassingly true. After emerging from the cellar, the boy had been reunited with his mother and there had been more tears, as well as a hug for Danny. Until at last, Mr Jameson had brought out his wallet, and passed out enough coins for all the tears to turn to smiles. Even Alf Smarsden had looked pleased.

Mr Jameson puffed on the cigar again, although now it was little more than a stub between his fingers. 'Yes. I suppose you're right, William. I've just . . . well I've a lot on my mind.' He paused to blow out a cloud of smoke. 'You did well, Danny. Gettin' them both out of there safely . . . although you might have warned us before you jumped. Scared the life out of me, I can tell you.'

It wasn't the enthusiastic thank you that Danny had wished for, but for the first time in days, Mr Jameson wasn't shouting or scowling at him. And for that, he supposed he should be grateful. So once again, he pushed Larkin to the back of his mind. And let go of the idea of visiting the Longsight Hotel.

Unfortunately, Mr Jameson's good humour didn't last for long.

The shouts were the first warning of trouble. Danny heard them as soon as their carriage drew near the Hyde Road gate, less than an hour later.

'Belle Vue must close!'

'Shut the zoo now.'

A cluster of people stood by the entrance, brandishing banners and indignation. It wasn't a big group, but it was noisy, and right at the front was the Reverend Eustace Threlfall.

The protest was already attracting attention. A night coachman had pulled his omnibus to a standstill on the opposite side of the road – and his passengers were leaning out of the windows to gawk. The shouts only got louder.

'Manchester's menagerie must go!'

'Say no to Belle Vue!'

With a muttered curse, Mr Jameson stopped the carriage and marched across the street. Danny would have liked to follow but Mr Saddleworth held him back. 'No, Danny. Let him handle this.'

So instead, they sat and watched as Mr Jameson stalked towards the protesters. The vicar stepped forward and raised a hand. Abruptly, the angry chanting stopped. The tension thickened.

'Reverend. What's goin' on here?'

'I would think it's obvious, Jameson. We're protesting because you've refused to listen.'

'I'm always happy to listen, but my answer will stay the same. I'm not closin' the park on Sundays. Not for you. And not for anyone.'

Reverend Threlfall curled his hands around the sides of his jacket. His smile was small and thin. 'I'm afraid that's no longer what we want. Last week, you assured me that Belle Vue was safe. And yet, just a few days later, another animal managed to escape. It's become quite obvious that your menagerie is dangerous. That your staff are careless. And that *you* have no control.'

'How dare you!' Mr Jameson's chest rose.

But the vicar barely paused for breath. 'I dare because for the last few days, a lioness has been on the loose, endangering the public and terrifying an entire city. The newspapers are right to question whether you're a fit person to run a menagerie.'

Mr Jameson took a breath and managed a smile even though his jaw was tight. 'There's really no need to fuss, Vicar. We've found Victoria, and she's on her way back to Belle Vue as we speak. So, you see, no one got hurt.' He raised his voice in the direction of the other protesters.

'Now, you can all pack up and go home!'

'I'm afraid it's not that simple, Jameson. I'd already heard the animal had been found and recaptured . . . but only after she trapped a young boy in a cellar, terrified him half to death and very nearly savaged him.'

Mr Jameson glowered. 'Rumours and exaggeration! Nothin' more.'

'I think not! The Frog and Bucket public house is in my parish, and I had the whole story from two of its best customers. Petrified, they were.' The vicar rocked back on his heels, and now his smile was neither small nor thin. 'This seems a good time to tell you. I've spoken to the Manchester Corporation and the councillors are meeting tomorrow to discuss closing you down. Not just on Sundays, but . . .' He paused to draw out the word. '. . . permanently.'

Chapter Seventeen

The official council letter arrived by messenger at breakfast the next morning. It was short. And to the point.

To Mr James Jameson. You are requested to attend an emergency meeting of the Manchester Corporation this afternoon at two o'clock in the town hall. Members are to consider an application to close the establishment known as the Belle Vue Zoological Gardens. You must confirm your attendance at the earliest opportunity.

Mr Jameson gripped the letter with both hands and tore it in half. And then in half again. And again. Danny watched the pieces flutter to the floor. 'That's what they can do with their bleedin' summons. Orderin' me around – for all the world like I was a puppet in a side show. Well they can think again!'

'Jamie! What do you think you're doing?' Mrs Jameson scooped up the ripped fragments and tried to knit them back together, but Danny could tell it was a hopeless task. 'We can't afford to make enemies of these people. They could shut us down!'

'No one would dare!'

'Yes, they would! The newspapers have stirred up a great deal of fear. And Reverend Threlfall's protest hasn't helped. But as well as all that, we've the bank watching for any sign of trouble.' She sighed. 'Listen to me, Jamie. You have to go. Who's going to fight for Belle Vue unless you do? There's no one else.'

'But they're fools, Ethel May. The lot of them, especially that pompous windbag who thinks the world should stop on Sundays. Don't they understand what we bring to this city? How many jobs? Without us there'd be whole families out of work. Entire streets.'

'You're right, Jamie. Of course, you are.' Mrs Jameson smoothed a hand down her husband's arm, much like the way Danny would gentle Maharajah. 'But if you don't go to this meeting, who's going to tell them that?'

'They should know already! Belle Vue is the most

famous pleasure park in the country! It'll last a lot longer than any one of them. And I'll be happy to tell them that – right to their faces.'

'So you *will* go to the meeting then?'

Mr Jameson's face softened. 'Yes, me dove.' He kissed his wife's forehead. 'Because you're right, as always. I'll go. In fact, we'll all go. You, me and Danny. And if it's a fight they want, then they'll get one.'

Manchester Town Hall was a solid, serious building propped up by four grey pillars. It was exactly the sort of place where Danny imagined solid, serious decisions were made.

The thought jabbed at his conscience. He needed to tell the Jamesons about Charles Larkin. He'd waited too long already. But it wasn't until they stood in the large marbled foyer of the entrance hall that he found the courage.

'There's something... something I need to tell you.' He cleared his throat. 'I met—'

'Not now, Danny.' Mr Jameson squeezed a finger under his shirt collar as if to loosen it. 'Unless it's more important than what's about to happen inside these four walls, then now's not the time. Tell me later.'

'But—'

'Didn't you hear, Danny? He said later!' Frowning, Mrs Jameson leant forward and tugged Danny's tie straight. Then she did the same for her husband, even though she'd already done it twice before. 'There, that's better. Now, do pay attention. The clerk's calling us. And remember your manners. Both of you!'

The clerk ushered them along a corridor before opening a door at the far end. The committee room was wood-panelled with a high ceiling and ugly curtains. It smelt of old books and furniture wax.

A long rectangular table took up most of the floor. Seated on one side was Reverend Threlfall, looking far more comfortable than Danny would have liked. Opposite him sat three men, but only the figure in the middle stood out. Sharp-featured with deep-set eyes, he looked younger than the others. More intelligent. Less patient.

It was Harold Goadsby, the Lord Mayor of Manchester. The man who'd seen Maharajah come to church; who'd watched him eat Mrs Smalley's hat and heard the screams of the congregation.

Danny's heart stuttered. Under his breath, Mr Jameson muttered a curse. Wordlessly, Mrs Jameson clutched at his hand and then let go. They slipped into the empty seats next to the vicar.

Naturally, the Lord Mayor was the first to speak. 'For those of you who don't know, I'm Harold Goadsby and I've the honour of being chairman of this committee.' He tapped his fingers against the table. 'And now that we're all finally here, perhaps we can begin. Reverend Threlfall, please explain your reasons for bringing this application.'

Immediately, the vicar sprang up, chest puffed out and feet braced apart, in much the same way as Danny had seen him deliver a sermon from the pulpit.

'It's quite simple, sir. The management of the Belle Vue Zoological Gardens is blundering and incompetent – and has been for some time.' He curled his hands around both jacket lapels. 'I'm here to demand that the park be shut down.'

Danny flicked his eyes towards Mr Goadsby. He was relieved to see the Lord Mayor appeared unimpressed. 'I'm afraid you'll have to give us more detail than that, Reverend. We cannot close an entire business on your opinion alone.'

'Of course, sir, I quite understand. Which is why I organized a petition.' The vicar pulled a sheaf of papers from his jacket and pushed it across the table. 'Take a look. You'll find it's signed by several hundred of my parishioners . . . all of them demanding the park close down.'

Beside Danny, Mr Jameson flinched in his chair but before he could jump to his feet, his wife clamped a hand on his arm. Her warning glare was enough to keep Mr Jameson sitting. But his shredded patience only seemed to worsen with each word out of the vicar's mouth.

'As for more detail, I can give you several reasons to close Belle Vue. You've already seen for yourself how unreasonable Jameson can be. Bringing an elephant to church! But it gets worse. In the last week alone, two animals have escaped. The first was a rare emu – the last of its kind, I believe. While the second was a dangerous lioness found in the cellar of a public house, terrifying a young boy. If I may,

I'll begin with the first incident . . .'

It seemed to take a long time for Reverend Threlfall to recount every detail of Emerald's escape, and even longer to tell the story of Victoria. Danny wasn't even sure whether half the facts were true.

But when he finally finished his evidence, the vicar sat down with an air of triumph. And then, it was Mr Jameson's turn.

'What do you say to these accusations, sir?'

'Poppycock!' Mr Jameson jumped to his feet with the speed of a cork coming out of a bottle. 'That's what I say. I've never heard such utter nonsense as has just been uttered in this room.'

Mr Goadsby's brows lowered. 'That sort of attitude is not going to win you any friends, Mr Jameson. Please keep your answer to facts. Otherwise I shall have to ask you to leave.'

'Very well. I'll give you some facts. I employ more than two hundred people at Belle Vue, each of them earnin' around one pound a week. And in the high season, I take on many more workers than that. I've everyone from black-smiths to beer brewers on my staff. There's an ice house, a firework factory and plenty of other businesses besides.'

Lifting his chin, he stuck his thumbs into his waistcoat pockets. 'And then there's my menagerie. Belle Vue has the finest zoological collection in the whole of the country. In the whole of the empire! In fact, the Queen herself is a great admirer of my animals.'

Once again, Mr Goadsby drummed his fingers on the table. The noise echoed around the room. 'That may be true. But what have you done to ensure your menagerie is secure? And that people are safe? You've some powerful animals in your care, animals that are not always easy to control.'

Danny winced. It was clearly a reference to what had happened outside St Mark's Church. But Mr Jameson seemed undeterred.

'Sir, I've done plenty. My keepers are workin' in pairs – one to lock the enclosures, the other to make sure it's done right. I've put extra staff on overnight to keep watch. And my blacksmith's been round and checked the padlocks on all the animal pens.' He jabbed a finger in the air. 'And I can tell you, Lord Mayor, we're safer than Buckingham Palace.'

'And what about the fireworks? Pyrotechnics is a dangerous business. It's not simply about noise, there are safety concerns as well.'

Mr Jameson scowled. 'Everything's workin' fine. We've just finished the final testin' for our summer show, and it couldn't have gone better. It's goin' to be the biggest and best you ever saw.' He paused. 'In fact, I'll make this promise to you. If there's any problems, I'll close Belle Vue myself.'

'I see.' Mr Goadsby placed the tips of his fingers together and leant back in his chair. It creaked a little under the strain. 'Thank you, Mr Jameson. I've no more questions.' He looked at the men sitting on either side of him; they nodded back. 'I think we've heard enough. You may wait outside.'

Danny sat with Mr and Mrs Jameson on the hard stone benches in the corridor. Underneath his feet, black and white tiles fanned out across the floor. He stared at the chessboard pattern until his eyes blurred. And when he lifted his head, a carved scroll glared back at him from the wall. Down the centre, picked out in gold leaf, were rows of names and dates.

Danny wondered if the list included Harold Goadsby, and what a person had to do to be included. And then he wondered if, one day, his name might be up there too. But the idea was so ridiculous that he didn't bother lingering over it.

An hour later, they were called back inside.

Mr Goadsby wasted no time on polite greetings. 'We've listened to both sides of the arguments. Mr Jameson is perfectly correct that his business brings money and jobs to Manchester. But Reverend Threlfall is also right to be concerned about noise, and safety. Two escaped animals are two animals too many. So we're ordering Belle Vue to close . . .'

Danny sucked in a breath. Beside him, Mr Jameson half rose from his seat, his fists opening and closing.

'. . . to close each Sunday. For the rest of the week, the park may stay open as usual. But on one condition – if there are any problems, the committee has given me the power to shut Belle Vue immediately. There'll be no coming back to the Corporation with more excuses. My decision will be final. Do you agree to these terms?'

A pause. Mr Jameson had turned an angry shade of red. He seemed incapable of speech. Finally, Mrs Jameson nudged her husband in the ribs. 'Yes,' he said. Another nudge. 'Sir.'

'Very good, I'm glad we're in agreement.' Goadsby paused. 'And Mr Jameson . . .'

'Yes, Lord Mayor?'

'Do be careful. Belle Vue is a valuable asset to this city. We'd hate to lose it.'

By the time they'd made their way out of the town hall, a swarm of newspaper men had already gathered on the stone steps, yelling and shouting.

'Mr Jameson, what have you to say?'

'A day's closure. This must be another blow?'

'Can your business survive this, sir?'

'Gentlemen! Gentlemen! Please.' Mr Jameson waited a moment for silence to settle, his smile broad. No one would have guessed that he'd cursed every step of his way out of the building. 'Just as I expected, the Corporation have seen sense and are lettin' Belle Vue carry on as usual. There's just a small change on Sundays. Nothin' that causes me a great deal of concern.'

He followed Mrs Jameson and Danny towards the waiting carriage but he stopped before climbing on board. 'And of course, the good gentlemen of the press are welcome to Belle Vue in three days' time – for the biggest, most fantastical show you've ever seen. It'll be free entry to you all.

Now, if you'll forgive me, I have a business to run.'

He shut the carriage door with a slam and dropped down into the seat next to his wife. She tucked her hand into his arm as they pulled away. 'There you are, Jamie. That wasn't so bad, was it? I must say, I couldn't believe it when I saw the Lord Mayor sitting there! But he seemed reasonable enough, don't you think?'

The smile that Mr Jameson had pasted on for the newspaper reporters faded. 'I wouldn't say that, Ethel May. We've lost a day's business every week. And for as long as the Corporation's watchin', everythin' at Belle Vue has to work smoother than butter on hot toast.' Across the carriage he caught Danny's eye and his warning was clear. 'So absolutely nothin' can go wrong.'

Chapter Eighteen

'D anny! DANNY!'

Danny lifted his head. It was the day after the town hall meeting, and he was crouched behind a pile of luggage at Longsight Train Station. Hiding.

Mr Saddleworth was due to leave for Paris this morning, and Danny had come to the station in yet another attempt to see Hetty. There was so much he wanted to tell her but, most importantly of all, he needed her advice. Because he still didn't know what to do about Charles Larkin – or his incredible story.

Unfortunately, shortly after arriving at the station, Danny had realized there'd be little chance of talking to Hetty. She was too closely guarded by her aunt. Miss Carkettle seemed to have eyes everywhere, and the protective instincts of a grizzly bear. Still, he was going to wait as long as he could – just in case.

'Danny!'

The shout came again and Danny peered out from his hiding place. Further along the platform, Mr Saddleworth was weaving through the waiting passengers towards him. He caught Danny's eye and waved.

'I thought it was you! Didn't you hear me, lad? I've been shouting for a good five minutes.'

Shaking his head, Danny stepped away from the luggage pile.

'Well, I'm glad you're here. I'd hoped to catch a word before I left Belle Vue.' Lightly, Mr Saddleworth placed a hand on Danny's shoulder. 'While I'm gone, I want you to look after Maharajah. He'll be your responsibility. There's no one I trust more.'

'Me?' Danny's surprise must have been obvious because the grip on his shoulder only tightened.

'Yes. Of course! Why would I ask anyone else?' A sudden glimmer of understanding sparked in Mr Saddleworth's eyes. 'Look, however Victoria managed to escape, I don't believe it was your fault. And I've told Mr Jameson that. You just have to be patient. Let him calm down. It's a busy time – and he's got a lot on his mind.'

Yes. Danny knew that better than most. Not only had the Manchester Corporation closed Belle Vue on Sundays, but last night a water pipe had burst in the new tea rooms, flooding the ground floor and destroying the stockpile of food.

It was likely to take several days for the building to dry out – and almost as long to replace the hoard of hams, pies and currant cakes stored in the waterlogged larder. With thousands of extra visitors expected in just two days, the flood was not only unfortunate, it was a disaster.

And it also meant that once again, Danny had still not been able to speak to Mr Jameson. The menagerist had hardly been home. And if he was honest, Danny was glad. Every time he'd imagined telling the Jamesons about Larkin, his stomach cramped. It was far easier not to say anything at all.

He looked at Mr Saddleworth. 'Yes,' he said. 'I'll take care of Maharajah.'

'Good. I didn't doubt it for a moment.'

Mr Saddleworth glanced across the platform to where Hetty was standing with her aunt, and his face softened. Miss Carkettle was fussing over a loose curl that had come unpinned, but Hetty was refusing to stand long enough for her hair to be put right.

'And be a good friend to Hetty, won't you?' he said. 'I don't think she's quite forgiven me for inviting Aunt Augusta to Belle Vue.'

'Yes, sir. I will. I promise.'

'Thank you. I knew I could rely on you.'

Striding back to his daughter, Mr Saddleworth pulled Hetty into a last embrace and whispered something into her ear. She smiled, nodded then kissed his cheek. And a few moments later, as the train steamed out of the station,

Hetty stood and waved until it disappeared from sight.

As he watched, Danny felt a stab of envy. Hetty and her father didn't always agree – but there was be no doubting the bond between them. And it seemed to him that his hopes of finding something similar were as far away as ever.

Later that night, standing underneath Hetty's bedroom window at Kirkmanshulme Cottage, Danny remembered the promises he'd made to Mr Saddleworth.

To take care of Maharajah.

To be a good friend to Hetty.

And to face Mr Jameson's temper with more patience.

And he wondered whether Mr Saddleworth would approve of what he planned to do. Although, it was too late to change his mind now. Danny had already been here a half-hour, waiting for the household to go to bed, and working out how to attract Hetty's attention when it did.

Another hour passed. Finally, the cottage settled into silence. Stooping, Danny grabbed some stones and threw them at a small window tucked under the eaves. The pebbles spattered against the glass. He waited in the darkness, counting off the seconds slowly. And, just as he was about to scoop up another handful, the window slid open.

'Who is it?'

'Me!' The hiss emerged far louder than Danny expected, and he had to lower his voice to carry on. 'Hurry up! I thought you wanted to be in the show? We're going to be late for rehearsal.'

The flash of a smile was his only answer, then Hetty ducked away from the window and disappeared from sight. Danny waited, far less patiently than before, and although it was probably only a few minutes until she returned, it felt much longer. 'Are you ready?'

Leaning across the window ledge, Hetty peered down. A red tasselled shawl hung loosely from her shoulders, and Danny realized she must have taken time to change into her show costume. 'Yes. Did you bring a ladder?'

Danny shook his head and his mouth curled up – they wouldn't be needing a ladder tonight.

Stepping back, he gave a sharp whistle. Immediately, Maharajah's solid outline emerged from the line of trees that shielded the cottage from the rest of Belle Vue. He stomped forward – as quietly as a fully grown elephant was able to – and stopped just below Hetty's window.

'Oh my word!' Hetty brought a hand to her open mouth, her eyes wide.

Danny wanted to laugh but he didn't dare risk the noise. Instead, he whispered, 'Come on. We have to go!'

'Fine! I'm coming.' Cautiously, Hetty slid one leg over the window frame. Her foot landed on the curve of Maharajah's back but he stayed steady as a mountain, not seeming to care about her fumbling.

Apparently satisfied with her foothold, Hetty swung her other leg across the ledge and, for a heartbeat, she stood, delicately balanced on Maharajah like a ballerina considering her first stage leap.

Abruptly, Maharajah stomped away from the cottage. And with a small, panicked squeak, Hetty fell forward, lying sprawled across the elephant's back, her hands clinging tight to the harness. Moments later, a lamp flickered on in one of the downstairs rooms.

'Quiet!' Heart drumming, Danny pushed back against the wall, and watched the small halo of light move from window to window, getting closer and closer. Until finally, the kitchen door cracked open, spilling light across the courtyard.

Danny held his breath. Why had he thought this was a good idea? It was almost as ridiculous as Mr Jameson taking Maharajah to church.

'Go on. Get away! Be gone!' Aunt Augusta's tart voice pierced the darkness. And with an indignant meow, a tabby cat stalked out of the cottage and along the garden path. Within moments, she'd disappeared among the trees, and the door slammed shut behind her.

Danny let out a breath. And then another. And another. But he didn't breathe easily until Maharajah knelt down and Hetty's feet finally touched solid ground.

She grinned at him. 'What are you waiting for? Let's go!'

Despite running, they were still late. Most of the red and blue soldiers had already trooped across the footbridge to Firework Island. And a trickle of Spanish villagers followed. It was to be the first official rehearsal of 'Prince Dandip and the Fight for Flamenca', and the air fizzed with nerves and excitement.

'Wait!' Hetty grabbed Danny's arm as the three of them reached the bridge. 'I want to thank you – for helping me, I mean. For keeping your promise about the show. For coming to get me tonight. I wouldn't be able to do this without you.'

Danny shrugged, embarrassed. 'It's nothing.'

'It isn't nothing to me.' She paused. 'I forgot to ask. What was it you wanted to talk to me about? The day Aunt Augusta arrived . . . you said it was important.'

Briefly, Danny cast his mind over all that he wanted to tell her. The shooting in the maze, Charles Larkin's revelation, and Danny's growing certainty that someone was making trouble for Belle Vue. But there wasn't near enough time to say everything he wanted to. And besides, over Hetty's shoulder, he could see Crimple's large figure hovering. The story would have to wait. 'I'll tell you later. After the rehearsal. Come on!'

Gripping the harness, Danny swung his leg across Maharajah then shuffled forward to sit in the dip behind the elephant's skull. It was as though the hollow had been made just for him. He leant forward, wrapping his arms as far as he could around Maharajah's neck, before burrowing his face against the rough skin.

Quickly, Hetty slid into the space behind him and looped her arms around his waist. He put out a hand to make sure she was secure, and the bright silk of her costume slid against his fingers. Looking up, he scanned the way ahead.

The bridge was wide enough to fit an elephant – but only just. It was built from a series of wooden planks balanced on brick columns that had been planted into the lake. Railings ran on either side, but Danny suspected they were more for show than for safety.

He was just about to urge Maharajah forward when a fist curled around the elephant's harness. Crimple was staring up at them. 'Why don't I lead him across? It looks narrow. Might be safer.'

'No!' Instinctively, Danny pulled the reins free, shaking his head. 'No, I can do it!'

He whistled sharply, and Maharajah stomped forward. The first few steps seemed easy enough. Maharajah's weight made the bridge sigh and sway slightly, but the planks held solidly. Below them, the water lapped against the bricks. Danny didn't look down.

Once, not so very long ago, he'd almost drowned; it had been Maharajah who'd saved him, striding into the river to scoop him up in the coils of his trunk. The rescue had sealed their friendship – and left Danny with a lasting fear of deep water.

Maharajah stomped a little further along the bridge. Now they were almost halfway across, and Danny couldn't help stiffening. The sway was getting stronger. He tried to force the tension from his arms and shoulders, but the jittery, uncomfortable feeling wouldn't go away.

Abruptly, Maharajah stopped stock-still and silent. Hetty leant sideways to peer around him. 'What's the matter? Why won't he move?'

Frowning, Danny shrugged. 'I don't know.'

He raised his ankus and whistled. Nothing. Then he whistled again, digging his knees into Maharajah's sides. The strange tension grew stronger. Danny pressed again. And slowly – almost reluctantly – Maharajah took another step.

That was all it took.

With an ugly snap, the wooden boards beneath their feet gave way. And in the gap between one breath and the next, all three of them plummeted downwards.

The ring of Hetty's terrified scream echoed in Danny's ears, alongside the panicked hitch of his own breath. Desperately, he struggled to hold on to the harness but it was no good. The leather slipped through his fingers and he was flung sideways, tossed like a leaf in the wind.

He landed heavily, air hissing from his lungs, and when he could breathe again, Danny realized he was lying on one of the broken planks – and it was slowly tilting towards the swirling water.

Frantically, he reached for the nearest support – one of the brick columns sticking upright from the lake. He locked his hands around it and clung on. Abruptly, the plank beneath him stopped sliding.

Spreading his legs wide apart for balance, Danny stood gingerly, and took in his first view of the damaged bridge. Half of it looked untouched, but the section nearest the island was in pieces. And while the supporting columns remained, most of the horizontal planks that criss-crossed the bridge had collapsed. Worse still, Maharajah lay sprawled on his side, slumped across the splintered wood.

But where was Hetty? *Where was she?*

Hastily, Danny scanned the chaos. His pulse began to speed up. He couldn't see any sign. Nothing at all – apart from the red tasselled shawl caught around Maharajah's trunk.

Danny looked again. Suddenly, the shawl moved, falling back to reveal gold curls and a pale face. And with dawning horror, he realized Hetty was dangling off the end of the bridge. And all that was stopping her falling was Maharajah's tight grip.

Abruptly, the bridge gave another groan, and Maharajah began sliding towards the water, taking Hetty with him. Danny's heart pounded. If they both fell, the chances were that Maharajah's great weight would crush her.

'Hold on. We're coming!' The shout came from the island, and Danny swung round. A handful of soldiers had begun edging their way across the broken boards.

'Stop! STOP!' Panicked, Danny held up his hand. 'You'll . . . you'll bring it down! All of it!' In the same moment, another timber crashed down into the lake, and Maharajah slid another few inches towards the water. Hastily, the men retreated.

Danny's chest heaved. Adjusting his balance, he examined the gap between him and Hetty. It looked possible, but only just. He knelt and stretched out carefully along the plank. It wobbled but held firm. He reached out an arm, making sure to keep focused on Hetty's face. Her skin was turned chalk-white, but her eyes were brave. 'Grab my hand. I'll pull you up!'

There was a long silence, then cautiously, Hetty loosened her arm from around Maharajah's trunk. She put out her hand but the distance between them was still too wide. 'I . . . I can't.'

'Yes, you can.' Danny wriggled along the board and leant out even further. Below him, the water swirled around the bridge columns. His heart thudded. 'Try again. Come on!'

This time, their fingertips touched and held. Slowly, Danny slid his palm across Hetty's, inch by inch, until finally, his fingers locked around her wrist. He tested the grip then pulled. With a deep groan, Hetty slid up, past Maharajah and across the boards.

Quickly, Danny crouched down beside her. 'Are you hurt?'

'I'm fine. My wrist's a little sore. That's all.' She flexed her hand. 'See! Perfectly fine.' Her glance flicked past him and he saw her eyes widen. 'But Danny . . . look!'

He spun round. Once Hetty had been pulled free, Danny had expected Maharajah to clamber to his feet easily. But he hadn't – because he couldn't. One of his tusks was impaled in the bridge. However much he tried, he couldn't seem to free himself.

Slipping the ankus from his belt, Danny raised the cane

and brought it down as hard as he could. The wood ripped. He did it again and again, and the crack widened. Then Danny was on his knees, pulling at the timber with his fingers. Splinters dug into his skin but he ignored them. And finally, the board pulled free.

Jerkily, Maharajah climbed upright. The bridge swayed and groaned, and this time none of them bothered being careful. Pelting across the boards, they ran back to the safety of solid ground. Behind them, the rest of the bridge collapsed into the swirling water.

'Oh my heavens!' Hetty panted, staring at the chaos.

Danny let out an unsteady breath and smoothed a hand along Maharajah's face. But when he took his fingers away, they were red. Blood was dripping from the base of Maharajah's left tusk.

Chapter Nineteen

'Hetty, there's some iodine in the keeper's cupboard. Top shelf. Fetch it, please.'

'Crimple, I need some water. And rags. But make sure they're clean.'

'And someone fetch a saw. Now!'

Danny threw out the commands quickly, and for once the words came easily and fluently. He didn't stumble at all. Perhaps that was the reason no one argued. Or maybe it was because his fear was obvious. If they didn't treat the wound properly then the chance of infection was high. And with the chance of infection came the possibility of death.

He and Hetty had brought Maharajah to the elephant house immediately after discovering the bleeding tusk. It had seemed the best place to work out what to do. Crimple had followed shortly afterwards, and this time Danny was grateful to see him. Another pair of hands might prove useful.

Lifting one of the lanterns from a hook on the wall, Danny turned to face Maharajah and drew the ankus from his belt. His whistle was a soft hiss. Obediently Maharajah lowered his heavy frame to the floor then rolled on to his side like a cat waiting to be stroked.

In this position, the broken tusk faced upwards. Danny knelt to take a closer look.

The sight stopped his breath.

The top half of the tusk was sliced almost clean through. Cracks ran down the remaining length, from the tip close to the root. And around the base, blood leaked from the circle of skin.

With sudden, vivid clarity, Danny remembered the last time Maharajah had been injured. Now the same sick feeling ballooned in his stomach. But this time, there was one important difference. Because this time, the injury was his fault. No one else's. He had made this happen, just as surely as if he'd used a knife.

Why had he forced Maharajah to continue over the bridge? Why hadn't he trusted him enough to know something was wrong – that there was a good reason for Maharajah to hesitate? And an even better reason to stop?

'Do you think he's in pain?' Hetty had moved to stand by his shoulder. Her voice was a low whisper in the dark.

'I don't know.' Danny cleared the roughness from his throat. 'Maybe. Yes.'

He closed his eyes and desperately tried to remember all that he'd learnt over the last few weeks. Mr Saddleworth had taught him so much but now, when the information was so vital, he struggled to recall any of it.

Gradually, pieces filtered through. An elephant's tusk was similar to a human tooth, Mr Saddleworth had said. The root was anchored deep within the skull, leaving about two thirds still visible – the tusk. Inside, near the root, there was a knot of blood and nerves that kept the tusk healthy and growing. If the cracks had reached that tissue, then Maharajah would be hurting. And worse still, there would be a strong chance of infection.

Danny's eyelids flew open. His unease heightened. Normally, it would be Mr Saddleworth standing here, making the decisions. But Hetty's father wouldn't be back for at least another week and by then it would be too late. Besides, he'd trusted Maharajah into Danny's care. Maharajah was his responsibility. No one else's. His heart slammed against his ribs.

'We need to get rid of the broken tusk first. Saw it off. Then clean around the root.'

Hetty examined his face. 'Who's going to—'

'I'll do it,' Danny said quickly. He tried to force as much confidence into his voice as he could. But inside, he trembled.

'Are you sure?'

'Yes.'

'Then how can I help?'

'Keep him calm. And hum. He . . . he likes that.' Turning his head, Danny raised his voice. 'Crimple, did you find a saw?'

'Here, lad.' The keeper handed him a small, jagged-edged blade, then patted him on the shoulder. It was a strangely comforting gesture from a man who had never been much of a friend. Danny wrapped his fingers around the handle and tested the weight.

'It'll do,' he said.

Carefully, he shuffled closer to Maharajah's side and lowered the blade. It sat just below the splinter line. There was no doubt that the broken tusk needed to be cut away, but he had to make sure not to slice through the cavity of blood and nerves. If he cut too low, there was a strong chance of that happening. Too high, and the tusk would continue to fracture.

In his head, Danny was certain he'd picked the right spot. But it seemed that knowing it was entirely different from believing it. Sweat dotted his forehead and he had to wipe it away with the back of his hand.

'Crimple, will you help hold his head? In case . . . in case . . .' He didn't finish the sentence but Crimple knelt down anyway.

The first drag of the blade was the worst. The cut released a cloud of white powder that rose into the air before settling on Danny's fingers. He managed a few more strokes, before stopping.

Hetty stopped humming and hooked a hand around his

arm. 'Danny, why don't you let Crimple do the rest? It might be easier.'

'No!' Furiously, Danny shook his head, tightening his grip just in case someone thought to pull the blade away. 'No. This is my fault.' He blinked his eyes against the sudden sting. 'I have to finish it . . .'

He angled the saw again, pulling it back until the teeth bit into the tusk. Then he pushed forward. Once again, a metallic whine grated through the air.

The blade was already more than halfway through to the other side. With a few more tugs, the broken tusk fell to the floor.

'Pass me the cloths and the water.'

Hetty gave him the bowl of rags and, carefully, Danny wiped around the base of the tusk. He was probably much gentler than he needed to be, but it made him feel better to take his time.

Grabbing the bottle, Danny splashed some iodine into the bowl and mixed it with a little water. The harsh smell pricked his nose. He dipped a dry cloth into the solution and began wiping around the blunt tusk. And every moment, Mr Saddleworth's instructions raced through his head.

Make certain there is no infection.

At last Danny stood back. The skin was clean and there was no sign of fresh blood.

'It's done,' he said.

The sawn-off tusk lay abandoned in the straw. Crimple

knelt to pick it up. It was almost as long as his arm. 'There's people that would pay good money for this. Those that want ivory trinkets. Jewellery and buttons and stuff. I reckon we should sell it. We'd make a fortune.'

'No!' The idea made Danny's stomach heave. He wasn't stupid. He knew there were poachers who killed elephants for their ivory, hacking through skulls to rip out tusks from their roots. But he wasn't like those people. Cruel and greedy and heartless. Maharajah was his friend. What sort of person would he be to make money out of this? 'No. Give that to me!'

He tore the tusk from Crimple's hands and threw it so far into the enclosure that he could no longer see it. When he turned back, Maharajah was struggling upright. They stared at each other. And Danny's heart stuttered.

It was strange to see this beautiful, powerful creature with a lopsided tilt to his face. Like a stately old man smiling through broken teeth.

Abruptly the gold eyes blinked and Maharajah's trunk hooked around Danny's waist, dragging him close. He lay against the rough skin and turned his face into the warmth.

'I'm sorry. I'm so sorry.' He couldn't stop saying it. It was though with every repetition, the words chipped away at the guilt. Mr Saddleworth had trusted him. He had trusted him to take care of Maharajah. And he had trusted him to be a good friend to Hetty. He had failed on both counts.

Somewhere behind him, Danny was dimly aware of a door opening. And then he was yanked back. Tom Dalton's face pushed into his. They were so close their breath mingled.

'So this is where you're hiding!'

'I'm not . . . hiding.'

'No, of course you aren't! You just ran off and left everyone to clear up your mess.' Tom curled his lip. 'Who do you think you are? You march around Belle Vue like you're someone important but people could've died today. And it would have been your fault.' He shoved his palm into the centre of Danny's chest and pushed. Then pushed again. 'Your fault!'

'Don't touch me.' Pulling away, Danny rolled his hands into fists. Hostility cracked between them like a whip.

'I don't know why I shouldn't. Everythin's gone wrong since you came. First you let a lioness loose around Manchester. Now Threlfall's kickin' off again – tryin' to close Belle Vue down! We could all lose our jobs! And tonight, this happens. You don't care about anythin' but yourself.'

The accusation hit Danny square in the stomach, the heavy weight of it seemed to spread into every corner.

But Tom still wasn't finished. 'I don't know why the Jamesons even brought you here. You're nothin' special. You're no better than where you came from. The slums of Edinburgh, wasn't it? Pickin' pockets and stealin' purses? Well, perhaps you should go back there! Because no one wants you!'

Later, Danny realized he must have thrown the first

punch. Because he heard the solid thud of flesh on flesh – and the painful vibration as contact was made. Then he saw Tom clutching the side of his face.

'You little runt!' Tom raised his fist, and Danny had no time to steel himself. The jab hit his nose with a crunch. He let the pain settle for a moment before swinging back. This wasn't over yet.

But the truth was neither of them was particularly good at fighting, missing far more than they hit. It didn't seem to matter. They were both stirred up and angry, like clockwork toys that had been wound up too tight and let go.

Danny's hair was stuck to his forehead. And blood and snot dripped from his nose. He wiped the trail away with the back of his hand then raised his fists to start again.

'Stop! Please!' Hetty had managed to squeeze between them, her arms outstretched and palms raised flat. The interruption was almost a relief. 'Stop it. How can you both be so stupid? This isn't going to help!'

Danny didn't answer. His chest heaved with the effort of drawing in air. A sudden cramp bent him double so that he had to rest his hands on his knees to stop himself from falling over. His head hung low. And somewhere in the background he heard the light tread of footsteps.

'Danny, listen to me.' Gently, Hetty laid a palm against his shoulder. 'Tom didn't mean what he said. I know he didn't. But you shouldn't have started a fight. What on earth were you thinking?'

Slowly, Danny pulled himself upright until Hetty was

forced to step back, and away. His heart beat painfully in his chest. 'You'd take his side, over me?'

'Of course not. I just meant—'

'And what he said . . . about where I came from.' Speech was getting difficult. 'How did he . . . how did he know all that?'

But Hetty didn't need to answer; her eyes had filled with guilt. 'I'm sorry. I shouldn't have—'

'It doesn't matter. Forget I ever wanted your help. Forget everything. You're no friend of mine. Just get out!' He waved his hand around the room. 'Get out. Get out all of you!'

Chapter Twenty

Charles Larkin was sitting in the hotel reception reading a newspaper when Danny sneaked inside. At first sight he appeared engrossed in the pages but Danny noticed that every time the front door opened, Larkin lifted his head to look.

It was the reason why Danny had slipped, unobserved, through the side entrance. He wanted to watch without being seen, because he still wasn't quite sure what he was doing here. Or what he was going to say.

He'd spent the night in the elephant house, curled up beside Maharajah's warm body. Not that he'd had much sleep. His body ached from the fight, and bruises had started to bloom across his skin. But even if there had been no pain, guilt would have stopped him from sleeping.

This was his fault. He'd made a mistake. And now

he'd made everything worse by pushing Hetty away. He'd regretted the angry words almost from the moment they'd left his mouth. But by then, everyone had gone.

At least Maharajah appeared unharmed. He'd slept as peacefully as any baby, breathing in slow even breaths with no sign of any pain or discomfort. At dawn, Danny had cleaned the skin around the broken tusk for the third time, dabbing the mix of water and iodine along the root. And by the time he'd finished, one of the elephant keepers had arrived for the day shift.

Reluctantly, Danny had said goodbye, but only because there was nothing left for him to do. Maharajah had seemed perfectly content. And Danny had known he needed to go home. The Jamesons must be wondering where he was – although no doubt Crimple had already told them the full, shameful story.

But when Danny finally walked out of the elephant enclosure, he hadn't taken the right fork towards Belle Vue House. Instead, he'd followed the opposite path towards the Longsight entrance. And then – expressly against Mr Jameson's orders – he'd sneaked out of the park alone.

Larkin's hotel was just a short distance away, along Redgate Lane, and it had been easy enough to slip through the side door. But now that he was here, Danny wasn't sure what to do.

He lifted his head and looked at the man who claimed to be his father. If anything, Larkin was even more finely dressed today. His boots were polished to a glossy sheen, and he wore gold cufflinks in the sleeves of his crisp white shirt.

He looked like a man who didn't work. But more importantly, he looked like a man who didn't need to. Danny wouldn't have come otherwise. Past experience had taught him not to trust anyone who looked like they needed money. They were usually willing to do anything to get it.

For a long time, Danny did nothing but watch – and Larkin continued to inspect each new arrival. Danny wondered how long it would take before he gave up. And then he wondered how long it would be before he did too. And after a while, he was surprised to find his mouth was dry and his palms were damp.

Swallowing, he wiped his hands down the front of his jacket. Perhaps the movement alerted Larkin because he turned abruptly. Their eyes locked.

'You came.' Larkin lifted out of the chair. 'I wasn't sure if you would. It's been five days.'

Danny said nothing but he raised his chin to show he was listening. Hesitantly, Larkin walked nearer, his eyes flicking over Danny's face and clothes. 'You look as though you've had a difficult night.'

Danny nodded again, but he still didn't say anything. He'd no intention of explaining all that had happened over the last few hours. His feelings were already far too confused. But, to his relief, Larkin didn't ask.

'So, have you eaten? Maybe we could talk over breakfast?'

The dining room opened off the hotel's reception hall. Larkin pulled the door ajar and waved Danny inside. They settled at a table set with silver cutlery. A vase of yellow roses stood in the centre. And it occurred to Danny that, despite the fine surroundings, Larkin didn't seem to care that his dining companion was rumpled, dirty and had obviously been in a fight. It was one mark in his favour.

A waitress brought them a pot of tea and some toast, then another fetched a plate of eggs and some boiled ham. Danny's mouth watered. He hadn't eaten since yesterday afternoon, and the smell alone was enough to set his stomach rumbling.

He gulped down the food with embarrassing haste. And it was only when he'd finished that he realized Larkin's breakfast remained untouched, and that, instead of eating, he must have been watching the entire time.

'So, I assume you want to know the whole story.'

Carefully, Danny placed the knife and fork on his empty plate, and then he nodded.

'Very well.' Larkin leant forward and tugged at his shirt sleeves. 'My name is Charles Edward Larkin. My family comes from Stirling. I'm the youngest of three brothers. My father made his money from woollen mills. I suppose most people would probably say we're wealthy.'

Deliberately, Danny kept his face blank. At the next table, a young couple settled into their chairs. Their excited chatter filled a long pause.

'It was always expected that I would go into the family

business, get married, raise children. But I was young and enjoyed my freedom a little too much to settle down. Then one day I met your mother. She was at the market. I couldn't take my eyes from her. She was the most beautiful thing I'd ever seen. Then or since.'

Danny saw him smile at the memory and, without warning, a picture flashed into his head. A woman – young and pretty with kind, dark eyes, and skin the same colour as his own. He recognized her from his dreams. She'd sing to him – and always the same sad tune. He wished he knew who she was, and if the image in Larkin's head was the same.

'I wanted to marry her, but my family didn't approve. They didn't think an Indian housemaid was a suitable match for their son. So, we married in secret. I thought eventually I'd be able to persuade my parents. But when I told them, they were furious and we argued.' Larkin tugged again at his shirt cuffs. 'And then later, I argued with her. That night she disappeared and I never saw her again.'

A waitress came to clear the table, stacking the plates and dishes with careful precision before picking up the empty teapot. Danny wanted to shout at her to go away. Instead, he waited while Larkin thanked her politely.

'And then?' he asked, when she had gone. 'What happened then?'

'And then things changed. Both my parents died, and there was nothing to stop us from being together. I started searching. Following her trail to Edinburgh. And to Cowgate. That's where I met the Dilworths.'

Danny jolted, surprised. Larkin was watching him intently. 'You remember them? They lived in the same building as your mother. From what they told me, they helped her after you were born.'

That was not how Danny remembered it. Mr and Mrs Dilworth may have looked after him, but only because he was small enough to be useful. It had been the Dilworths who'd forced him to crawl through coal holes to steal from people's homes. But later, when he'd grown bigger, they'd replaced him with a younger, smaller boy. And he'd learnt to pickpocket to survive.

Danny set his face and nodded. Larkin must have taken it as a signal to carry on, except now he didn't sound so calm.

'And then, they told . . . they told me she'd died. And nothing mattered any more. I couldn't believe I wouldn't have known.' His voice faded and he cleared his throat. 'But after that I found out about you. My son. It changed everything. And I've been looking for you ever since.'

Larkin lifted his arms, waving them in much the same way that a magician would perform a conjuring trick. 'So here you are. Here *we* are.'

Danny said nothing. The thought came to him that this was exactly like a magic show. And that he was sitting here, trying desperately to work out how the trick had been achieved – and not quite believing in the illusion.

'So?' Larkin let his arms drop back to his sides. 'Don't you have anything to ask me? Anything at all?'

'My name?' The question burst out, as much of a surprise to him as it was to Larkin. 'What's my real name?'

'You mean you don't know?'

Danny shook his head. 'Mr Jameson called me Daniel. He said it was his grandfather's name. Before that...' To his embarrassment, his voice cracked a little. 'Before that no one called me anything.'

It wasn't quite true – but all the other names had been crude and ugly. Strangely, it had been Frank Scatcherd who'd called him 'Boy'. And while Danny had lived in Edinburgh, it had been the only name he would answer to.

'Good Lord, I didn't realize. I didn't think . . .' Larkin studied Danny's face. 'Your mother called you Edward. And her name . . . her name was Anaya.'

Anaya. The sound was delicate and beautiful, as soft as rain on a petal. Danny repeated it in his head, over and over again.

Anaya.

Anaya.

Anaya.

And then he tried his own name. Edward. But it didn't seem to work as well. Maybe because he didn't feel like Edward. He felt like Danny.

He pushed back from the table and stared at Larkin. Was any of this story true? And if it wasn't, why would Larkin go to such lengths to lie? Why would anyone want to pretend to be his father? It made no sense.

'Look. I wish we hadn't argued. I wish I'd gone after her

straight away. I was wrong. And I will regret that to my dying day. You must believe me.'

Danny's gaze flickered to the roses in the middle of the table. The yellow petals looked even brighter against the whiteness of the tablecloth. Reaching across, he snatched them from the vase.

'What are you doing?'

He stood. 'I have to apologize to someone.'

'I see.' Larkin said, even though he couldn't possibly understand. 'It must be important?'

'Yes. It is.'

'And will I see you again?'

Danny stayed silent for a moment and then he nodded. 'Yes. I'd like to.'

Larkin smiled. 'Then we will.'

Chapter Twenty-one

The maid answered the door to the Saddleworths' house but only after Danny had knocked so loudly that the hinges rattled.

'I'm here to see Hetty.'

She scowled, obviously annoyed at his abruptness. 'I'll go and ask. *You* stay here. And don't you dare move.'

Danny waited impatiently on the doorstep. The yellow roses were already wilting in his hand. He shoved them behind his back as brisk footsteps sounded down the hallway.

'Come on. I'm to take you to the parlour.' But when Danny followed the maid into the room, there was no sign of Hetty. Instead, Miss Carkettle sat, ramrod-straight, on the edge of the plump sofa.

His throat dried. 'Where's Hetty?'

'*Henrietta* is in her room, reflecting on last night's behaviour. I expect that she will be there for some time.'

'Can I talk to her?' A yellow petal floated from the flowers and on to the hearthrug. Danny tightened his hold around the stems. 'Please?'

For a moment, Miss Carkettle stared at the fallen petal, and her expression seemed to soften. But just when Danny thought she might give in, her shoulders stiffened.

'No!' she said. 'I've forbidden Henrietta from seeing you. She knew my wishes. I made it quite clear that I didn't approve of this show, or of her taking part. But last night she crept out – dressed in little more than her undergarments from what I've seen – with every intention of joining the rehearsal. If it hadn't been for Mr Crimple seeing her home, I might never have found out.' A pause. 'So no, you cannot see my great-niece. And at the moment, I cannot imagine a time when you will be able to do so.'

She rose from her seat and nodded to the maid. 'Please see the boy out. And this time, don't allow him back in.'

And when the cottage door slammed shut behind him, Danny was still clutching the flowers.

As soon as he was able, Danny threw the roses into Belle Vue Lake and watched the water close around them. The surface rippled briefly then smoothed flat until it was impossible to tell that anything had been there at all.

He knew this was his own fault. He should have held on to his temper. Not swung a fist at Tom Dalton or lashed out at Hetty. And he certainly shouldn't have forced Maharajah to continue over the bridge.

He walked a little further along the path and then wished he hadn't. Guilt punched a hole in his chest. A team of carpenters were working on the broken footbridge, their hammers beating rhythmically against the new wood. One of the men looked up, shielding his eyes against the summer sun. 'Oi, lad! You seen Mr Jameson?'

Danny shook his head. 'No.'

'Pity. We found this. Thought he should know.' The man held up a piece of wood. It was wide enough to be one of the planks that had criss-crossed the footbridge. But Danny could see nothing about it that looked either important or remarkable.

'See the top side, it's splintered right across. But underneath, you just look . . .' The carpenter twisted the plank so the other surface was visible. 'The board's not ripped, it's been sawn, part way through.' He shrugged. 'Just seemed odd that's all.'

Danny froze. And in his head, suspicions shifted, stirred and struggled to life – prodded into consciousness like one of the menagerie's great Russian bears waking from sleep. He worked it through logically.

Last night, everyone else had walked over to the island safely. But he, Hetty and Maharajah had been the last ones to cross the bridge. It had groaned under their weight. Then suddenly, halfway along, the wooden planks had snapped – and they'd all come crashing down.

The accident had been no accident. Someone had made certain the boards would be weak enough to break.

For a moment, Danny see-sawed between incredulity and rage. And then the balance tipped. He was tired of letting things happen. He was going to find out what was going on. Because there was only one man he could think of who wanted Belle Vue to fail. The Reverend Eustace Threlfall.

There was no sign of Reverend Threlfall at the church, so Danny tried the vicarage. The house stood next door to St Mark's, surrounded by a large garden overflowing with flowers. And standing in the middle of them was Constance Threlfall. It was the first time Danny had seen her without her brother.

'Hello!' He slipped through the gate and walked along the path. 'Hello,' he called again, keeping his voice soft.

Tilting her head, Constance turned slowly. She was holding her arms at waist height, hands cupped together as though holding something infinitely precious.

'Oh, it's you.' Her smile was as bright as the first time they'd met. 'I'm glad it's you. Look what I've found.' She moved her fingers apart and Danny realized why she was being so careful. Trembling in the centre of her palm was a blue butterfly, fragile as a flower and just as beautiful. 'Isn't she marvellous?'

Danny nodded, stepping closer. And he realized the butterfly was more lavender than blue, with veins of purple threading through each delicate wing. He had the sudden, strongest urge to trace a finger along each fine line. But just as the thought formed, the butterfly came to life. Spreading her wings, she lifted into the sky and rippled upwards. They both watched until she'd disappeared.

Constance smiled. 'She's gone now.'

'Yes. She has.'

Together, they turned towards the house. Now that her hands were empty, Constance swung her arms like a child. There was a freedom to her movements that Danny had never seen in another adult. It made him want to do the same. Instead, he forced himself to remember the reason for his visit.

'I was calling for your brother. Is he home?'

'No. Eustace said he had some important business in Manchester.'

'Oh.' Danny wasn't sure whether to be disappointed or glad. Anger had driven him here, but he hadn't really thought what he might do once he arrived. Had he been expecting to force a confession from the vicar? It seemed stupid now. 'Your brother doesn't like the menagerie, does he?'

'No. Eustace says the animals are noisy. And dirty. And he hates them being so close to the church.'

It was nothing that Danny didn't know already, but the information hardened his suspicions. They'd reached the end of the lawn and ahead, winding up to the vicarage, was a sloping path lined with hollyhocks and catmint. The flowers' sweet scent filled the air as they walked, and the warm sun pressed colour into Danny's cheeks. He let out a sigh. Being with Constance was oddly peaceful.

'And what do *you* think? Of the menagerie?'

'Me? Oh, I love the animals.' If Constance's smile had been bright before, it was brilliant now. 'Sometimes I go to Belle Vue just to sit and watch. The capuchin monkeys are my favourites, but the tigers are beautiful too.' Abruptly, she spun round to face him. Distress had replaced the joy. 'But you won't tell Eustace, will you? I don't think he would like it. I don't think he would like it at all!'

Surprised, Danny shook his head. 'No. I won't tell him.'

His promise seemed to soothe Constance. Her shoulders relaxed and the normal serene expression returned. Even so, Danny was still wary about asking his next question.

'Constance, do you think your brother would let the animals loose? Maybe even . . . even help them escape?'

'Oh no. Eustace wouldn't do that. He's a good person. Not like—' She stopped then bent to pluck one of the blush-pink hollyhocks, twisting the stem anxiously between her fingers.

'Not like who?' Danny fought to keep the urgency out of his voice but he wasn't sure he quite succeeded. Constance's eyes dropped to the flower in her hand. She didn't look up. 'Not like who, Constance?'

'I meant that he's good, not like other people.'

Danny stepped nearer. 'Is that really—?'

'Constance!' They both turned. Reverend Threlfall

was striding towards them. As usual, his clothes fit close to the bone, but today a long black cape swirled from his shoulders. He looked less like an angel, Danny thought, and more like a medieval crusader from one of Hetty's history books.

'I see we have a visitor. To what do we owe this pleasure? Don't tell me – Jameson has seen the light and decided to close Belle Vue?'

Danny didn't smile. 'No, sir.'

'No? Well, I imagine he's been busy enough. I hear you and the elephant had an unfortunate accident on the bridge. I can't say I'm surprised. This is exactly the sort of carelessness I've been warning against.'

An uncomfortable prickle stung the back of Danny's neck. 'How did you know ... about the bridge?'

The vicar shrugged, and the edges of his cloak curled back to reveal the scarlet lining. 'News spreads quickly around Gorton, especially about Belle Vue.' His mouth twisted. 'In fact, by now, I'm sure the story has reached the ears of the Lord Mayor. How unfortunate for you.'

Danny drew a sharp breath. 'The carpenters say the bridge was damaged. Someone sawed through the planks ... before the rehearsal. Did you know?' He could hear the sound of his voice rising. His chest was getting tighter. 'Did you know about it ... before last night?'

The vicar's eyes narrowed. 'I'm going to pretend, for your sake, that you didn't just ask me that. Making such accusations can be dangerous.' He hooked a hand around his sister's arm and drew her away from the flowers. 'Now I'm afraid you must excuse us. Constance and I have a quiet day planned. Please let yourself out.'

And as brother and sister disappeared into the house, Danny was left standing by the garden gate, a swarm of questions buzzing in his head.

Chapter Twenty-two

Mr Jameson was in his study, bent over a large pile of papers and bills on his desk. He was so absorbed, he didn't hear the door open, so for several heartbeats, Danny was able to simply stand and watch.

Only this morning, he'd studied Charles Larkin in almost the same way. And just like then, he didn't know how to begin this conversation – even though there was so much to say.

He wanted to pour out all his worries. The guilt he felt about Maharajah's injury, his fear that someone was laying the blame for the disasters at his door, and his suspicions about Reverend Threlfall. But most of all, he wanted to pour out all his muddled feelings about the man who claimed to be his father.

He cleared his throat, and Mr Jameson looked up. For a brief moment, Danny was certain his expression held only relief and gratitude. But he must have been wrong because the first words out of his mouth were furious.

'What in the blue blazes were you thinkin', lad? You've been gone all night. Ethel May's been worried sick! And it's only because I made sure Crimple kept an eye on you that we knew where you were.'

Danny stiffened. At least one mystery was solved. Nelson Crimple had been turning up like a bad penny whenever he rounded a corner. It appeared that Mr Jameson had sent a spy.

'And there's no need to look at me like that. If Crimple's been followin' you it was only to make sure you were safe. And I'm not goin' to apologize for it.' Despite the words, Mr Jameson's eyes flickered guiltily. 'Anyhow, from what I hear, there's every reason to be worried. I'm told you started a fight with Tom Dalton. And don't try to deny it, because you've obviously been brawlin'. Just look at you!'

Danny resisted the urge to touch the bruises on his face but he didn't think Mr Jameson expected an answer so he said nothing.

'And I haven't even got started on the bridge collapsin'. Lord knows, Danny, I don't expect much. All I asked is for you to keep your head down and look after Maharajah. You know he's our biggest attraction. Now, thanks to your carelessness, he's a laughin' stock. An elephant with only one tusk.'

Danny's anger bubbled to a boil. 'Didn't . . . didn't you say there's no such thing as bad publicity?' He could feel his throat closing up and he made himself slow down. 'You said that as long as . . . as long as people are talking about us . . . it's good . . . it's good for Belle Vue.'

Scowling, Mr Jameson pushed back his chair and got to his feet. 'Don't try to be clever with me, lad. One or two interestin' stories might bring in the crowds but all we've had lately are disasters. Escaped animals trying to eat children. Protests and banners at the gate! The Manchester Corporation talkin' about closin' us down. The newspapers are rippin' us apart. And what's worse – the investors don't like it. I've had Snade bendin' my ear already.'

He grabbed one of the papers from the desk and waved it at Danny. 'And to cap it all, this came by messenger. A letter from Goadsby. He heard about the accident on the bridge and he's comin' to inspect the park. Of course, we won't know when because it's goin' to be a surprise visit!'

He crumpled the paper into a ball and tossed it into the fire. Danny watched the page blacken at the edges before sparking into flames.

'Do you understand what you've done, lad? This could cost us everythin'. Everythin'.'

Danny lifted his gaze from the fire. The tightness in his throat had worsened, and now he didn't think he could have spoken, even to whisper. Curling his hands into fists, he spun on his heels and was out of the door before Mr Jameson could react.

'Danny! You come back here! Right this minute. Come back! DANNY!'

But he was already down the path and out of the garden gate, Mr Jameson's voice fading to an indistinct rumble in the distance.

Outside the Longsight Hotel, Danny made sure to find a hiding place where he could see the front entrance. Once again, he'd slipped out of Belle Vue, directly against Mr Jameson's orders. But he no longer cared. There were too many other things to worry about.

Luckily, Danny didn't have long to wait. Larkin emerged from the hotel less than an hour later. As usual, he was dressed as if meeting royalty – spotless and flawless from the collar of his frock coat to the tips of his leather gloves.

Hastily, Danny pushed away from the shadow of the hotel wall. 'Do you still want to talk?' The question emerged more abruptly than he'd intended, and for a moment, Larkin looked startled to see him.

'Yes. Yes, of course. I just didn't expect you so soon.' Carefully, he studied Danny's face. 'Naturally, I'd be delighted to talk. The question is – do you?'

'I–I just want ... I want to know more about you. About everything.' Danny straightened his shoulders and Larkin smiled.

'Well then, it's a beautiful day, and I was about to go for a stroll. Why don't you show me Belle Vue?'

In silence, they followed the road to the Longsight gate

where Larkin handed over the shilling entrance fee and took one of the small metal tokens that gave them access to every attraction in the park.

They didn't need to buy the halfpenny guide map from Mr Cogwell. Instead Danny led the way to the ape house where the capuchin monkeys were using their long tails to cartwheel around their enclosure. Swinging down from the rafters, one grabbed a child's hat and another stole a lady's handkerchief. Then they chased back up to their high perch to examine their treasures.

For once, Danny couldn't manage a smile at their antics. Nerves had begun tumbling in his stomach. Maybe this wasn't such a good idea; perhaps he should have talked to the Jamesons first. Or tried again to speak to Hetty.

So he said nothing as they reached Belle Vue Lake; and still nothing when they passed the sea lions sunbathing on the rocks; and very little when they swerved to avoid a party of schoolchildren, squealing over their lemon-flavoured ices.

Instead, he stuffed his hands into his pockets and tried to look confident, even though his throat was dry with uncertainty.

At the lakeside, one of the pleasure boats was pulling out across the water, just in front of the footbridge. And Danny saw that the carpenters must have finished their repairs, because the pale new wood showed up against the old, battered boards.

A little further ahead, a cluster of pebbles banded the

shore. Abruptly, Mr Larkin stopped and scooped up a stone. He turned it in his hands, as if feeling the weight and shape.

'Good enough,' he said, before turning towards the lake. He flicked his wrist and the pebble skimmed across the water. It bounced. Once. Twice. Three times. And then just when Danny thought it had run out of energy, it did it again. And again.

His eyes widened. 'Can you teach me?'

'Yes. Of course.'

They searched the shore, looking for the perfect stone. It had to be wide and flat, Mr Larkin said. Smooth as an egg shell, and just as light.

'Here's one.' He tossed it into Danny's palm. 'Hold it flat between your fingers. Like this.' He reached and adjusted Danny's grip. 'Now flick your wrist. The quicker the better.'

Carefully, Danny balanced the stone then threw it. The stone skimmed the water. Once, then twice. He looked up and caught Larkin's eye. They exchanged a grin.

'Good. But I reckon you can do even more. Try again.'

They stayed for a while longer, flicking the stones across the water, but not talking overly much. The sun was beginning to dip in the sky as they walked back. And Danny was surprised to find the afternoon had run on without them.

'I hoped you'd come back, I wasn't sure you would. But I'm glad you did.'

'So am I.'

It hadn't mattered that they'd not talked about anything

important. There had been no more stories about Danny's mother, or Larkin's family, or any other subjects they might have discussed. Instead, they'd searched for stones, and skimmed pebbles across the lake and talked about very little. It had been exactly what Danny had needed, without him even knowing it.

'Is that one of your friends?'

Danny looked up. Hetty and her aunt were walking towards them, and Larkin was watching them with interest.

'Yes. That's Hetty . . . I mean Miss Henrietta Saddleworth. And her aunt, Miss Carkettle.'

'I see.' Larkin slid him a sharp glance. 'And is Hetty the person you wanted to apologizc to earlier?'

'Yes. But I didn't get to see her.' He scuffed his boot on the ground. 'Her aunt thinks I'm a bad influence.'

Larkin grinned. 'All the best people are. Just leave it to me.'

Miss Carkettle had already started shepherding her niece in the opposite direction when Larkin swept into their path. His bow was low and graceful.

'Miss Carkettle. Miss Henrietta. How delightful to meet you. Please forgive my presumption, but I've heard so much about you both it seems I know you already.'

'I wish I could say the same, sir. But I'm afraid I can't.' Miss Carkettle arched an eyebrow. At her side, Hetty stared at Danny then scowled and looked away. She didn't turn back.

'That is certainly my loss, madam. I'm Charles Larkin.

My late father was Sir Edward Larkin. You may have heard of him. A cousin to Lord Henry Larkin of the Cheshire Larkins?'

Danny could see a slight flicker of interest in Miss Carkettle's face. 'Perhaps the name is vaguely familiar. Where did you say you came from?'

'From Scotland, madam. My family live in Melrose Hall, just outside Stirling. But of course, we have a home in Edinburgh and another in London.'

Miss Carkettle's mouth pinched. 'That's a great number of houses, Mr Larkin. I suppose, given how widespread your family appears to be, it is just possible our paths may have crossed.' She paused. 'Although I certainly don't remember it.'

'Well, yes . . . My young friend here would like a few words with Miss Henrietta. However, I understand you have some concerns. I would never dream of going against your authority but if I give you my word as a gentleman . . .'

Larkin let the request hang, perfectly poised, between them. It was like watching a fisherman baiting a hook, and Danny was almost sure Miss Carkettle would bite.

He was wrong.

'That is all very well, Mr Larkin. However, the boy not only encouraged my niece to defy me, but he helped her to do it. And I don't believe such behaviour should be rewarded. Not unless we wish to become as headstrong as the Americans.' She hooked a gloved hand around Hetty's arm. 'Come along, Henrietta. Let's go home.'

As they walked away, Danny willed Hetty to look back. To give him the smallest sign that he'd been forgiven. But she didn't. Perhaps she was still as angry with him, as he was with himself. He stayed watching until they turned the bend.

Larkin came to stand beside him. 'I'm sorry. It was worth a try.'

Danny shrugged as if he didn't care, even though his heart felt as though it had been scooped from his chest. An arm circled his shoulder.

'Look, in my experience, friends come and go. The only people you can really rely on are your flesh and blood. Wouldn't you agree?'

Chapter Twenty-three

The final rehearsal began far less dramatically than the last. This time, there was no sudden plunge down towards the water. No dramatic rescue from the bridge. All the same, as Danny walked across to Firework Island, he felt a tug of trepidation.

He was on foot, leading the way ahead of Maharajah. The rest of the cast followed behind, dressed in their brightly coloured show costumes. And although Danny knew the chances of Hetty being allowed to come were small, he looked for her anyway. And when he didn't see her, his disappointment was just as fierce as if she'd promised to be there.

Instead, as he guided Maharajah up the path to the top of the hill, it was Tom Dalton who trooped past. For several long moments, they stared at one another over the heads of the other soldiers. And Danny was near enough to see the large bruise covering Tom's cheek. His chest filled with a mix of shame and satisfaction.

And then he looked up, and saw the blunt stump of Maharajah's left tusk, and guilt replaced everything else. Stretching tall, he traced his fingers along the sawn tusk and then around Maharajah's gold eyes where the skin was as soft and delicate as paper.

With all his heart, Danny wished there was some sign that he'd been forgiven. Because it didn't matter who had caused the damage to the footbridge. Or sawed through the boards. Or stood back to watch the disaster unfold. Because this was his fault. Mr Saddleworth had asked him to look after Maharajah – and he'd failed.

Suddenly, a rough grip curled around Danny's neck and chest, and Maharajah was pulling him close. Close enough that the two of them might merge together. They stood there, swaying gently for the space of several heartbeats. And it seemed to Danny that, as always, Maharajah had known exactly what he needed. And when.

'Listen! All of you! Gather round.'

Danny raised his head. Mr Jameson stood on the brow of the hill, gesturing for everyone to move closer. Obediently, soldiers and villagers shuffled into a circle around him. But Danny held back, glad to have Maharajah as an excuse to stay on the fringes.

'Now I need to run through what's happenin' tomorrow night. So, you all listen carefully – and make sure you remember.' Mr Jameson's gaze circled the group. 'At the openin' of the show the music will start. Softly at first, then louder and louder. We'll have a few fireworks firin' off. Lightin' up the island from above. Whippin' up excitement. The audience will be over there on the mainland.'

Mr Jameson pointed across the lake to a wooden platform jutting out on to the water. It was where Snade and the other bankers had been standing when Maharajah had sprayed them with his trunk. Since then, rows of seats had been built in tiers to form a spectators' gallery, and more chairs were being arranged on either side of the shore.

'There's twenty thousand tickets been sold at the last count. And more likely to be bought tomorrow. So, expect a lot of noise.'

Danny's throat dried. He remembered how nervous he'd first felt at the thought of all those people. How terrified he had been of making a mistake. He didn't feel so very different now.

'And then the fightin' will start on the island. The British soldiers on this side, the French on the other. And caught between them, a Spanish village sittin' right up on the hill.'

Mr Jameson swept a hand towards the painted backdrops outlined against the horizon. The canvas scenery had been brought to the island a few days ago and fixed to large wooden frames. And Danny had to admit, that from a distance, it looked like rows of Spanish houses had been dropped into the centre of Belle Vue.

'Then suddenly, Prince Dandip and Maharajah will

appear at the top of the hill.' Mr Jameson lifted his head and searched for Danny until their eyes met.

'When the first explosion goes off, that's your signal to move, Danny. The fuses are linked, so once one starts, the others will follow, one after another. All you have to do is hold Maharajah steady and walk him down towards the shore.' A pause. 'Can you manage that?'

Danny pressed his lips together and nodded. He didn't dare speak, because he was certain that whatever emerged from his mouth would be angry. He'd already been blamed for the bridge accident. Now it seemed Mr Jameson didn't even trust him to ride Maharajah in a straight line.

'Well, let's hope so.' Mr Jameson's nod was curt. Turning back, he lifted his hands like the conductor of an orchestra. 'There'll be rockets, and lanterns and firecrackers lightin' up the island.' His fingers swirled through the air. 'And the music will get even louder. Suddenly, Maharajah will sound out a trumpet call and everythin' will fall silent. The soldiers will lay down their guns, and there'll be dancin' and singin'. And right at the end, Her Majesty's face will be lit up against the sky in fireworks. Then everyone'll line up along the water's edge for the final bow.' He lowered his arms to his sides. 'Have you got that?'

Like everyone else, Danny nodded. The story still sounded as ridiculous as the first time he'd heard it. But there was no denying that if all went to plan, the show was certain to be a success. It had everything. Battles, explosions, music and fireworks. Even a prince and his elephant.

'Good!' For the first time tonight, Mr Jameson looked pleased. 'And let me assure you, there's no need to worry about the pyrotechnics. There'll be a few bangs and lots of smoke, but it's all for show. Nothin' that can do anyone any harm.' He raised his voice so it rang across the island. 'Isn't that right, George?'

'Aye.' Down on the shore, George Dalton waved in acknowledgement, but he didn't stop to say anything more. He was too busy supervising the horse and cart carrying the barrels of gunpowder and coils of fuses across the bridge. Strapped to the top, Danny could just see the outline of Queen Victoria's face, her profile pinned out on to a large wooden board. The broken frame had obviously been rebuilt in time. But to Danny, it was yet another reminder of being accused of something he hadn't done.

Mr Jameson clapped his hands. 'Excellent. So, you get to your places – and let's run through it from the beginnin'. Make sure you all know exactly what you're doin'.'

The practice went surprisingly smoothly. The French and British soldiers fought with enthusiasm, and the Spanish peasants fled their village so loudly that their screaming must have been heard all across Belle Vue.

And much to Danny's relief, Maharajah didn't waver from the path; or flinch at the sound of the small explosion; or stomp into the water. And when he sounded out a trumpet call, it thundered resoundingly around the lake.

This time, the rehearsal for 'Prince Dandip and the Fight for Flamenca' had run like clockwork.

It was past eight o'clock in the evening when Mr Jameson
and Danny returned to Belle Vue House. Their journey
home had been conducted mostly in silence, and Danny
was glad when Mrs Jameson opened the door to greet
them.

'You've a visitor, Danny. *A gentleman.* I put him in
the front parlour. He didn't give his name, but he asked
particularly for you.'

She lifted her brows in a half-question but Danny didn't
answer. An unwelcome suspicion stirred in the back of his
mind. He only hoped he was wrong.

In the hallway, the parlour door was slightly ajar, and
Danny peered through the gap cautiously. Just as he'd
suspected, leaning against the fireplace was Charles Larkin.
He'd propped his hat and walking stick against the arm of
the sofa, and was staring into the fire. There was every indi-
cation that he'd been waiting for some time.

Straightening his shoulders, Danny pushed open the
door. Larkin turned. 'At last! Thank goodness! I came to
find out how you were. You seemed so upset this afternoon
and I was worried.'

'You can't come here!' The words burst from Danny's
mouth more forcefully than he'd intended. 'You can't ... *be*
here.'

Anxiously, he flicked a glance over his shoulder but the
parlour door had swung closed behind him. And he wondered how long it would take to encourage Larkin out of

the house. And if he could do it without the Jamesons knowing.

Larkin's mouth flattened. 'I wasn't sure what else to do, or how I could get in touch with you. Coming here seemed to be the only option. But I'm sorry if it causes you a problem.'

'I would have come to you. At the hotel.'

'Yes. I'm sure you would … eventually.' Larkin's voice was wry. 'Look, I know you still have doubts, but surely by now you must believe me. I'm telling the truth. *I am your father*. I know it's difficult but—'

The crash of crockery hitting the floor interrupted him. Danny spun round. Mrs Jameson stood in the doorway, her face chalk-white and fragile. A tray of china cups lay at her feet, the teapot leaking steadily across the rug.

A fraction of a moment later, Mr Jameson burst into the room behind her. 'Ethel May! What is it? What's the matter?'

But his wife said nothing, and when he didn't get an immediate reply, Mr Jameson turned to Danny. 'What's goin' on, lad? Who's this man? And what's he doin' here upsettin' Ethel May? Cos if he's causin' trouble, I don't care if he's a king, he can get out now.'

Danny swallowed. He looked around the room, at the different expressions on all three faces. And he knew a moment's panic. He was trapped inside a barrel rolling downhill and gaining speed, being tossed from rock to rock, and back again. And the chances were very strong that at the bottom, the barrel would crack open and fall apart. 'He's . . . he's . . .'

But it was Larkin who stepped forward. 'You must be Mr James Jameson. My name's Charles Larkin.' He stretched out a hand. 'I'm Danny's father.'

Mr Jameson made an inarticulate noise and ignored the offered handshake. Instead, he slipped an arm around his wife and pulled her close. She curled into his chest.

Larkin dropped his hand. 'I'm sorry. I thought you both knew. I was sure Danny would have mentioned me by now.'

'No.' Unlike his wife, Mr Jameson's face held no hint of how he felt. 'No, he didn't.'

'Well then, I must apologize. If I'd known . . . well I certainly wouldn't have broken the news like that. It was never my intention to cause any upset.'

'You didn't succeed then, did you? Cos this seems like a great deal of upset to me.' Mr Jameson turned to Danny. 'When were you goin' to tell us, lad?'

'I . . . I tried to.' His tongue felt heavy, and once again his throat was closing up. 'But it never seemed like a good time.' Even to his own ears, the excuse sounded feeble.

'No. I don't imagine it did.'

Abruptly, Mrs Jameson pushed away from her husband's chest. Her face was still pale and she blinked rapidly, but when she spoke, her voice was firm. 'Well, Mr Larkin. I think you'd better stay to dinner. We're having chicken.'

Chapter Twenty-four

Dinner was a disaster – much like an accident that everyone can see is about to happen, yet no one knows how to stop.

Although it started well enough. The best dinner service had been laid out on the dining room table; Danny recognized the pattern of pink roses and gold swirls. And the kitchen maid had fetched the Jamesons' wedding crystal from the dresser. She'd even made an apple tart, with thick cream custard, to follow the roasted chicken and buttered potatoes.

But the elegant china did nothing to make up for the awkward tension as they settled at the table. And when Mr Jameson began sharpening the knife to carve the meat, it seemed to Danny that the noise was particularly loud.

'So where are you from, Mr Larkin?' Mrs Jameson asked

politely. Her cheeks had almost recovered their colour. 'Perhaps you can tell us a little about yourself?'

'From the Stirling area of Scotland, ma'am. My father was Sir Edward Larkin, of Melrose Hall.'

The Jamesons exchanged a look that was difficult to decipher, and Danny wished he knew what they were thinking. But neither of them had said a great deal since Larkin's announcement.

'I see. And is that where you met Danny's mother? At Melrose Hall?'

'No, ma'am. I met her at the fruit market in Stirling. She was buying oranges. We married three months later, even though my family didn't approve. Sadly, in the end, my parents managed to drive us apart. It was only after their deaths that I was able to begin searching for my wife.' He paused and sipped his wine. 'And of course, that search led me to my son. Edward.'

The story was a much shorter version of the one that Larkin had told Danny. But maybe Mrs Jameson understood enough to fill in the gaps because she didn't ask any more. In the silence, everyone ate their chicken. Then Mr Jameson put down his fork. 'The boy's name is Danny.'

Larkin's gaze flicked towards Danny and away again. 'Now it is. But when he was born, he was christened Edward. I believe my wife named him after my father.'

'Well, he's Danny to us. And that's all that matters.'

'If you say so.' Larkin inclined his head and stabbed at another piece of chicken.

Scowling, Mr Jameson leant across the table. 'Listen to me, Larkin. Don't think you can come here and start taking over. For the last two months, we've looked after that boy. We've fed him, clothed him. Brought him into our house. Given him a home. A name!'

Danny could feel a flush rising up his face. He wanted to be anywhere but in this room. He stopped pretending to eat and pushed back his chair.

'Do you know how he was livin' before?' Mr Jameson had picked up the carving knife again. He was using it like a sword, jabbing the air as he made each point. 'Do you? Well, I'll tell you, shall I? He was stealin'. Anythin' he could find to sell. Just so he could eat. And have you seen his scars?'

Leaning across the table, he tugged at Danny's sleeve with his free hand. The crude letters 'FS' were clearly visible. 'There – that should tell you what his life was like. Not pretty, is it?'

With more care than was necessary, Larkin put down his cutlery, and wiped his mouth with the napkin. 'I came to Manchester as soon as I could. As soon as I knew I had a son. And as soon as I heard he was here at Belle Vue.'

'Well that wasn't soon enough, was it?'

'Jamie, please! This is not the time, or the place, for this discussion!' Mrs Jameson's face was as pale as pearl, and she'd curled her fingers into fists on her lap.

Larkin must have noticed her distress, because his voice gentled. 'It's quite all right, Mrs Jameson. I understand that this is a difficult situation for us all. But with your permission, I'd like to stay at Belle Vue a little longer and get to know my son. I hope you have no objection?'

Mrs Jameson took a breath. 'Of course you must get to know each other. If you're Danny's father then you have every right.'

'But that's the point, isn't it? How do we know you are who you say?' Mr Jameson had still not put down the knife. 'We only have your word for it. You might be a con man . . . A swindler. A thief. You could be anyone!'

Deliberately, Larkin pushed back his chair and rose to his feet. 'I think I'd better leave now, Mr Jameson. Before we both say something we regret. Mrs Jameson, thank you for the dinner. It was most kind.'

In a few swift strides, he was out of the door. Hastily, Danny scrambled to his feet. 'I'll go and say goodbye.'

Mr Jameson opened his mouth as if to argue, but his wife grabbed his hand first, and silenced him with a look.

'Very well, Danny, go if you wish . . .' She paused. 'But please come back . . . won't you?'

Larkin was shrugging into his coat when Danny caught up with him in the hall. He flicked an impatient glance in the direction of the dining room. 'That could have gone better. They're not exactly reasonable people. He practically accused me of lying.'

'They're just upset. It's a shock. I–I should have told them earlier.' Danny was surprised by the strength of his need to defend the Jamesons.

'Yes. I suppose so.' Distractedly, Larkin fastened the last of his coat buttons then snatched up his hat. 'Listen, Danny. I want to stay in Manchester and get to know you better. But if it's going to cause trouble, maybe it's best if I didn't.'

'No! Don't go.' The reply was instinctive. For most of his life Danny had only ever travelled in one direction because he'd never had any other choice. But now his path had led quite unexpectedly to a crossroads, and there was more than one road. He had the strongest desire to see where the other routes might lead. 'Please. I want you to stay.'

'Are you certain?'

Heart thumping, Danny nodded.

Larkin smiled. 'Then meet me tomorrow, at the elephant house. Let's make it early. Eight o'clock. We can talk again then.'

Chapter Twenty-five

There were no crowds clustering around the elephant house at eight o'clock the next morning. It was too early for visitors, and Danny was glad of the quiet.

He'd arrived well before the arranged meeting time so he could feed and clean Maharajah but mostly so he could check the broken tusk once again. It was a relief to find that the injury was still free from infection.

'Good morning!' The shout filtered into the enclosure from the outdoor paddock. 'Are you in there?'

Danny set down the bowl of cleaning cloths and went outside. Larkin stood by the gate, as elegantly dressed as ever. Today, he wore a top hat of shiny silk and a shirt with a high starched collar and long cuffs. A silver-headed walking stick swung from one gloved hand.

Once again, Danny was struck by the differences

between them. It was still astonishing to him that this man could be his father. And yet, for some reason, it didn't seem quite so unlikely as it once had.

Stepping through the mud, Danny walked across the paddock to unlock the gate. And, as he lifted the latch, it occurred to him that Larkin had not yet met Maharajah. So instead of slipping outside, he let the gate swing open. 'Would you like to come in? I could introduce you to Maharajah.'

'I'd be honoured.' Larkin tucked his hat beneath his arm and brushed back the curl from his forehead. 'If you'd care to show me.'

Inside, Maharajah was chewing through a batch of sugar cane, using his trunk to grab the sticks and curl them up to his mouth. The canes crunched noisily between his teeth. Slowly, Larkin circled the pen, not seeming to care about the dirt and straw muddying his polished boots.

'He's big. Even bigger than I imagined.'

'Yes. But he's gentle.' Danny rubbed his palm along Maharajah's side, knowing exactly which spot would bring the most comfort. Almost immediately, a throaty rumble vibrated through skin and bone and muscle. Although perhaps, Danny thought, it wasn't a sound so much as a feeling.

'You're good with him.'

Danny felt a swell of pride. He was always at his most confident around Maharajah.

'Does he understand you?'

'Yes. Everything. Sandev always said elephants are the cleverest of all the animals.'

Larkin stopped circling and raised his eyebrows. 'Sandev?'

'He used to be Maharajah's keeper before Maharajah came to Belle Vue. Sandev was the one who taught me. In India, they called him a mahout. Someone who trains elephants.' Danny picked up the ankus that he'd propped against one wall. They had done this many times before, but he'd never got over the wonder of it. 'Look. I'll show you.'

Lifting the cane, he gave a sharp whistle. Obediently, Maharajah sank to the ground, his head resting low on his front legs. Danny pulled an apple from the jacket pocket where he kept a store of treats.

He sat the fruit in his hand and held it out. Instinctively, Maharajah started towards it, but with one short signal, Danny told him to wait. They stared at each for almost a full minute. And then Danny whistled again. With one graceful movement, Maharajah reached out and snatched up the apple. He munched it noisily.

And then – just as Danny had known he would – Maharajah turned the tables. He climbed to his feet, stretched out his trunk and grabbed the ankus from Danny's hand. Lifting it out of reach, he waved it like a magician would wave a wand.

Danny grinned – he knew exactly what was expected of him. He knelt, raising his arms up. And as soon as his knees touched the floor, Maharajah dropped the ankus into his outstretched palms.

Larkin released a laugh, admiration clear on his face. It felt good. 'How incredible! I'd never have believed it unless I'd seen it with my own eyes. It's as though you can read each other's minds.'

'Yes. Sometimes . . .' Danny hesitated. He'd never voiced the thought out loud for fear of sounding ridiculous. 'Sometimes . . .' he tried again. 'I'm certain Maharajah knows exactly how I feel. And what I think. But . . .' Danny trailed off. Larkin waited and said nothing. 'But I let him down. I didn't trust him . . . not like he trusted me.'

'I don't understand. Why would you think that?' Larkin frowned.

'There was an accident on the bridge . . . his tusk was broken . . . it was my fault. Maharajah stopped. He didn't want to move further on, but I made him. If it hadn't been for me—'

'No. I'm certain that's not true.'

Danny blinked. 'And it's not the only reason. Everything is going wrong. Everything I *do* is wrong!'

'What do you mean?' Lightly, Larkin placed an arm around Danny's shoulders. 'Look if there's something bothering you, tell me. I might be able to help.'

Danny hesitated. He'd spent most of his life keeping himself apart. And even now there were only a handful of people he trusted. But in the last few days, this man had saved him from a gunman, tried to mend his friendship with Hetty, and taught him to skim stones on Belle Vue Lake. Talking was little enough to give him in return.

And suddenly, all his worries poured out. From his first disastrous meeting with Snade and the other investors, to Victoria's unexplained escape, and his accident at the firework factory. He even found himself revealing his suspicions about the padlock on Emerald's cage. It was everything that he'd wanted to tell Mr Jameson – and hadn't.

Larkin didn't say very much but he listened, in that intent way that a few people do, showing that he heard every word – and not only did he hear, he also understood.

Finally, Danny took a breath.

'And the shooting in the maze . . . when I first met you? Do you think that's part of it?'

'Yes. It has to be.'

'And so you think someone is deliberately causing problems for Belle Vue?'

'Yes.' Now that Danny had laid out each detail, it seemed even more obvious.

'Why?'

'I think someone wants Belle Vue to fail. I think they want it to fail badly. And I think they want me to get the blame. The accidents always seem to happen when I'm nearby. Or . . . or in place where I've just been.'

Larkin's eyes widened. He drew in a sharp breath, and his arm dropped from Danny's shoulders. 'So who do you think it is?'

'It sounds ridiculous.'

'Tell me anyway.'

Danny swallowed. 'I think it must be Reverend Threlfall. He's the only one who wants Belle Vue to close . . . I just don't have any proof.'

Larkin's grip tightened on his walking stick. Swinging it, he paced away for a few steps. And when he turned back, his expression was determined.

'Look. I didn't want to say anything before, but after what you've just told me maybe now is the right time.' He dragged a hand across his jaw. 'When I leave, I want you to come with me. We could travel. Anywhere you choose. Point to a place on a map, and that's where we'll go. Paris, Rome. Madrid. Further away if you'd like. It'll just be you and me.'

Stunned, Danny let his mouth drop loose. How many times had he wished for that? When he was scraping a living on the streets of Edinburgh, he would have done anything to escape. But it was different now. Now he had a home at Belle Vue. Didn't he?

'I have some savings. Although, not a great deal. My brothers run the family business, and most of the money's tied up in that. But they give me an allowance so I've enough to get us started.'

Danny stayed silent. And perhaps Larkin thought more persuasion was needed because he walked a little closer, his stick making pockmarks in the dirt.

'Besides, what's keeping you here? Jameson seems obsessed with his business. His wife always takes her husband's side. Your friend, Hetty, is not even speaking to you.

And as for her aunt . . . well, she obviously doesn't approve of you at all.' He stabbed the ground with his stick. 'So, tell me: who is there to stop you from leaving?'

Maharajah. It was the first name that came into Danny's head. The only friend who wasn't lined up against him. But then just as quickly, Danny remembered the accident on the bridge, and the bleeding, splintered tusk.

Maybe Maharajah would be better off without him. Maybe they all would. Hetty, the Jamesons, Mr Saddleworth. Even Tom Dalton. And maybe when he was gone, all the disasters that had plagued Belle Vue would stop.

'I have money.' Danny spoke quickly. He was flinging himself off a high cliff not knowing if he would land safely. He felt a little sick. 'Mr Jameson put it into the bank for me. And he said it was mine. To spend however I wanted.'

'Did he?' Larkin didn't look as pleased as he might. His gloved hand opened and closed around his walking stick. 'I see. That does make a difference. Maybe you might be better staying here after all.'

Danny jerked. 'Why?'

'The Jamesons have done right by you, given you an inheritance. Perhaps, in time, they mean for you to take over Belle Vue. Compared to that, what can I offer you? The Larkin mill isn't even mine to give.'

'But . . . but you're my father.' It was the first time Danny had admitted the possibility, and he was certain he shocked both of them by saying it. Nervously, he cleared his throat and when his voice finally emerged, it was small and frayed and broken. 'Aren't you?'

'Yes. Yes, I am.' Larkin's mouth curled up at the edges. 'So why don't you come with me? Father and son together.'

Chapter Twenty-six

'So, we're agreed. You're coming?'

'Yes.'

'And we'll leave tonight? After the performance?'

'Yes.'

'Good!' The satisfaction was clear in Larkin's voice. Brandishing his walking stick, he paced across the enclosure floor. Now that the decision had been made, he seemed different. Bigger. Bolder. More animated – as if he'd thrown off a heavy weight that had been pinning him down. 'We'll need to make plans.'

'Yes.' It was the third time that Danny had nodded his agreement. And a knot was beginning to form in his throat. Blocking the air, making his head spin dizzily.

He watched Larkin pivot on his boot heels. 'I'm still not entirely sure why you feel the need to take part in the show, but I suppose it'll work in our favour. Everybody will be so busy they won't notice that we've gone.'

He pivoted again. 'Pack a bag today, then hide it somewhere. Somewhere outside the Jamesons' house but in a place that you can get to easily. Then as soon as the show finishes, we'll pick it up and leave. I'll meet you at the footbridge straight after the final scene.' His eyes locked on Danny. 'Agreed?'

'Yes.'

'Excellent. And Danny . . . ?' Larkin's eyes were bright with something that was far more than excitement. 'You've made the right decision. We're going to have such amazing adventures, you and I! Don't you think?'

'Yes.' The knot loosened. 'I do.'

And so, Danny thought later, how easy it had been to steer his life into a new direction with just a handful of words.

The Jamesons' house was quiet when Danny let himself inside, but the smell of baking lingered in the air. Mrs Jameson must have been busy all morning, and he knew there'd likely be a plate of fresh biscuits on the kitchen table, waiting just for him.

For a moment, he let the thought drift. The comfort of home-cooked food would be one of the many things he'd miss when he was gone.

'Danny?'

He turned. Mrs Jameson was standing in the hall, wiping

her hands on her apron repeatedly, even though they looked quite clean. And he wondered how long she'd been waiting there, watching out for him.

'I hoped it was you. I wanted to make sure all was well after last night. I'm afraid Mr Jameson's temper got the better of him. It was rather a shock, you see. For both of us. And he's been under such strain. With all the new attractions and the building work and the expansions. And of course, it's very important that he keeps the investors happy because otherwise . . .' She stopped, took a breath and dropped the apron. 'Well, that's a story for another time. Anyway, are you quite well?'

'Yes, ma'am. I'm fine.'

'Good. Good.' Her smile held more than a touch of relief. 'Now all we need is for the show to go smoothly, and everything will be exactly as it was. Life will return to normal.' She stopped as though a possibility had only just occurred to her. 'You will be there, won't you? In costume? As Prince Dandip? You've not changed your mind?'

Guilt hit Danny's chest with the force of a fist. 'Yes. I'll be there,' he said. It was the truth but not all of the truth – because by the end of the night, he'd be gone.

'Oh. I am glad. And Mr Jameson will be pleased.' This time the smile was deep and heartfelt. 'Just make sure you're back here by eight o'clock so we can get you dressed and ready in time.' She stepped nearer. 'And don't worry about Mr Larkin. If he is your father, he's welcome here for as long as he wishes to stay.'

The guilt punched again. Hastily, Danny nodded and moved towards the stairs.

'Oh, wait. Just a moment!' Reaching out, Mrs Jameson smoothed a gentle hand over his hair. And Danny knew the cow's lick curl must have fallen down, across his forehead. 'There that's better. Go on then. Off with you! I'm sure you've jobs to do.'

Danny took the stairs two at a time, and ran the rest of the way to his room. And when he was safely inside, he closed the door firmly before sliding the bolt across.

Now the guilt wasn't a fist, it was a giant hammer pounding away at his insides. For a moment, he thought he might be sick. And then he set his jaw and thought of all the reasons why he needed to go. And of all the reasons he'd decided not to stay.

Crouching, Danny pulled a suitcase from underneath his bed. The hinges creaked as he lifted the lid. The last time he'd tried running away – on the walk from Edinburgh to Manchester – he'd packed every belonging that he owned, but it hadn't been very much.

This time, there was a lot more to take. An entire wardrobe of clothes; the silver-backed brush that Mrs Jameson have given him; the poster of Maharajah from his old circus days; and a newspaper cutting about the Edinburgh auction – the day that he'd first met Maharajah.

When the suitcase was full, Danny had trouble closing the lid. But eventually, it clicked shut. Grabbing the ankus, he slid it into his belt. He would need it later. And after the show, he would find a safe place to leave it – for someone else to use. The thought sent his stomach dipping to his toes.

He knew he had to leave a note, but he wasn't sure what to say. And when he thought of some words that might have worked, he didn't know how to write them. Hetty's lessons had covered only the most basic of sentences.

So, in the end, he picked up the pen and carefully scrawled: 'Thank you.' Because he knew the shape of those words. And then after a long pause he wrote his name: 'Danny'. Because he knew that too.

The message seemed absurdly small and miserly for what the Jamesons had given him. The queasy feeling in his stomach worsened. And once again, he tried to remember how he'd felt earlier, when he'd been making plans with Larkin. How, in that moment, leaving Belle Vue had seemed not only the right choice, but also the only one.

He'd found his father – and more importantly, his father had found him. Nothing had changed in the last few hours, so why did he feel far less certain? Far more unsure of the step he was about to take?

He pushed the doubts away and folded the paper in half. Carefully, he placed it on the mantelpiece above the hearth so Mrs Jameson would be certain to see it – but not too soon. Then he picked up the suitcase and closed the door quietly behind him.

This time, no one heard him leave.

And now that everything else was done, there was

only one more task left. It was the one he was dreading the most.

It didn't take long to walk to the elephant house. Maharajah was awake, standing alone in his stall almost as though he'd been waiting. As Danny drew nearer, the gold eyes watched him steadily.

Sliding a hand into his jacket, Danny searched for an apple. Then he offered up the fruit on his palm like a gift. Maharajah swept it up with his trunk. And it occurred to Danny that it would be the last time he would do this. The last time that it would just be the two of them, alone together.

Almost from the beginning, there had been a bond. And the connection had only grown stronger over the weeks and months since. Around Maharajah, he always felt safe and known and understood.

He stroked the warm, rough skin – as he had done many times before – and laid his head against Maharajah's side. A rush of warm breath tickled his cheek. And he felt the ebb and flow of breathing. In and out. Out and in. For long, painful moments, the only sound was the beat of Danny's heart, and Maharajah's faint throaty rumble.

'I won't get a chance later. Not properly, there'll be too many people around. So ... so I wanted to do this now when it's just you and me.' His throat tightened and when the words finally emerged, they were threadbare. 'I wanted to say thank you. And goodbye.'

Chapter Twenty-seven

Danny's heart was heavy when he left the elephant house a few hours later, and his feet dragged on the ground as if they were made of bricks. He hadn't imagined that it would hurt this much. That the ties that bound him and Maharajah together, would feel taut and twisted with the strain of being pulled apart.

But he had made his decision. And there was no going back. If there was a place where he belonged, surely it must be with his real father? The father who wanted him.

So, after waiting for as long as he could, he forced himself to leave the enclosure. And to take the path across the paddock. And unlock the gate. And walk through. And even though, every step of the way, he wanted to turn around, he didn't. Because he couldn't afford to swing back and forth like a button on a loose thread.

At his side, the suitcase banged against his legs. His next job was to find a place to hide it. He found the right spot under the Belle Vue bandstand. And after tucking the case out of sight, he checked the clock tower on the dance hall roof. It was almost eight o'clock. Mrs Jameson would be expecting him.

But when Danny turned along the path towards Belle Vue House, he couldn't stop a gasp. Hundreds of people were pouring in through the gates. The steady trickle of visitors had become a torrent. Desperately, he tried to push through the crowds. He needed to get back to the Jamesons.

'Watch it!'

'Have a care.'

'Don't push so!'

But Danny ignored the angry protests and charged on. He wasn't the only one. A few steps ahead, another visitor, wrapped in a long dark cloak, was also pressing steadily through the crowd. But this man seemed oddly separate from everyone else. Not part of a family, or a group of friends, or even one half of a couple.

Curious, Danny jostled a little nearer. There was something about the visitor that was oddly familiar but the man had drawn his cape so tightly around himself that it was impossible to see a face or figure. Suddenly, he stumbled and the cloak flew wide, exposing its bright scarlet lining.

And Danny felt another jolt of recognition. But it wasn't the person that had set his instincts flaring. It was the cape.

Because it was identical to the one Reverend Threlfall had been wearing on the day Danny had visited the vicarage.

His heart thudded against his ribs. Why would the vicar come to the show? Why was he keeping himself hidden among the crowds? And why was he alone? There were a hundred different questions spinning in his head but Danny was certain the answer to each one of them was the same.

Reverend Threlfall was here to cause trouble.

In the end, the decision to follow the vicar was easy because Danny knew there was little choice if he wanted answers. But more than that: he owed the Jamesons the truth before he said goodbye – to them and to Belle Vue.

Ahead, the cloaked figure had battled to the edge of the crowd, and was now walking more quickly, with the purpose of someone who knew exactly where they were going. Cautiously, Danny followed. Pacing himself, so that each footstep matched the steps of the man ahead.

They skirted past the maze and the glass hothouses; and then the dance hall where the clock tower now read fifteen minutes past eight. But instead of veering towards Belle Vue Lake with the rest of the spectators, the figure peeled away along the path towards the aviary.

Danny slipped into the shadows and headed in the same direction. He was careful – probably more careful than he needed to be because Threlfall didn't once look back. Silently, they zigzagged through the cages – following almost exactly the same path as Danny and Hetty had taken just over a week ago. And for a moment, Danny wondered if they were heading towards Emerald's pen.

But instead of stopping at the emu enclosure, the vicar continued on along the track. Now there could be only one possible destination: the reptile house.

Danny could have sung with relief. The reptile enclosure was always secure, with high, barred windows and padlocks on the door. There were simply too many dangerous creatures inside to take risks. Not only was it home to Cleopatra, but there were puff adders, poison dart frogs and funnel-web spiders. Any one of them could be deadly.

So, if Threlfall was hoping to release another animal, this time he wouldn't succeed. Besides, after Victoria's escape Mr Jameson had promised to hire extra guards.

At the reptile house, the figure stopped outside the door, curving his body around the padlocks as though to hide them from view. Danny ducked behind a tree and watched.

Time ticked on. His breath see-sawed in and out of his chest impatiently. Surely one of the keepers would patrol along shortly? Maybe Nelson Crimple might appear, sent by the Jamesons to track him down.

But no one came. And then Danny realized why. Most of Belle Vue's staff were on the other side of the park – taking tickets and controlling the crowds. And the rest were part of the show.

In this moment, he was entirely on his own.

Abruptly, a series of metallic clicks broke the silence, and three padlocks clattered loudly to the floor. The enclosure door moved, just a fraction, and the cloaked figure slipped through the gap and disappeared.

Danny's heart stuttered. Quietly, he slid from his hiding place and crept towards the building. The door was still slightly ajar. He pushed it wider and stepped into the darkness.

Inside, the reptile house was dark but not silent. A purring growl vibrated between the walls, mingling with the hisses, snarls and croaks of the other reptiles. But among all the animal noises, Danny could distinctly hear another, far more human sound. The light tread of footsteps.

He stopped, raising his head to listen. The footsteps sounded again, pacing around one of the exhibition halls just off the main corridor. The intruder was with the snakes.

Edging around the corner, Danny scanned the room. Glass cabinets lined the walls, each one housing a different group of snakes – pythons, vipers, boas and mambas. But it was the cobras that seemed to interest the cloaked figure. He'd lit a gas lamp above their cabinet and was staring inside, apparently fascinated.

Danny edged closer, careful to keep to the shadows.

Then with one impatient gesture, the figure pushed back the hood of his cape. And Danny's mouth fell open; his world tipped sideways. Because it wasn't Reverend Eustace Threlfall. It was someone entirely and utterly unexpected.

It was the vicar's sister, Constance.

'Constance?'

She straightened, moving away from the glass case. 'Danny? Is that you?'

'Yes.' He stepped nearer, and now he could see that the cabinet lid was wide open. A set of keys dangled from the lock. 'What are you doing?'

'I'm setting the animals free. I've thought about it. And they shouldn't be locked up. It's not right.'

'Why not?'

'Animals shouldn't be in cages. They should be in fields. And skies. And rivers. They should be free.'

Of all the explanations Danny had expected, this was not one of them. He'd been certain that whoever was setting the animals loose was doing it to hurt Belle Vue. It had never occurred to him that there could be another reason.

'But the animals are safe here. And warm. And well fed. And if they get ill, Mr Saddleworth makes them better.' Danny could hear his own confusion. 'This is their home, Constance. This is where they're looked after. Where they're protected. Why would you want to let them loose?'

Slowly, Constance tilted her head. It was as though she were carefully considering all that he'd said and was working through every argument. Finally, she said, 'Would you want to be locked up?'

The question was so simple, it felt like a trap. With sudden vivid clarity, Danny remembered the lavender-blue butterfly caught between Constance's cupped hands. He could still picture the tremble of its veined wings. And how those wings had spread and strengthened with the sudden joy of being set free. And then he remembered how they'd both watched as the butterfly had soared into the sky – and disappeared.

But he didn't answer the question, because he didn't know how to.

Instead, he changed tack. 'Was it you who broke the padlock on Emerald's cage?'

'Yes. With a hammer.' Constance seemed surprised to be asked.

'And what about Victoria . . . the lioness . . . was that you as well?'

'Yes. Of course. I did tell you it wasn't my brother. Eustace is a good person. He obeys the rules. But sometimes, the rules aren't right.' For the first time, she looked worried. Lines creased the plain circle of her face. 'He'd be cross with me if he found out. You won't tell him, will you?'

'I have to, Constance. You can't let animals roam around loose. It's dangerous. What if they got hurt? Or what if they hurt someone?' Deliberately, Danny gentled his voice. He was struggling to make certain his words made sense. 'Remember when Victoria escaped? Did you know we found her in a cellar? Trapped inside with a young boy? He was . . . he was terrified.'

Constance frowned. She looked to be travelling along a series of complicated paths in her mind. 'I hadn't thought of that. I wouldn't like the animals to harm people. Or scare anyone. I just want them to be free.'

'I think maybe . . .' Danny's mouth dried. Inside the cabinet, a king cobra, thick as a blacksmith's arm, was unravelling slowly from its coil. It was a sign of his shock that he'd forgotten where they were. And how dangerous it could be.

Cautiously, he stepped to one side. 'Constance. Stay exactly where you are. *Don't move.*'

'But—'

'Stay still!'

He watched the cobra lift slowly upright, holding its head high above the opened lid, then unfurl its tongue from between thin lips.

And a warning rang in his head louder than a church bell.

There's enough poison in one bite to kill twenty people.

He breathed out slowly. Beside him, Constance twitched.

Suddenly, the loose skin around the cobra's neck flared into a hood, its bronze and black scales standing out like warning signs. And Danny knew he only had one moment.

Reaching out, he slammed a fist against the cabinet lid, just as the cobra's mouth opened into a wide, pink hollow. The lid fell with a crash – knocking the snake back into the case. Sulkily, it slid away and curled into a corner.

Heart pounding, Danny twisted the key in the lock. 'Freedom is wonderful,' he said. 'But, so is being safe.'

Chapter Twenty-eight

Constance didn't protest when Danny suggested that he walk her home. He certainly couldn't leave her here. And he reckoned that, if he was quick, he still had just enough time to get ready for the show.

But before they left the reptile house, Danny made sure to pull the door shut and click the padlocks securely back into place. Then he slipped the bunch of keys he'd taken from the snake cabinet back into his pocket. There were too many dangerous animals inside not to be careful.

At the vicarage, Reverend Threlfall answered the door with a speed that suggested he'd been pacing the floor. His stiff collar hung loose around his neck, and his hair looked as though fingers had been driven through it.

'Constance, where have you been? You know I don't like you walking around at night.' He glared at Danny. 'And what in heaven's name are *you* doing here?'

Danny hesitated. He'd spent the last fifteen minutes wondering what to say to Reverend Threlfall. How to explain the full story. But he needn't have worried, because Constance spoke first. As usual, her words were simple, straightforward and honest.

'It was me, Eustace. I let the animals escape. I did it.'

'What are you talking about, Constance? I don't understand.' The vicar frowned, obviously confused. 'Is the boy putting you up to this? Planting stories in your head?' His face tightened. 'Or is this one of Jameson's schemes? I should have known. That man can't be trusted!'

Danny forced himself to keep calm. 'No, sir. This isn't a trick. And it has nothing to do with Mr Jameson. But I think . . . I think you need to speak to your sister. Alone.'

Lightly, he touched Constance's arm and waited until she turned to look at him. 'I have to go now, Constance. The show is due to start soon and I have to be there. But just tell your brother exactly what you told me. I'm sure he'll understand.'

'Yes, Danny. I will. I promise.'

She smiled her sweet smile, and Danny couldn't help smiling back. He raised his eyes to look at the vicar. 'Please don't be angry. I think your sister is just about the kindest person I know.'

But as Danny left the vicarage and sprinted back towards Belle Vue, he was aware of something niggling at him, as irritating and persistent as a splinter. Although it wasn't until he reached the Longsight gate that he realized what it was.

Spinning on his heels, he ran back towards St Mark's, pushing his arms and legs as fast as they would go. At the house, a shaft of light spilt out on to the front step. He knocked loudly but this time it took far longer for Reverend Threlfall to yank open the door.

Danny didn't bother with polite greetings. 'I need to speak to your sister again.'

'I'm sorry. I think there's been enough drama for this evening, don't you? Mr and Mrs Jameson will have my apology in the morning. As will you.'

The door began to close. Hastily, Danny stuck his foot into the gap. 'I don't want an apology. I just need to speak to Constance.' He softened his voice. 'Please. I'll be quick. I wouldn't ask if it wasn't important.'

The vicar stared unblinkingly at him. 'Very well,' he said at last. 'If it's so urgent. She's through there – in the parlour. But please be brief. This evening has been most upsetting. For both of us.'

Constance showed no surprise at his return. 'Danny. How lovely! I've been telling Eustace all about the animals, just like you said.'

'I know, Constance. That's good.' He sat next to her, and slipped the keys from his pocket on to the sofa. 'But I want to ask you about these. The keys you had in your hand when I saw you at the reptile house. Who gave them to you?'

'Those?' Constance shrugged. 'A man gave them to me.

He said I should keep them. To open the cages, and that I shouldn't use the hammer again, on the padlocks. He wanted me to let the animals go free. He said it was a good thing. And that I should carry on.'

Danny's heart thumped in his chest, but he made his voice calm. 'What did the man look like, Constance?'

She sighed. 'Just a man.'

'Do you know his name?'

'No. I'm sorry.' And then her eyes widened, and when she answered it was as though she was presenting him with a gift. 'But you must know him, Danny. He's the man with the missing finger.'

Chapter Twenty-nine

The man with the missing finger.

It could only be George Dalton. There was no one else Danny knew who matched the description. But why would Dalton want to make trouble for Belle Vue? And why, just before the biggest night of the year, had he handed over a set of keys to Constance Threlfall, and encouraged her to let loose a cabinet of venomous snakes?

It made no sense. Unless… unless, all this time he'd been blaming the wrong person. An uncomfortable suspicion slithered along Danny's spine like the trail of a cold fingertip. 'What's the time?'

Something about his desperation must have shown because Reverend Threlfall simply pulled out a pocket watch from his waistcoat. 'Nearly nine o'clock. Why?'

Danny didn't answer. The show was due to start in a

little over an hour. The edgy suspicion grew stronger.

'I have to go. Take care of Constance!' Spinning on his heels, he raced out of the parlour and back through the house, leaving the vicar staring after him, the pocket watch still dangling from his fingers.

The Belle Vue firework factory was the obvious place to look for answers – and for George Dalton. But by the time Danny had battled through the crowds again, the building looked empty. And when he tried the handle, the door was locked.

He cursed, picturing the set of keys lying where he'd left them – on the sofa next to Constance. How could he have been so stupid? So careless?

He rattled the door handle again. Should he keep trying? Or look elsewhere? Or maybe it would be best to find the Jamesons. They must already be wondering why he was so late. And yet he couldn't leave the factory without making certain Dalton wasn't inside.

Twisting sideways, Danny shoved against the door. It buckled, bowed but held solid. He tried again, slamming the wooden panels so hard that he was sure at least one would break. But nothing gave.

Heart drumming, he forced himself to think. He'd been a thief, a pickpocket and a housebreaker. Only a few days ago, he'd squeezed through a coal hole into the cellar of the Frog and Bucket. There had to be a way into this building.

Stepping back, he scanned the walls. A little to the left,

just a few feet above head height, was a narrow rectangular window. It would have to do.

He paced backwards then ran straight at the wall, arms stretched as far as they could reach. Barely a breath away, he jumped. The tips of his fingers caught on the ledge of the window. And held. Tightening his grip, he took the weight of his body on both arms, boots scrambling for purchase on the bricks below. And just as he thought he'd have to let go, he found the right angle and heaved himself up on to the ledge. He'd done it!

The window latch was not particularly complicated so it didn't take long to unfasten. Pushing against the wooden frame, Danny wriggled through the gap. Inside, the jump down was far easier because one of the workbenches had been shoved against the wall. Lightly, he hopped to the floor then looked around.

The factory was almost empty. Every box of fireworks had been stripped from the workroom, leaving only dust and dirt and the faint, unpleasant smell of sulphur. The bare shelves weren't particularly surprising. 'Prince Dandip and the Fight for Flamenca' was set to be the biggest show Belle Vue had ever seen. Every firework, rocket and shell would be needed tonight.

No. That didn't particularly worry Danny. But what tipped his uneasiness into blind panic was the fact that every single barrel of gunpowder was gone.

What had Tom said? *There's enough gunpowder here to blow up the island.*

. . . to blow up the island.
'. . . to blow up the island!'
His blood turned cold.

Danny left the same way he'd entered, clambering on to the workbench and out through the window. Outside, half-formed fragments of music drifted across the lake, mixing with the laughter and hum of the crowd. The orchestra was tuning up. The show was about to start. And soon the entire cast would be parading across to Firework Island to take up their positions. But Danny wasn't going to be with them.

Because every instinct – every sixth sense for trouble – was screaming that something was wrong. That tonight, another disaster was about to strike Belle Vue. And if he did nothing, there would be no one else to stop it.

But his only clue was the identity of the man with the missing finger – George Dalton.

He'd already searched the factory. Now the most obvious place to look was on Firework Island. Dalton had spent the last few days rigging the complicated system of explosions that would turn Mr Jameson's ideas into reality. Tonight of all nights, the pyrotechnist had to be there.

Frantically, Danny headed towards the lake, trying to keep from being caught up in the crowds. But it was impossible. Every route across Belle Vue was packed with people. He could only move at a snail's pace. It wasn't fast enough.

With rising panic, he tried to remember the shortcuts

through the park. Somewhere there was a path that cut behind the lake and ran parallel to Kirkmanshulme Lane. It was narrow and so overgrown that hardly anyone used it. But it was probably his best chance.

When Danny found the track, it was wilder than he remembered, with weeds up to his knees and thorny bushes that tugged at his clothes. And now that dusk had fallen, it was almost completely dark.

He pushed on anyway, finding his way more by touch than by sight. And suddenly, as if conjured from his imagination, there was George Dalton. Not on Firework Island. But here, on this overgrown, isolated track. Far away from the crowds.

Instinct stopped Danny from crying out – from moving any nearer. Instead, he tucked himself low to the ground and watched. Dalton appeared to be talking to someone. But while Dalton's face was lit by lantern light, his companion was nothing but shadow.

'What d'you want? I've not much time.' Dalton sounded surly; whoever he was meeting, Danny didn't think there could be much affection between them.

'I want your promise that everything's ready. I've been waiting weeks for this.'

Danny's blood jumped. He knew that voice. He'd listened to it for several hours in a committee room at Manchester Town Hall. It was the crisp, no-nonsense tones of Manchester's Lord Mayor. Mr Harold Goadsby.

'Of course it's ready. I rigged it up meself. There's twenty barrels, in three separate stockpiles on top of the hill. Enough to blow up the whole island. Once the fuse is lit, they'll explode one by one. Only needs a single match.'

'I'm not interested in how you've done it, only that it's going to work.'

'It'll work.' A little defensiveness had crept in amongst the gruffness. 'But I'll be needin' to light the fuse in the next few minutes . . . while there's no one on the island. Because once it starts, it'll be quick. Even I'm not goin' to have much time to get clear. And I won't risk people bein' hurt. My grandson's in that show.'

'Yes, you've already told me. Several times. I'm not a fool.' Goadsby's words were laced with impatience. 'But remember, the whole point is to have an audience. I want the maximum effect. And I want it in public. I don't want anyone to ever forget tonight.'

'Don't worry. Nobody will.'

'Good. And after that, Belle Vue should be ripe for the picking. No one will want to be part of a business plagued with so many unfortunate accidents.' He drew out the word. 'Animal escapes. Bridge collapses. Protests. Explosions. Jameson's investors will be desperate for their money back. He'll have to sell.'

Danny's pulse began to jump in his neck. He'd heard enough. He may have been wrong about *who* was causing the accidents – but he'd been right about *why*. Goadsby wanted to damage Belle Vue so badly that it would never survive.

He needed to find Mr Jameson and raise the alarm.

Carefully, Danny edged back, making sure to keep his breathing slow and steady. No sudden moves. No loud and unexpected noises. And maybe – just maybe – he might have been able to sneak away, undetected. But suddenly, a firework shot into the sky, exploding into bright bursts of colour. For a moment, it seemed to light up the whole of Belle Vue. And when it died away, George Dalton was staring straight at Danny.

'It's the Jameson boy!'

'Then what are you waiting for? Get him after him!'

Danny spun on his heels and ran, tearing a trail through the long grasses and overgrown ferns. Leaves and thorns clung to his clothes and scraped at his skin. Even so, he wasn't worried. He could easily outrun Dalton. The pyrotechnist wasn't a young man, and Danny had desperation on his side.

Within a few minutes, the rough track emerged on to one of the cinder paths, and Danny could have sung with relief. He knew this area well – all the shortcuts and all the hiding places. There was no chance of Dalton catching him now.

Ploughing down the side of the elephant paddock, he raced through the copse of trees and around the pond. Already the beat of Dalton's footsteps was growing fainter and fainter as Danny sprinted further and further away.

Ahead, a fence blocked the path. Curling his hand around one of the posts, Danny took a jump and landed solidly on the other side. Relieved, he raced towards the keepers' hut, turned the corner – and ran straight into the barrel of a gun.

'Stay where you are!' The order was followed by the unmistakable click of a trigger being pulled back. And Goadsby stepped out from the side of the hut, a small ornamental pistol cradled in one hand. Its pearl handle glinted cruelly.

Danny stopped, chest heaving. The mayor smiled. 'Good. And just in case you're wondering, boy, I'm quite prepared to shoot. And tonight, nobody will come running to help you. After all, what's one gunshot amongst all this noise?'

Heavy footsteps thudded on the path behind them and for one moment Danny felt a jolt of hope – but then Dalton appeared from around the corner. He was breathing heavily.

'You took your time,' Goadsby sneered. 'I thought we'd lost you. It's just lucky you ran in a near complete circle, otherwise I might not have tracked you down.'

Dalton scowled but he was too busy trying to catch his breath to reply.

'Still, I suppose it's better if I deal with the problem myself.' Staring at Danny, Goadsby used the pistol to motion towards the hut. 'Get inside, boy. Now!'

For a moment, Danny hesitated. His first instinct was to run but Goadsby was holding the gun with surprising confidence. Perhaps it would be better to play for time while he worked out a plan.

Slowly, he shuffled across the threshold. The two men followed. The hut was small, with only a few sticks of furniture – a table and two chairs, plus a small metal brazier that the keepers only ever lit in the winter months.

'Get over there. And sit on the floor.' Goadsby gestured with his gun once again, and Danny sank to the ground near the table.

'What we goin' to do with him?' Dalton looked unhappy. Sweat had plastered the grey curls to his skull, and his mouth was set in a sullen line. 'You never told me I'd have to deal with anythin' like this. I was just to start a few explosions and light a fuse! That's what you said. That's what we agreed!'

'Oh, I don't think he's going to be a problem. In fact, it's all worked out rather perfectly.' Cunning sharpened Goadsby's face. 'We've already made sure the boy took the blame for most of the other accidents. So, it'll be easy to pin this on him as well. He's a former thief and a known troublemaker. And he paid at least one visit to the firework factory. One can only imagine the damage he did there . . .'

'But we can't—'

'And before you start fussing, Dalton, just think: if you're to set up on your own, your reputation needs to be faultless. No one will want to do business with the man who blew up half of Belle Vue. So . . .' He kicked a thin, polished boot into Danny's side. 'Here's your scapegoat. Right at our feet.'

Chapter Thirty

'Now, here's the plan.' Goadsby pushed the gun into Dalton's hand, and closed his fingers around the handle. 'You stay here with the boy. Knock him out. Kill him. I don't care. Just as long as he doesn't leave here and raise the alarm.'

'I can't kill him!' Danny heard the horror in Dalton's voice with something close to relief. The pyrotechnist might be a cheat and a liar but he was obviously not a murderer.

'I'm sure if you try hard enough, you'll manage to think of something. Because let me make this clear – if he gets free then the entire plan is worth nothing. Do you want that?'

'But why do I have to do it?'

It was a whine, and Goadsby did nothing to hide his contempt.

'I'm a member of the Manchester Corporation. Chairman of the licensing committee. And the city's Lord Mayor. I am a great many things. But what I am not – is a common thug. So, you take care of him. And before you start complaining, remember the only fingerprints on this whole business are yours. No one can tie me to anything. I've made very sure of that.'

'But it were all your idea! I only went along with it because—'

'Well, now you're up to your neck in it,' Goadsby interrupted. Beneath his words, a threat thrummed loudly. 'I'll go and make sure the fuse gets lit. I'll even put a match to it myself, if I have to. But you stay here and take care of the boy. Remember, you owe me. And you know what will happen if you fail.'

He left without waiting for a response, letting the hut door slam shut behind him. Dalton flicked an anxious look at Danny. The sweat that had dampened his forehead was now darkening his shirt collar.

Swallowing visibly, he used the pistol to point at the floor. 'You stay right where you are. Hands in front where I can see them. And no movin' about.'

Cautiously, Danny stretched out his arms and did as he was told. Dalton was a nervous man with a gun. It wasn't a good combination. If anything, he was more dangerous than someone who knew what they were doing. Warily, Danny watched as Dalton began pacing the floor.

'Any moment,' he muttered. 'Any moment – and that

explosion will sound. Any moment. And then this will all be over.' He grabbed one of the wooden chairs, and sat on the edge of the seat, rocking backwards and forwards. Then abruptly, he leapt up again, and resumed his pacing.

Nervously, Danny flicked a glance towards the door. It seemed a long way away. He was going to have to be patient and clever; distract Dalton long enough to make a move. 'Why? Why did you do it?' he asked.

For a moment, Danny didn't think Dalton would answer, but then he twisted on his boot heel and spat into the dirt.

'Goadsby made me.' He paused but Danny said nothing. More than anyone, he knew the value of silence. And finally, Dalton sighed.

'A while back, I did some work for him. Jameson never knew anythin' about it. It was a private job. Goadsby had been boastin' to his rich friends about becomin' Lord Mayor – and he wanted a fireworks show. Somethin' big and fancy. I said I'd do it. But it went wrong. One of the rockets exploded. It's how I lost my finger.'

He gave a half-laugh. 'But worse than that, the roof of Goadsby's house caught fire. Burnt down one gable end before they could stop the flames.'

Almost absent-mindedly, Dalton slumped back into the chair. 'He was furious. Said I'd been careless. Negligent, he called it. Said I'd go to prison for all the damage I'd caused. But he never told the police. Didn't even ask for any money. He just said that one day he'd want a favour. And whatever it was, I'd have to do it.'

So, it had been blackmail. Goadsby had forced Dalton to be part of his plan in return for staying quiet. But something told Danny it wasn't quite the full story.

'I still don't understand,' he said. Mentally, he measured the gap between them. If he was going to get closer, Danny needed to keep Dalton talking. 'Why would the Lord Mayor of Manchester want to ruin Belle Vue?'

'It's simple. Jameson is sittin' on a gold mine here. He's got more than a hundred acres of land and he's buildin' enough shops and factories to make a small town – a brewery, gasworks, blacksmiths, ice cream parlour, bakery, ballroom, and that's not even all of it. They make money all right, but Goadsby reckons they could bring in a lot more. With the right man to steer them.'

'What about the animals?' Carefully, Danny edged forward. He was getting closer. 'You didn't say anything about the menagerie?'

Dalton snorted. 'Goadsby doesn't want the menagerie. Too much hard work. And he couldn't care less about the animals. He'll sell them off once he gets his hands on this place. Use the land to build an empire. More shops. More factories. More profit. That's what he wants.'

Danny shuffled a little nearer, but Dalton didn't seem to notice.

'You see he's not stupid but he is mean. He wants Belle Vue and everythin' that goes with it – and he wants it cheap. Every disaster for Belle Vue, drives the value down. The investors are already gettin' nervous, threatenin' to take their money away. Soon all Jameson will have is debts and bills.'

'So it was you? Causing all that trouble?' Danny paused, unsure how much he could push Dalton before he refused to talk. But he needn't have worried. The pyrotechnist leant forward, resting his elbows on his knees as he played with the handle of the gun. He seemed in the mood to confess.

'The bridge collapse were easy. I didn't even have to do much, just saw through the planks underneath, make them weak enough to fail. And that accident at the firework factory, when you broke Queen Victoria . . . that were me too. I just gave Her Majesty a little shove. But they were the small things.'

Danny frowned. What else had happened that he didn't know about? Had there been other disasters that Mr Jameson had kept secret?

'It was Goadsby who made sure the gasworks didn't get the new licence. And he arranged it so the tea rooms flooded.' He gave a half-laugh. 'And Eustace Threlfall was a godsend. A vicar hell-bent on shuttin' the whole place down. He played right into Goadsby's hands, and the poor fool didn't even know it. I even got Threlfall's sister to let loose some of the animals. Although, she seemed happy enough to do it.'

Danny felt his temper flare but he tried to keep his face blank. 'And tonight? What's going to happen tonight?'

Dalton lifted his gaze from the pistol and flicked his eyes around the room. For the first time, he seemed reluctant to talk. 'Tonight, an explosion is goin' to destroy Firework Island. Right in front of most of Manchester. A big public disaster. And Jameson will lose everythin'. Goadsby's goin' to be able to snap up this place for next to nothin''.

It was making an odd sort of sense. 'So what do you get? For helping him?'

'I told you – I get to stay out of prison!'

'And?' Danny said. Instinct told him there was something more. 'What else? What else do you get?'

This time the pause was longer. 'And a parcel of land, with enough money to set up on my own. I'll have my name over the factory door. Be my own boss. All my life I've worked to put money into someone else's pocket. Now this is my chance. A chance to pass on somethin' to my family . . . to my grandson.' Dalton snapped, and Danny realized that what he had mistaken for gruff sullenness was actually a deep, resentful bitterness.

'I see.' He watched Dalton's hand relax around the polished handle of the gun. The barrel tilted towards the floor. Now it was close enough to touch.

'Remember what I told you, lad? About bein' a pyrotechnist? That all you need is the right amount of fear. Well, that's what this were all about. All I had to do was take a risk, climb a little higher – and then I'd be lookin' at the stars.'

This time Danny didn't ask another question. He made a grab for the gun. But just as his fingers brushed the barrel, the hut door swung open. Dalton jerked back, tightening his grip on the pistol and pulling away.

Danny cursed. Every gain he'd made was lost. He turned. Miss Carkettle stood in the doorway, her eyes locked – not on Dalton – but on Danny. And if she'd been angry with him before, she was furious now.

'I'm looking for Henrietta, and don't think to lie to me, young man. I know exactly what's going on. Despite my express wishes, she's run off to be in this ridiculous show. I demand you tell me where she's hiding!'

Danny opened his mouth but suddenly, Miss Carkettle seemed to notice someone else was in the room. She stared at Dalton and then at the small pistol in his palm. 'What on earth are you doing, sir? Put that gun down at once. You could hurt someone.'

'I'm afraid I can't do that, ma'am.' Hastily, Dalton lurched upright, holding the pistol at arm's length. The movement must have given him time to think. 'I . . . I caught the boy stealin'.'

Instinctively, Danny jerked his head. 'No! That's not—'

'Stealing? Well, I can't say that's much of a surprise.' Miss Carkettle's lips thinned. 'However, regardless of his actions, I don't approve of firearms, so I must insist you put the gun down. It really is quite dangerous.'

Dalton shifted uneasily but he didn't drop his hand. The silence lengthened, and Danny wondered if there was still a chance to grab the gun. Then Miss Carkettle released a sigh. 'Very well. I shall fetch Mr Jameson myself. The boy is his responsibility. He can deal with this. And afterwards, perhaps you could help me find my niece.' She turned on her heel and marched back across the hut.

'No! You stay where you are! You can't leave 'ere.' Dalton's shout stopped Miss Carkettle halfway to the door. She pivoted, her spine ramrod-straight, every muscle bristling. And for a moment, Danny found himself filled with admiration. She and Hetty had more in common than he'd first thought.

'What do you mean, I can't leave? Of course I can leave.'

'No. You're not goin' anywhere, ma'am.'

'Don't be ridiculous. I have no idea what is happening here, but I blame it on the reading of too much modern literature. This is not the Wild West. This is Manchester.'

'No one is leavin', ma'am. Not till this is all over. And it will be over, anytime now. We just have to wait a little longer. Just a minute more. That's all. Now, go and sit over there with the boy.'

'Really! This is too much! You cannot keep me here against my will.'

'I'm afraid I can, ma'am.' Horrified, Danny watched Dalton's hands twist nervously again and the pistol swung round to face Miss Carkettle. 'I've got a gun.'

'No! Don't!' Hastily, Danny scrambled to his feet. 'Please don't hurt her.' He sprinted across the floor until he stood directly in front of Hetty's aunt. Now the pistol was pointing at the hollow of his spine. He swallowed. 'This isn't about me stealing anything, Miss Carkettle, I promise. Mr Dalton and Mayor Goadsby are planning to—'

'Shut up!' With one panicked movement, Dalton swung his hand and hit Danny across the back of the head with the gun.

It seemed to surprise them both, and for a moment, Danny froze. Then pain ricocheted around his skull, sending agonizing waves through his temple. And his teeth. And his throat. Letting his knees soften, Danny sank to the floor and closed his eyes.

'Good heavens! You've killed him!' The shock in Miss Carkettle's voice didn't quite hide a tremor of fear.

Dimly, Danny heard footsteps then Dalton was leaning over him, so close that the bristles of his beard left scratch marks. Trapping a breath behind his teeth, Danny stayed as still as stone. His heart beat frantically in his chest.

'No. He's just knocked out cold. That'll save me a job.' Dalton drew back. Mentally, Danny counted the steps as he walked away. He reckoned he had one chance – and *only* one chance. And this was it.

Twisting suddenly, Danny rolled to his side and raised one leg. Then using his hip as a pivot, he kicked out as hard as he could. His boot caught Dalton exactly where he'd intended – right on the back of the knees, just where the flesh was softest. With a cry, Dalton crashed forward, sprawling full-length in the dirt. The pistol slipped from his hands and skidded across the floor.

Danny clambered to his feet, wincing as pain stabbed through his head. But he didn't have time to give in to it. Dalton was already trying to get up. Quickly, Danny stepped closer and kicked a boot between his shoulder blades, feeling absurdly grateful when Dalton slumped unresisting to the floor.

He looked around the hut. Behind Miss Carkettle, a coil of thick cord lay abandoned in a corner. 'The rope! Pass me the rope. Quickly!'

But Miss Carkettle didn't move. She was staring at Dalton, with the dazed blankness of someone in deep shock. 'The rope!' Danny called again. And this time she blinked rapidly.

'Really! There's no need to shout.' Drawing herself up, she reached out and grabbed the cord. 'Here.'

Without ceremony, Danny yanked Dalton's hands behind his back and wrapped the rope around his wrists. Over his shoulder, he felt Miss Carkettle step nearer and he braced himself for criticism. But Hetty's aunt was full of surprises.

'Wrap the cord in a figure of eight, Daniel. Around each arm and crossed in the middle. That'll make it tighter.'

Wordlessly, Danny did as she instructed, and Dalton groaned as the rope pulled taut. Then he scooped the pistol from the floor and handed it to Miss Carkettle.

'I need to go now. I have to raise the alarm. But I'll send help when I can. You'll have to stay here. Keep the gun on him. And make sure he doesn't move.' He paused. 'Do you understand?'

Her eyes sparked. 'Of course I understand, young man. I'm a Carkettle.' She raised the pistol so it was in a perfect line with her right shoulder. 'If he moves, I'll shoot him.'

Chapter Thirty-one

Danny ran. He ran as fast and as hard as he was able. And every step of the way he waited for an explosion. A blast that would rock Belle Vue to its foundations and destroy the place he called home.

But it didn't happen.

Instead, the air seemed to pulse with excitement; the sort of giddy anticipation that comes before a long-awaited celebration. The noise rolled and surged like a sea at high tide.

Already, the spectators' gallery was full. Each seat on every tier had been taken. And the remaining crowds were spreading out along the shore facing the island.

Next to the gallery, an orchestra had begun to play – soft music that rose in delicate layers to circle the park. And suddenly, a series of fireworks soared from the grass in a brief staccato burst. One. Two. Three. Four. Before exploding into shimmering fountains that filled the sky with colour. The music swelled even louder.

If it had been any other time, Danny would have marvelled at the beauty of the scene. But not tonight. Tonight, he prayed for it all to stop. For everyone to stand, turn and disappear into the darkness.

Of course, no one did. Instead, people were still flooding through the park gates. Their heads bobbing and dipping in the moving stream. Danny tried to push against the tide, knocking against knees and arms and ankles. But he kept being flung back, tossed like a piece of driftwood. And then, in the distance, a sight sent his panic soaring.

Soldiers were marching across the footbridge, smart and splendid in their red and blue uniforms. Behind them were the Spanish peasants, illuminated by a chain of paper lanterns held on long hooks above their heads. One village girl led the way; long, loose curls spiralling across her shoulders, her butter-yellow skirt swinging with each step.

And right at the back, towering over everyone, Danny saw an elephant; twelve feet tall, with gold eyes and one sawn-off tusk. His heart drummed heavily in his chest. Had he been too slow? Was Goadsby on the island? Was he already lighting the fuse?

But the clock on the dance hall roof said there were still fifteen minutes before ten o'clock.

Surely he had time to stop this? To warn everybody? After all, Goadsby didn't know Belle Vue like Danny did, and the crowds would probably have slowed his progress. Simply finding the fuse would cause a delay.

Yes, there was still time.

Sucking in a breath, Danny pushed harder through the press of people, using his elbows and kicking with his feet. He wasn't going to turn back now. Even though he might already be too late.

The procession was finished by the time Danny reached the footbridge. The soldiers and villagers were already spreading out across the island to take up their positions for the opening scene. Overhead, fireworks trailed across the sky, and the music rose steadily – just as Mr Jameson had said it would. 'Prince Dandip and the Fight for Flamenca' was about to begin.

Heart slamming, Danny raced across the bridge. In the centre of the island, the hill rose above him and, silhouetted against the horizon, were the painted backdrops of the Spanish village.

Danny sprinted up the path, pushing until his muscles stung with the effort. At last he turned the final bend. The track opened out on to a flat strip of land, just below the brow of the hill. It was where Mr Jameson was kneeling next to a coil of fuses. An open box of matches lay at his feet.

'STOP! STOP!' Danny didn't think he could shout any louder.

Hastily, Mr Jameson scrambled upright. 'Danny! Where

in the blue blazes have you been? It's bad enough that George Dalton didn't show. But you? I thought I could rely on you!' For a moment they stared at each other, then Mr Jameson turned his back and knelt down again. 'It's too late now. I'll do it myself.'

He picked up the box and pulled out one of the matches.

'No! Stop! Please. PLEASE!' Danny's heart was pounding so fiercely he thought it might burst from his chest. He sucked in a breath. He had to make sure he was understood; that he didn't stumble over the words. 'Don't . . . light . . . the . . . fuse.'

'What are you talkin' about? The show's about five minutes from starting. I can't hang around for you to get ready. You had your chance. And now it's gone.' Mr Jameson's voice had dropped to a whisper. And Danny was surprised to hear that he sounded more sad than angry. 'You get home. And we'll talk about this later.'

'No! You don't understand.' The panic was starting to bite. His chest was getting tighter. The words were getting more difficult to say. 'If you light that fuse, you'll blow up the whole island. People . . . people might get hurt. Or worse.'

'What? Don't be ridiculous!' Mr Jameson frowned. 'Dalton said everything was perfectly safe. He rigged it all himself, and he knows what he's doin'. I reckon someone's been tellin' you tales, lad.'

The fear rose another notch. But it was a different sort of fear than before. Before Danny had been terrified he might not arrive on time; what he hadn't considered is that he might not be believed.

'Please! You have to—'

'What's going on here, Jameson? The boy giving you trouble again? I just wonder what mischief he'll get up to next.'

Horrified, Danny looked down the hill to see a man picking his way up the path towards them. It was Harold Goadsby.

Slowly, Mr Jameson stood, a smile pasted to his face. 'Lord Mayor! What are you doin' here, sir? Only my staff are allowed on the island tonight. You'd better get back over the bridge. Watch the show from across the water with all the other visitors. You'll enjoy it more.'

But Goadsby continued on towards them. Now he was close enough not to have to shout. 'Oh, you mustn't mind me, Jameson. I just wanted to make sure everything's in order. Remember I warned you there'd be an inspection? Well, tonight seemed as good a night as any.' He waved his hand carelessly in the direction of the fuse. 'But you carry on. I promise I won't get in the way.'

Stopping, he rested one foot on a rock and dropped his hat on the path next to it. He looked relaxed. Composed. And entirely confident. And Danny knew, with complete certainty, that this is what he'd planned all along.

Goadsby had never intended for Dalton to light the fuse early. He hadn't wanted Firework Island to be empty and deserted.

No.

He wanted the explosion to happen when the island was full of people; watched by thousands of spectators; and on the night of the biggest show Manchester had ever seen. Because he wanted the disaster to be as public and as catastrophic as possible. And if some people died, then it would be worth the risk. Because Belle Vue would never, ever recover.

'Don't. Please don't!' Danny's words emerged in short, tight sentences. 'There are stockpiles of gunpowder. On the hill. Enough to blow up the island. Maybe worse. Goadsby and Dalton are in it together. They've rigged it so the island will blow up. I don't know how. I just know . . .' Speech was getting harder. 'I just know you shouldn't light that fuse.'

Goadsby laughed, nonchalantly. And if Danny hadn't heard the plans with his own ears, doubt would have taken hold.

'What nonsense! Why on earth would I want to sabotage the show? Put people at risk of harm? Including myself? It makes no sense.'

'Danny?' Mr Jameson looked bewildered. 'What in the blue blazes are you talkin' about?'

'Mr Goadsby is the one who's been causing all the trouble for Belle Vue. He wants the park to fail . . . for people to stop coming . . . so he can buy it up cheap. All the businesses . . . all the attractions . . . all the land.'

'Really, Jameson, you can't possibly believe this? The boy is obviously trying to turn attention away from himself. It's a fairy tale from start to finish.'

But Mr Jameson ignored him. All his attention was centred on Danny. 'You realize how serious this is. I'll have to cancel tonight's show. Delay it, if we're lucky. People are goin' to be angry. I could lose . . .' He paused. '*We* could lose everything.'

'Yes.' Danny was proud that his voice sounded so steady. 'I know.'

Mr Jameson raised his hand. The dry match was still pinched between two fingers. 'And you still want me to throw this away?'

'I do. Yes.'

For several moments, Mr Jameson examined Danny's face and then he stared down at the match. And for the first time, Goadsby's confidence seemed to slip. He made an instinctive move forward before checking himself. Now his smile looked forced.

'Don't be stupid, Jameson. The boy's a liar and a thief. If the show doesn't go ahead tonight, you might never be able to stage it again. Your investors could take away their money. All your efforts would be wasted.'

Mr Jameson said nothing. Then without any particular haste, he struck the match and waited until the flame flickered in his hand. Danny's heart beat in rapid, erratic bursts. He swallowed. It felt like standing on a clifftop, looking down and knowing that one movement would change everything.

'You make a good point, Lord Mayor.' Thoughtfully, Mr

Jameson patted his jacket before pulling out a cigar. Leaning forward, he lit it. And a cloud of smoke drifted into Goadsby's face. 'But don't call my son a liar. Or a thief. I don't like it.' And then he lifted his hand and blew out the match.

The breath that Danny hadn't known he was holding, rushed out. And a surge of bubbling lightness welled up from somewhere deep inside. Despite everything, Mr Jameson had believed him. And in that moment, he realized his mistake.

He couldn't leave Belle Vue. This world that he was only just beginning to explore and to understand. He couldn't leave the people who had taken him in and given him a home. And he couldn't leave Maharajah or the friends that he had made.

And even if that meant saying goodbye to his father, he was going to stay. Here at Belle Vue. And he was going to prove to Mr and Mrs Jameson that they had not made a mistake in bringing him here. The decision must have been the right one because he felt the certainty of it settle in his bones.

Mr Jameson puffed on his cigar. 'Danny. It looks like the show's off.'

'You fool! You stupid, half-witted fool.' Fury distorted Goadsby's face. His cheeks flushed red, and angry lines made dents in his forehead. 'I can't believe you'd take his word over mine.'

'Well, you should believe it, Lord Mayor, because that

what's happenin'. Now if you don't mind, I'd like *you* to get off *my* property.'

Goadsby swallowed, his eyes moved shiftily between them. Slowly, he leant to pick up his hat, before stomping off down the path. In silence, they watched him go. Then Mr Jameson knelt beside the fuse and yanked at the coils. They came away in his hands.

'That'll sort it. There's no point in riskin' him comin' back.' He took a deep breath, as if he'd just realized the enormity of his decision. 'You better stay on the island and spread the word. I'll go and break the news to that lot over there.' He gestured across the water towards the crowds. 'And Danny?' His voice was soft. 'I don't know how you found out about this. I don't even understand why. But thank you for comin' back!'

Danny grinned. Despite all that had happened, the relief of finally being believed was overwhelming. He watched Mr Jameson disappear down the hill before turning back to inspect the fuses. And it was then that he made a discovery that sent his blood cold.

The box of matches that had been lying on the ground was gone.

Harold Goadsby had taken them.

Chapter Thirty-two

Danny had been frightened before, but this feeling was more than that. It was as if a hollow had opened up in the pit of his stomach.

Goadsby had the matches. He must have grabbed them when he picked up his hat from the path. But it wasn't the theft that bothered him. It was another, far more terrifying thought.

Mr Jameson had ripped out the coil of fuses, but Goadsby did not need to light the fuse to set off the explosion. He just needed to start a fire. The flames would do the rest – because George Dalton had planted enough gunpowder on the island to blow every piece of it apart.

Goadsby hadn't abandoned his plans. He still had every intention of destroying Belle Vue.

Danny began to run.

He spotted two of the French soldiers first. They were lying in one of the hollows in the hillside, waiting for the signal to start fighting.

'You have to go now.' Danny cupped his hands around his mouth to make his voice carry. 'Get off the island. It's not safe. The show's over!'

But the men only laughed. Across the lake, music was still drifting out across the water. And a single firework soared upwards, before exploding lazily. There was no sign at all that Mr Jameson had managed to raise the alarm.

Danny tried again. 'Please listen. You have to leave! Now!'

With a sigh, one of the soldiers propped himself up on his elbows. 'Look, lad. This is the easiest money we'll make in a year. We're not goin' anywhere. Not till it's over and we get paid. Now if you want my advice – you'll shut up and move on.'

Horrified, Danny watched him lie back down. How was he going to spread the word when no one wanted to listen? How could he save people when they didn't believe they needed saving? And how was he going to make certain Hetty and Maharajah stayed safe?

Spinning on his heels, Danny lurched down the path towards the shore. At the water's edge, a group of Spanish peasants were waiting for the performance to start. Stretching on to his toes, Danny waved at them furiously and pointed towards the bridge. 'Go, now! Quickly!'

But the villagers looked more confused than frightened.

Danny dropped his hands. His chest felt tight. His heart drummed manically. Suddenly, further along the bank, a flash of bright yellow broke through the darkness. He scrambled down towards it.

On the shore, a girl with wild curls stood next to a boy in a red soldier's jacket. 'Hetty!' he shouted. 'HETTY!'

'Danny?' She turned so quickly that her skirts flew out. 'Where have you been? You should have been here hours ago. The Jamesons were so upset. Mrs Jameson was almost in tears. How could you do this to them? How could you!'

'I can explain. But not now. We have to get everyone off the island.'

'What are you talking about? The show's about to start.' Narrowing her eyes, she lifted her hands to her hips. 'Is this something to do with your new friend? Mr Larkin, wasn't it?'

'No. No! Please, you have to listen. Just trust me.' His words were starting to stick and slide against each other. And he wasn't sure if he was making any sense. 'There's going to be an explosion. Everything . . . the island . . . the people . . . it'll be destroyed.'

'Don't listen to him, Miss Henrietta.' Tom stepped nearer. Deliberately, he lifted his rifle on to one shoulder and balanced it between both hands. 'This is another one of his stories.'

'No! No, it's not!'

But Tom continued as though Danny wasn't there. 'He's a troublemaker. A clumsy halfwit. And now on top of everythin' else, he's trying to make sure the show fails as well. I don't reckon he can help himself.'

'No, it's not like that. Just listen.' Desperation made Danny's voice splinter. He grabbed Hetty's elbow, swinging her round until she was forced to look into his eyes. 'I'm telling you the truth, Hetty. I am. I promise you – on Maharajah's life, I am. Everybody has to get off the island. Now!'

Hetty stared at him, and it seemed to Danny that a whole lifetime passed before she spoke. He wondered if she could hear his heart. 'If Danny says it's true, then it is.'

The relief was so intense that his whole body shuddered. Tom scowled and swung his rifle a little higher. 'No, I don't reckon he's—'

And suddenly, on the horizon, Danny saw a flare of bright, burning orange. Flames were licking across the roofs of the Spanish village. The painted scenery was on fire.

'Look!' He stabbed a finger towards the top of the hill. 'LOOK!'

They turned. And almost unconsciously, Hetty lifted a hand to her mouth. 'Oh, good heavens!'

But it was Tom Dalton who looked the most horrified. 'The gunpowder! We can't let the flames reach those barrels.'

Hetty dropped her hand. 'What do you need us to do, Danny? How can we help?'

For a brief moment, Danny stared at the flames. And oddly, it was George Dalton's words that came back to him.

'All you need is the right amount of fear.'

The right amount of fear.

He could do this.

'You two spread the word,' he said. 'Get everyone off the island. As quickly as you can. I'm . . . I'm going to find Maharajah. And see if I can stop the fire.'

Danny was already halfway up the slope when he realized someone was hard on his heels. He turned; Tom Dalton glared back at him, defiantly. But Danny didn't stop running. This wasn't the time for arguments.

And then, just as they reached the brow of the hill, he heard the noise he'd been dreading. A deafening cry. Raw, wounded and terrified.

Maharajah. But where was he?

Desperately, Danny scanned the island. Soldiers and villagers were swarming along the shore, scrambling down the hillside and running towards the footbridge. Hetty had obviously managed to raise the alarm – although the sight of flames shooting across the sky probably helped. Now no one could be unaware of the danger.

The painted village was already scorched and blackened. And the blaze was spreading towards the thicket of trees on top of the hill. It reminded Danny of another fire, in another place. And he knew Maharajah's fear would be paralysing.

Once again, a frightened bellow sounded out across the island. It was coming from the other side of the burning scenery. But before Danny could move, Tom's urgent shout pulled him back.

'Oi. Over here! Quickly.' He was standing on a strip of grass, close to the bend in the path before its last steep climb to the top. It was the same spot where Mr Jameson had been kneeling, just a little earlier.

'This is where Grandpa rigged the explosives. Someone's already pulled out the fuses but the gunpowder's still here. Over by the bend. And there's more barrels than I thought. Four altogether. Enough to cause a big blast if the fire gets near.'

'What if . . .' Carefully, Danny let the thought unfold. 'What if we could move the barrels. Roll them downhill . . . and into the lake?'

'I suppose it could work. The water would stop the gunpowder from explodin'.' Tom frowned. 'But I don't know how we'd do it. The barrels are heavy. Grandpa used a horse and cart to carry them up here.'

Abruptly, another terrified roar shredded the night air. And a plume of black smoke ballooned across the hillside. And when it lifted, the outline of a large animal was silhouetted against the burning horizon. Danny's heart lifted.

'*We* might not be able to do it,' he said. 'But I know who can.'

Chapter Thirty-three

The bitter taste of smoke stung Danny's throat. He tugged off his jacket and bundled it over his mouth. Carefully, he inched closer. Maharajah stood in front of the flames, rocking his head, ears flapping. But his huge body was frozen. He didn't seem able to move.

Danny stared into the gold eyes – and saw the depth of his terror. He reached out and gently stroked his palm along the rough ridges of skin, feeling each dip and bump beneath his fingers. 'It's going to be fine, I promise. I promise you!'

From the moment he'd recovered his voice, Danny had talked to Maharajah. Gentle words designed to coax and comfort. It had never felt odd because he was always sure Maharajah understood. But this time, he couldn't just repeat the same old reassurances. He had to persuade Maharajah to fight his fear.

Moving closer, Danny pressed his face into the hollow below the broken tusk. 'I need your help. You're the only one who can do this. But you won't be on your own. We'll do it together.'

The gold eyes stared back at him, and for a moment every emotion seemed magnified between them. Every fear. Every worry. Every anxiety. And then Maharajah blinked. Curled his trunk around Danny's neck. And calmed.

Danny didn't think he'd ever been so grateful in his life. 'Thank you,' he whispered. 'Thank you.'

Carefully, he led Maharajah down towards the strip of grass where Tom was standing beside a small pyramid of barrels. Above them, the fire snapped and snarled, filling the air with smoke and ash. The heat was close to stifling. But now they were far enough away not to be in any immediate danger. Danny just wasn't sure how long that would last.

Tom was watching Maharajah warily. 'Can you make him to do it?'

'I can't force him.' Danny looked up into the clear, gold eyes. 'But he'll do it because he wants to help.'

Instinctively, he reached for the ankus tucked into his belt and whistled. The noise was piercing so he gentled it a little.

Reaching out, Maharajah pushed the first barrel. It toppled to the grass with a thud then tipped on to its side. Danny whistled again. And Maharajah gave the drum another hard shove. The path ahead was clear and it bounced along the ground, poised briefly on the lip of the hill before tumbling over the edge. Standing on the slope, Danny watched it splash into the lake, then disappear.

He swiped a hand across his damp forehead and turned back towards the fire. Maharajah was silhouetted against the flames. For a long moment, the gold eyes locked on his. And Danny knew all that kept him here was the bond between them. He just hoped it was enough.

'That was good,' he said. 'Now we have to do the rest.'

Obediently, Maharajah rammed his trunk against the next barrel, and it followed the same path into the water. Then he did the same again. And again. Until finally, the last barrel sank beneath the surface of the lake.

'That's it.' Tom looked down the slope, panting. 'We've done it.'

'Not yet. That was four. But there are more. Twenty barrels altogether . . . in three separate piles.'

Tom's mouth twisted. 'Don't be stupid! I don't know where you heard that, but it's nonsense. Grandpa wouldn't have brought any more here. He didn't have to. There was already more gunpowder than he needed. It would have been too dangerous.'

'I know.' Danny walked further along the grass slope. Despite the heat and the flames, he kept his eyes trained on the ground. Searching for any trace of the other stockpiles. His chest tightened. 'But he did it anyway.'

Frowning, Tom marched closer and grabbed his arm. 'What are you tryin' to tell me? That my grandpa rigged this on purpose?'

'I'm not trying to tell you anything. I just know there's more gunpowder here. That's all.' Danny jerked away until Tom was forced to drop his hands. They curled into fists.

'You're lyin'. I know you are. This is another one of your stories.'

'No, it's not—'

'Danny! Tom! Thank heavens.' They turned. Hetty was sprinting up the path towards them, cheeks flushed. She looked as though she'd run the entire length of the island. 'We need to go. Another fire's started down by the bridge. We have to be quick. Most people have already gone . . . and the rest are following. Come on!'

She spun on her heels to leave and Tom moved to go after her. But Danny stayed where he was. 'I can't go.'

'Don't be stupid. Of course, you can. You have to!'

'Not yet. There are more explosives around here some-where. Enough to destroy the island. I have to find them. I need to make sure everyone's safe.'

'I've already told you. There aren't any more barrels!' Tom's eyes had narrowed. 'You're makin' the whole thing up.'

'No. I don't think he is, Tom.' Hetty stood on the path, staring at a circle of rocks a little further downhill. 'Otherwise, what's that?'

At first, Danny couldn't see where she was pointing. But when they scrambled along the slope, the edge of a wooden drum came into view, peeking out from behind the biggest rock. And just beyond it, partially hidden by the stone circle, more barrels were packed into neat, tight rows. Tom's face paled.

Danny banged a fist against the nearest barrel and heard the answering thud. It was full. 'I'm staying. Someone has to get these out of reach of the fire.'

Twisting around, he whistled to Maharajah before kneeling down to clear the ground. One or two of the largest stones would have to be moved before the barrels could be pushed away. And besides, he didn't want to stand and watch Hetty and Tom leave. His eyes prickled, and he swiped a hand across his face.

Suddenly, someone was crouching in the dirt beside him. And then another person was kneeling at his other side. And two pairs of hands were scrabbling in the soil alongside him.

'Did you think we'd go without you?' Hetty shouted over the crackle of the fire. 'Don't be so stupid!'

This time, the stockpile took longer for them to clear. Maharajah had to push away the rocks then roll each barrel up and across the ridge before gravity sent them tumbling down into the lake.

The fire had reached its peak, and the heat was close to blistering. Danny could feel his lungs cramp, and the smoke had left his throat raw. He wasn't the only one. Tom and Hetty were obviously struggling. Finally, they stared down at the lake.

'I reckon altogether that must be fifteen,' Tom coughed into his sleeve.

Quickly, Danny pulled away from the edge. 'Then there are five more. I need to find them.'

'No, Danny. You've done enough.' Hetty grabbed his arm. The smoke had almost rubbed away her voice. It was now no more than a whisper. 'Even if the fire reaches the rest of the gunpowder, the worst of this is over. And there's no one left on the island.'

'Let me go.' Danny pulled back, tugging so hard he almost lost his balance. 'You don't understand. I've got to do it! The Jamesons . . . I have to show them . . .'

'No! We haven't any more time.' Furiously, Hetty pulled him round so he was forced to face her. To look into her eyes.

'Danny, listen to me. You've done as much as you can. Everyone's safe. And the rest of it . . . it's just dirt and rocks. The Jamesons wouldn't want you to risk your life for this. They wouldn't want you to risk your life at all. We have to go!'

Chapter Thirty-four

'Danny? Aren't you listening? I said come on!'

Hetty shook his arm. On her other side, Danny could see Tom, hair sweat-stuck to his forehead, one sleeve of his red jacket ripped from the seam. Behind them Maharajah swayed nervously.

Every face seemed to be turned in his direction, as if waiting for some signal that only he could give.

And suddenly, Danny felt the haze lift. Everything was clear again. 'Everyone's safe? You promise?'

Hetty nodded. 'Yes. Everyone. There's no one left on the island. Except us. We need to leave!'

'Yes. I can go now.'

'Then come on!'

Together they raced down the path towards the shore. Boots slipping on the rocks and stones. Maharajah stomping behind.

But when they circled round to the other side of the island, they were forced to stop. Just as Hetty had warned, the fire had reached the footbridge. Flames were licking through the new wood.

'Now what are we goin' to do?' Tom's question echoed the one screaming in Danny's head. But Hetty simply lifted her chin.

'We'll have to go into the water, of course. We can't risk staying here if there are more explosives.'

Danny's stomach dipped. Bile rose up in his throat. He thought of all that he'd faced tonight – the chase through Belle Vue, the kidnapping, the gun threats, the escape from Dalton and his confrontation with Goadsby. But right at this moment, none of it seemed as terrifying as stepping out into the lake.

Hetty's face softened. Gently, she put her hand on his shoulder. 'We've no choice, Danny. Maharajah can carry us across. It'll be fine, I promise. We'll do it together.'

He almost laughed. Her words were a near echo of the ones he'd used to coax Maharajah away from the fire. And he knew that if Maharajah had been able to face his fears, then so could he.

He sucked in a breath. 'Yes. Let's go.'

Without giving himself time to change his mind, Danny whistled. Maharajah sank to the ground. Quickly, he slid one leg across his back, and slipped into the dip behind his ears. Hetty swung up next to him, linking her arms around him as she had done many times before.

'Tom?'

Danny leant down and stretched out a palm. They stared at one another for a long moment then Tom reached up and grasped the offered hand. He settled into the curve behind Hetty, and almost immediately, Maharajah rose to his feet. Lifting his head, Maharajah sounded out one long trumpet call, and strode into the water.

The lake was deeper than it looked, and it was certainly far colder. And within a few steps, it was swirling around Maharajah's knees.

'Further out, Danny!' Hetty shouted in his ear. 'We have to get right out into the lake, away from the island!'

Danny nodded, trying to look calm but inside, his heart beat frantically in his chest. Obediently, Maharajah waded even further, and the water rose even higher. Thick, bitter smoke filled the night sky but there was enough light from the fire to see.

'You can stop now! I think we're safe.'

Lined up along Maharajah's back, the three of them turned to watch. Flames were licking across the island. Now nothing remained of the Spanish village or the footbridge or the thicket of trees. But suddenly, quite unexpectedly, Queen Victoria's face appeared, lit up against the darkness. The bright outline lasted barely a moment. And then with a giant crack, Her Majesty tilted forward and fell into the fire.

'I don't think that's how Mr Jameson imagined it,' Hetty said. And for the first time that night, Danny smiled.

But almost immediately, an explosion ripped through the night, blasting rocks and stones and branches into the air. They rained down on to the lake, falling like cannon-balls around them. The flames had reached the remaining gunpowder.

With a wild, terrified roar, Maharajah lifted up out of the water. And for a moment, all Danny could hear were the frightened noises of every animal in the park. Bellows and growls and screeches. And then Maharajah plunged back down again – and Danny heard nothing at all. His grip on the harness slipped away, and he fell into the lake.

The water closed over his head. He twisted, pitched, floated for an instant. Then flipped again. Panic spread through his body with the speed of spilt ink. He'd been here before, but this time he might not be so lucky.

Suddenly, an arm hooked around his chest and he was lifted upwards, his face breaking the surface of the lake on a loud gasp.

'Stop struggling. And hold still.' Danny barely heard the words, but the tone made sense. He forced himself to stop fighting, to let his body drift loosely in the water. He didn't have the energy to do much else.

'That's better,' the voice said. And they were the last words Danny remembered before the blackness took over.

Danny lay on the grass. Clouds of smoke blocked out the moon and stars so the sky was little more than a black blanket above him. The fire was still burning on the island.

But he was alive.

He was alive!

For a moment, Danny let the euphoria overwhelm him. And then he lifted his head. Where was he? It was somewhere quiet, maybe on the shore near the disused track. But Hetty and Tom weren't with him, and neither was Maharajah.

Suddenly, on the other side of the lake, a trumpet call echoed through the dark, and then another. And he knew with complete certainty that Maharajah was safe. That they were all safe.

He looked across to where Charles Larkin was stretched out beside him, water dripping from his wet clothes. He must have pulled off his jacket and boots before diving into the water, because he was dressed in only his trousers and a cotton shirt. The gold cufflinks had disappeared, and his sleeves had been pushed up to his elbows. It was the first time Danny had seen Larkin look less than perfect.

A sudden overwhelming rush of gratitude rose up from somewhere deep inside. This man – his father – had saved him. He wanted to reach out to thank him. To pour out every heartfelt emotion rising to the surface.

Instinctively, Danny moved forwards. Then he stopped. Numb with disbelief.

At first, he thought he must be wrong. That the confusion of being underwater had left his mind muddled. But when he leant closer, he knew there was no mistake. No mistake at all.

Carved across Larkin's left wrist – on the pale strip of skin uncovered by his wet shirtsleeves – were two letters.

FS.

The gashes were deep and ugly. And Danny knew they must have hurt like the devil. Because they were a perfect match for the letters branded on his own wrist. And that could only mean that they were made by the same person.

Frank Scatcherd. The King of Cowgate. Leader of the Leith Brotherhood.

Blood rushed away from Danny's head. His stomach twisted and he only just stopped himself from retching.

'It was a lie, wasn't it? Everything was a lie.'

Slowly, Larkin turned to look at him. But he didn't speak. Angry hurt pinched Danny's chest. His skin felt like glass, so fragile that it might shatter with one touch.

'You're not my father. Are you?'

And then because Larkin didn't answer, he shouted it again.

'ARE YOU?'

Chapter Thirty-five

Danny wanted the answer, and yet at the same time he wished he could put his hands over his ears to block out the words. 'Are you my father?' he asked again.

Silently, Larkin lifted to sit upright. Staring out across the lake, he pushed his fingers through his wet hair. The curls slicked back from his forehead.

'No,' he said. 'No, I'm not.'

Pain spiked through Danny, forcing all the giddiness away. With the greatest of effort, he stopped himself from crying out. He pulled his knees up to his chest and wrapped his arms tightly around his body. Every muscle shivered but whether it was from damp or shock, he didn't know.

The silence lengthened, and then Larkin said. 'How did you know?'

'Your wrist.'

Larkin's eyes flicked down and, almost absent-mindedly, he smoothed a thumb across the knot of scars. 'How careless of me. It's not a mistake I'd normally make. Good tailoring and long sleeves tend to hide a great deal.' His accent was no longer so finely cut, something rough had crept around the edges, blunting each word. 'But I suppose tonight I wasn't entirely thinking of myself.'

'Weren't you?' Danny hadn't known he could sound so cold, and Larkin's head pulled back sharply.

'Don't forget. I helped save your life tonight. You might have drowned.'

'You lied to me. You've lied to me every single time we've met.' Danny's mind filtered back through the events of the last few days. There had been one particular episode that had never seemed to fit with Goadsby's plan. 'That first night,' he said. 'In the maze. Someone was shooting at me. You arranged that . . . didn't you?'

'Yes. Of course.' Larkin shrugged.

'Why?'

'Anyone in my line of business knows you have to gain people's trust. Once you have trust, you can make a person believe almost anything. You thought you were in danger and I helped you. It was as simple as that.'

Horrified, Danny sucked in a breath. He'd been a fool. A stupid, gullible fool who'd believed the lie because deep down, he'd wanted to believe it.

'But perhaps after tonight, we're even. A lie for a life.'

'Do you think so?' Danny snapped. Cold had seeped into his bones. His wet clothes clung to his skin, and light tremors were running up and down his body. But he didn't move. He wanted to dig out the truth – here and now – however painful.

'So how do you know him?' Danny didn't need to say Scatcherd's name, Larkin knew exactly who he meant.

'I grew up with him in Cowgate. We joined the Leith Brotherhood together. Being part of a gang was the only choice for boys like us. And I thought we were friends. Sadly, I was wrong.'

Larkin drew in a breath. 'When he took over the Brotherhood, everything changed. He became . . .' There was a slight pause. '. . . unnecessarily cruel. And I think he enjoyed the cruelty.'

His fingers moved over the scars again. 'These were a souvenir when I disagreed with him. He wanted to make sure I knew who held all the power. Shortly afterwards, I left the Brotherhood – and made my own way. But we stayed in touch. It doesn't pay to get on the wrong side of Frank Scatcherd.'

Danny swallowed hard. Anger and betrayal were struggling for the same space in his chest. 'Did he send you . . . did he send you here?'

'Yes. I suppose you might say that.' Larkin's mouth twisted. 'About a month ago, I visited him in prison. More out of curiosity than anything else. I couldn't believe he was finally behind bars. And he told me about you. Ordered me to come to Belle Vue. To find some means of drawing you away.'

Danny said nothing, but he was certain his heart pulsed faster.

'There didn't seem much point at the time. He offered me good money but he was hardly in a position to pay. Only once he escaped from Calton Jail, I got to thinking that I should come and see what had him so obsessed. Why he hates you so much.'

Danny flinched. The reasons behind Scatcherd's hatred had never been a secret. Thanks to Danny, the King of Cowgate had lost everything. His money. His power. Even his freedom.

Larkin turned to stare across the lake. 'At first, the plan was to gain your confidence, lure you away then hand you over to Scatcherd . . . for a price. But later, I thought maybe the Jamesons were a better bet. I saw the way they are with you. I reckon they'd have given me the keys to Belle Vue to get you back.'

Danny couldn't help an involuntary start. He only wished that it were true.

'But now I'm wondering whether we wouldn't make a good team – you and me. You're quick. You're clever. You're loyal. And you've not let anything beat you. And if I did have a son, I'd want him to be exactly like you.'

Larkin slid him a sideways glance. 'Look, Danny. I'm not a cruel man – not like Scatcherd. I simply make the most of every opportunity. Just like you. Why do you think you ended up here, at Belle Vue? You saw a chance and you grabbed it.'

He plucked a stone from the shore and threw it across the water. Danny watched it bounce then disappear into the darkness. 'So, the offer's still there. Come with me. We could travel. Explore the world. Just like I said.'

'You mean con people.' It wasn't a question.

'If you want to call it that.' Larkin's mouth lifted into a half-smile. 'So how about it? I've a feeling we'd work well together.'

'NO!'

Danny turned. Mr Jameson was running across the shore towards them.

'He's not going anywhere. He's stayin' right here.'

'Jameson.' Almost casually, Larkin climbed to his feet. 'Don't you think the boy should decide for himself?'

Mr Jameson staggered to a stop, only a short distance away. For a moment he looked unsure. 'Well, Danny? Are you stayin' here? Or goin' with him?'

Danny looked between them, even though there was no choice to make. Belle Vue was home, and always would be. He should never have considered leaving.

'I'm staying,' he said.

Mr Jameson took off his jacket and knelt to wrap it around Danny's shoulders. 'Come along then. Let's go home.'

Chapter Thirty-six

At Belle Vue House, Danny was bundled into bed, wrapped in blankets and propped up with pillows. Someone had brought an old rocking chair into the room. And whenever Danny opened his eyes Mrs Jameson was sitting at his bedside, using one foot to tilt backwards and forwards. She didn't say a great deal but a soft hum filled the air as she sorted through a bundle of sewing. And more often than not, the sound lulled Danny back to sleep. He was exhausted.

The next time he woke up, he thought it was probably morning, although it might not have been. Hetty had burst into the room, bringing with her a wave of sunshine and energy. Tom Dalton followed a few steps behind, but he stayed near the door as though unsure of his welcome.

Hastily, Danny pushed himself upright and slumped

back against the pillows. He tried to smile, even though it was difficult.

'You look well,' Hetty said, plumping herself down on the bed. It was a lie. Every part of Danny's body felt battered and bruised, but he didn't argue.

'The whole of Belle Vue is talking about you. People think you're a hero.' Hetty grinned. 'Even Aunt Augusta is impressed. "*That boy has the courage of a Carkettle!*"' Her impression sounded so much like Miss Carkettle that Danny smiled again, and this time it was easier.

Hetty chattered away, updating him on all the news. He managed to make sense of most of it. The fire had destroyed part of the island, but not all. And it would certainly have been a lot worse had they not managed to clear so much of the gunpowder. And, apart from one twisted ankle, everyone had escaped safely.

Later, when Maharajah had plunged beneath the water, both Hetty and Tom had lost their grip on the harness. But thankfully they'd been near enough to swim to shore without too much trouble.

And as for those behind the plot – Mr Goadsby and George Dalton were in the hands of the Manchester City Police. But while Dalton had confessed to everything, Goadsby had so far stayed silent, and it had been Mr Jameson who'd had to fill in the gaps. He'd even managed to persuade the Manchester Corporation to lift the order about Sunday closing.

Finally, Hetty seemed to run out of news. '. . . I think

that's about all. Oh, I nearly forgot. Tom has something to say to you.' She looked over her shoulder and motioned furiously. 'Isn't that right?'

With obvious reluctance, Tom moved nearer to the bed and stared at a point somewhere over Danny's left shoulder.

'So I reckon I was wrong . . . about you. And . . .' He swallowed visibly. 'And I'm sorry.'

The apology had obviously been difficult to make, but there was still a part of Danny that wanted nothing more than to throw it back in his face.

And then he remembered how Tom had run up the hill alongside him. And how they'd worked together to move the gunpowder barrels away from the fire. And how he'd stayed on the island, even when he could have escaped.

So when their eyes locked, Danny leant back against the pillows and nodded an acknowledgement. He wasn't sure they'd ever be friends, but in Tom's place maybe he would have done the same.

'I'm going back home to Bolton to stay with my mam and dad, for a bit. Just until everythin's died down. But Mr Jameson reckons there'll be work here for me one day.'

'And you mustn't worry about Maharajah either.' Hetty said quickly. 'Everyone's been looking after him. And Mr Jameson was so grateful that he gave him the biggest pile of apples you ever saw. He was so grateful.' She smiled. 'So you see, Danny. Everything's fine. You just need to rest and get better.'

Hetty would probably have continued talking but

Mrs Jameson put down her sewing and ushered them both out.

And then at last, Mr Jameson came to see him. The visit that Danny had both hoped for and been dreading.

'Danny. How you feelin'?'

He paced across the room to the window, lifted the lace curtain to stare outside and then dropped it again when it seemed that the view hadn't changed.

'Fine,' Danny said.

'Good. Good.' Mr Jameson swivelled on his heels, then tucked his thumbs into his waistcoat pockets. There was a long silence.

Danny plucked at the bed sheets nervously. To his shame, he felt his eyes prickle, and he had to blink hard to make them stop. 'I'm sorry,' he said. 'I let you down.'

'No! No, you didn't.' Mr Jameson looked panicked. 'Don't ever say that!'

'But all the money you lost on the show . . . and I couldn't even stop the explosion. If I'd got there quicker, I might have . . . I could have . . .' Embarrassed, Danny swiped the back of his hand across his face.

'No! You saved people. That's what's important. And if anyone's made a mess of this, it's been me.' In a few hasty steps, Mr Jameson reached the side of the bed. He stood hovering for a moment, then almost hesitantly sat down. 'Listen, Danny. I need to explain somethin' to you. And I want you to listen carefully because some of it might not make a great deal of sense.'

Danny waited.

'When I was young, I was just like you. I had nothing. No money. No family. But I was clever. And I had ideas. I started work here at Belle Vue. It was much smaller then, barely five acres. On my first day, I met the owner's daughter – Ethel May. Fell for her like a sack of spuds, I did, but I never thought I was good enough for her. She had to practically twist my arm to get married.'

Danny's mouth curled up. He could just picture Mrs Jameson manoeuvring Mr Jameson into making a proposal, and then not allowing him a chance for any second thoughts.

'Later, when her parents died, her brother wasn't interested in runnin' Belle Vue so I took over. At first, we didn't do so well. But things got better. I built up the menagerie and the other entertainments. And people started comin'.' He smiled. 'And you know what happened when we bought Maharajah. He always did pull in the crowds.'

Danny nodded. 'Yes. I remember.'

'I worked hard. Always thinkin' of ways to make Belle Vue bigger and better. Tryin' to attract more people. Madcap schemes and ridiculous gimmicks, Ethel May called them. But I kept on pushin' because I never wanted to go back to that time when I didn't have any money or a home of my own.'

Abruptly, he got up again and paced around the room.

'Security, that's what I wanted. It's what I want for Ethel

May.' He paused. 'And it's what I want for you too. That's why I've been working so hard. Concentratin' on the business. Gettin' investors. Expandin' all the attractions.'

Danny stared down at the patchwork blanket stretched out across the bed. However hard he tried, he couldn't force his head to look up.

'But now I've come to realize somethin'. Just giving you a roof over your head – and pilin' up money – isn't enough. And workin' hard, without honest talkin' isn't any good either. Because it near broke Ethel May's heart when she thought you might leave us. And it near broke mine too.'

Danny lifted his eyes. Mr Jameson was looking at him steadily.

'So don't ever think that we don't want you here. Because we do. And that's what I'm tryin' to tell you.' A pause. 'Do you understand?'

Slowly, Danny nodded.

'So how about we make it official? First thing tomorrow, you, me and Ethel May will go down to the town hall and fill out every bit of paperwork that makes sure you're our son in the eyes of the law. And after that, maybe you can start callin' us Ma and Pa.'

Danny let the thought settle, testing it for size. Larkin's betrayal still hurt, and it was likely to do for some time. And there was every chance that he would never find out the names of his real parents. Or how he came to be abandoned. Or how he came to lose his voice.

But at that moment, none of that seemed to matter. He felt a light feeling bubbling deep inside. It was more than happiness. It was the feeling of having the whole world at his fingertips, with all the endless possibilities that came with it.

'Yes,' he said. 'I'd like that.'

Chapter Thirty-seven

Danny was allowed out of bed two days later – although he was forbidden to leave the house. Or do any work. Or talk too much. Or do anything else that might have been in the least bit interesting. And eventually, after an hour or two of Mrs Jameson's fussing, Mr Jameson took pity on him.

Their first call was to the elephant house – and Danny didn't think he would ever forget the look in Maharajah's gold eyes when he opened the door and whistled. In just a few steps, Maharajah was at his side, tugging until they were locked together. And Danny felt the familiar, happy rumble vibrate through every bone.

Mr Jameson laughed. 'He's missed you.'

'I've missed him,' Danny said, and pressed his face into the hollow just below the broken tusk. And it seemed to him that Maharajah pressed right back.

Later, after leaving Maharajah with a stick of sugar cane and some more apples, they hitched up the horse and cart and paid a visit to the Threlfalls. The vicar opened the door but if he was surprised to see them, he was careful not to show it.

'Well . . . I suppose you'd best come in. Perhaps you'd care for a cup of tea?'

Mr Jameson took off his hat and nodded. But Danny shook his head politely. Instead, he waited in the garden, watching the blue-winged butterflies dance from flower to flower. This time there were no raised voices from inside – and Danny didn't try to eavesdrop.

An hour or so later, when the two men emerged from the house, the vicar looked different. All of the hellfire and fury seemed to have been snuffed out; and there was a quietness to him that had not been there before. He shook Mr Jameson by the hand, and he and his sister stood in the doorway to say goodbye. Constance smiled her sweet smile and waved until they disappeared from sight.

On the way home, Mr Jameson let Danny take the reins of the horse and cart, then he leant back against the box seat to puff on his cigar.

'You can't hold grudges for long, Danny. And it takes a big man to apologize. I reckon the reverend is less of a windbag than I first thought.' He paused and something flickered in his eyes that might have been discomfort. 'And . . . and I owe you an apology too. I never should have thought – even for just one minute – that you'd be careless with the animals.'

Danny dipped his head to show he'd heard but inside his heart was singing.

'Although who'd have ever thought it was Constance Threlfall lettin' the animals loose?' Mr Jameson released another cloud of smoke. 'I can't imagine what she was thinkin'. If you hadn't been at the reptile house, Lord only knows what might have happened!'

Abruptly, Danny felt a memory shake loose: a brown-and-gold snake, thick as a blacksmith's arm, stretching its head high above the glass cabinet. And he remembered how the king cobra had fanned out its hood ready to attack; and how his heart had raced as he'd slammed down the lid; and how his hand had trembled as he turned the key.

'Do you think Constance was right . . . do you think the animals should be allowed to go free?' Danny blurted out the question before he could think to hold it back, and he wasn't entirely surprised when Mr Jameson let out a laugh.

'You're askin' that of a man who owns a menagerie! What d'you expect me to say, lad?'

Danny didn't answer. Instead, he let his hands loosen around the reins; the horses' pace didn't even slacken. They knew their way home.

'Very well, for what it's worth, I'll tell you what I believe.' Sighing, Mr Jameson leant forward and rested his elbows on his knees. 'Humans and animals have to live in this world together, which means we have to treat each other fairly. So here, at Belle Vue, we try to care for our animals properly. Look after them. Keep them healthy and safe. It's one of the reasons I hired William Saddleworth. The best animal doctor in the country, there's no question. But not only that, he's got ideas. Big, modern ideas.'

Mr Jameson paused long enough to puff on his cigar again. 'You take Emerald. She's probably one of the last Tasmanian emus alive in the world. By bringin' her to Belle Vue, we've saved her. And William's been writin' to other menageries – speakin' to all sorts of people – tryin' to find her a mate. And if he manages that, then there's a hope of saving an entire breed. An entire *species*. Just think of it!'

He slid Danny a sideways glance, and his eyes sparked. 'Of course, if I can get a little publicity for Belle Vue while we're doin' it, then so much the better. I've still a business to run.'

The corners of Danny's mouth lifted but he said nothing. He'd asked the question because he didn't know the right answer. And he suspected there wasn't one.

Some people would always believe that animals should be allowed to roam free, not locked inside cages or trapped behind fences and metal bars. While others would argue that menageries gave humans the chance to learn about the natural world. And to appreciate all the wonders of it. And that without such places, the gap in understanding would be too wide to ever bridge.

It might very well be impossible to reconcile the two sides.

'But no more fireworks? Or explosions?' Danny said. 'The animals don't like it.'

Mr Jameson's lips thinned for a moment then at last he shook his head. 'No. No more fireworks.' He paused. 'And if means that much to you – no more Prince Dandip either. Except maybe on special occasions. The rest of the time, you be yourself, lad. Daniel Jameson. Cos we don't need anyone else.'

By the time they reached Belle Vue House, Danny was exhausted. He slid down from the cart just as the front door opened. But it wasn't Mrs Jameson who stood impatiently on the step. It was Hetty.

'Papa's home!' she shouted, running down and grabbing Danny's hand. 'The auction was called off so he's back early. Come and see!'

In the parlour, Mr Saddleworth and Miss Carkettle sat on either side of the fireplace. He'd brought gifts from Paris for everyone. A silver locket for Hetty; some lace handkerchiefs for Mrs Jameson; a black shawl for Miss Carkettle; and a silk-lined cigar box for Mr Jameson.

'And I might not have managed to bring back a zebra for Belle Vue but I did get this.' Mr Saddleworth placed a small wooden carving in the centre of Danny's palm. An elephant – trunk raised and ears fanned out as if in greeting. The resemblance to Maharajah was remarkable. 'It's for you, Danny.'

'Thank you, sir.' He held up the figure to the light and

saw that each tiny tusk had been painted a pale, polished ivory. His chest tightened. 'It's beautiful.'

'Yes, the craftsmanship looks quite accomplished . . . even if it is French.' Miss Carkettle's tart voice rang from the corner. 'And thank you for my shawl, William. It'll be perfect for funerals.' Her eyes scanned the room. 'I must say this has certainly been an interesting visit. In fact, I doubt I shall ever forget it. However much I may try to.'

There was a short silence then Mr Jameson cleared his throat. 'Well, it's been an honour to have you, ma'am. Of course, next time you come, there might be a few changes here and there.'

'So I believe. In fact, I understand you're seeking some financial assistance for Belle Vue. Is that correct?'

'Yes ma'am. And I can't pretend it's not provin' difficult. Mr Snade and the other investors are runnin' scared after what's happened these last few days. They want their money back. But I've no doubt somethin' will come up. It always does.'

'I see.' Miss Carkettle sniffed. 'I assume your investors are business*men*, Mr Jameson. Perhaps, instead, you should talk to a business*woman*.'

He stared at her, frowning. 'I'm sorry, ma'am. I don't quite understand what you're meanin'. Perhaps you might spell it out for me.'

'Very well, if I have to.' She sighed deeply. 'When he died, my father left me his business. He was a manufacturer of soaps: Carkettle's Skincare Creams, you may have heard of us. Of course, I've expanded the company since then. It's now the biggest of its kind in the country.' Her lips pursed. 'So, what I'm suggesting, Mr Jameson, is that you should bring your request to *me*.'

'You'd be willin' to put money into Belle Vue?' Mr Jameson looked staggered. He reached an arm along the sofa to where his wife sat next to him. Mrs Jameson took his hand.

'But Miss Carkettle,' she said, 'I was under the impression you had no time for Belle Vue? I believe you told me it was an improper place to bring up children.'

'Well, a great deal has happened since then,' Miss Carkettle's gaze flicked to Danny and back to the Jamesons again. She lifted her chin. 'In particular, I owe your son a debt and I always honour my debts.'

'That's very generous of you, ma'am. Thank you.' It was Mrs Jameson who spoke again, because her husband seemed to have been struck dumb.

'However, I do have two conditions.'

Danny only just stopped himself from smiling. How like Miss Carkettle to make sure there were rules.

'I've been thinking for some time of creating a tribute to my father – the late Mr Humphrey Carkettle. Something that would bear his name. A legacy of sorts, I suppose. And he was a great lover of wildlife.'

Mr Jameson had finally recovered. 'You mean a bench?' he said. 'With a bronze plaque perhaps?'

'No. Too small.'

'A statue?'

'Too ordinary.'

'What about a giraffe . . . named Humphrey?'

'Certainly not, Mr Jameson!'

'An exhibition hall!' The idea came into Danny's head only a fraction of a moment before he opened his mouth. And in his excitement, he forgot to stumble or hesitate or slow down. 'A learning place where everyone can find out about the animals. Especially the ones in danger – like Emerald. With pictures and stories and information. Just like a museum, only for living things. Here at Belle Vue.'

Mr Jameson raised his eyebrows then lowered them again. His eyes sparked. 'Yes. You might have something there, Danny. Let me think . . .' He stared into the distance. 'We could call it the "Humphrey Carkettle Centre for Animal Welfare Education and Conservation".' He used his hands to trace the words in the air. 'The country's first zoological school. What d'you think, William?'

Mr Saddleworth grinned at Danny. 'A brilliant idea.'

'Yes. That's certainly sounds like an interesting possibility.' Miss Carkettle put her hand to her lips and Danny noticed her cheeks were a little pink. 'If you can draw up some plans, I'd like to hear more.'

Mr Jameson nodded. 'I see no problem with that. And the other condition?'

Miss Carkettle dropped her hand and lifted her chin. 'The other condition is that Belle Vue does not open before one o'clock on a Sunday. No one should have an excuse not to go to church. And you should be spending time with your family.'

Mr Jameson scowled, and then he looked at his wife and then at Danny, and his face relaxed. 'Fine. Let's agree to Sunday openings from midday, Miss Carkettle. And you have yourself a deal.'

'Very well, Mr Jameson. Midday.' Hetty's aunt inclined her head, with a speed that suggested she'd anticipated this all along. 'But I expect to see you *inside* church the next time I visit. Not outside.' She extended a gloved hand, and Mr Jameson took it and smiled. And so, with no more than a handshake, the deal was done.

Miss Carkettle rose to her feet and pulled on her gloves. 'Well, I must be going. My train is due to leave within the hour. I only hope the service has improved. Come here, Henrietta.' She offered one pale, powdered cheek to her niece, and dutifully, Hetty kissed it. Then to Danny's surprise, she summoned him forward.

'Daniel . . .' She leant nearer and he placed his lips on the same patch of powdered skin. She smelt of roses and lavender. 'Now, come and see me off.'

In the courtyard, Danny joined the others to say goodbye. And after Crimple had brought the luggage; and Miss Carkettle had inspected it; and every piece had been loaded to her satisfaction, she climbed on board and shut the door. The carriage rattled away.

Mr Jameson rubbed his hands. 'Didn't I tell you everything would come right?'

'Yes, Jamie, you did. Although, I'm not sure how you managed it.' Mrs Jameson hooked her fingers around her husband's arm and steered him back towards the house. The others trailed behind. 'William, perhaps you and Hetty would like to stay for supper? I'd love to hear more about Paris.'

'Oh, can we, Papa?' Hetty's face lit up. 'Please!'

'Very well, but only if you tell me all that's been happening here. I can't believe half of what I've heard. I hope you've been careful, Hetty...'

They trooped up the steps, but just as Danny turned to follow, something caught his eye. A man stood on the other side of the courtyard. He wore a top hat and gold cufflinks that glinted from beneath his jacket sleeves.

'Hello, Danny.' Larkin's voice carried easily across the yard. 'I wasn't sure whether you'd agree to see me, but I thought I should try anyway.'

Danny said nothing, but as Larkin walked nearer, sweat dampened his palms. And it was only when he was an arm's span away that it occurred to Danny to step back. It was like the odd dance they'd done when they'd first met.

The corner of Larkin's mouth tipped up. He stopped. 'You've no need to worry. I'm not going to waste my breath making another offer.' A pause. 'So, you didn't tell the police about me? I did wonder.'

'No. No, I didn't.' Danny shook his head. Of course, he'd thought about it, but when Mr Jameson had suggested contacting Constable Oversby, he'd resisted. What had

Larkin done? No crime had been committed. He'd told a lie then saved his life. And perhaps, one action did cancel out the other.

For a moment, they stood looking at each other. Then Larkin reached into his jacket pocket. 'Before I left, I wanted to give you something. My way of making it up to you, if you like.' He pulled out a parcel – no bigger than an envelope and only a little thicker. 'Go on. Take it. It belongs to you.'

Warily, Danny examined Larkin's face, but his expression gave nothing away. He edged forward and when he was near enough he snatched the package out of Larkin's hand and stepped back. Quickly.

'Well? Aren't you going to open it?'

Hesitantly, Danny looked down. The parcel was light, oval-shaped, and wrapped in faded floral paper. And as he tore back the layers his hands trembled. At last, he unwrapped the final sheet. The painting of a woman stared up at him. She was beautiful – dark-haired and soft-eyed. And he was almost certain she was the woman from his dreams.

'I stole it. From your friends, the Dilworths. But I'd bet everything I own that it belongs to you.' Larkin's eyes glinted. 'Only don't bother asking any questions because I don't know anything else.'

The warning was unnecessary because Danny couldn't speak. It was as though he'd been knocked sideways. Shock spread through his body, loosening the muscles from his bones.

Larkin was still watching him carefully. 'So, this is good-bye. Maybe our paths will cross again, one day. I'd like to think so.' He lifted his hat. 'But one more thing, Danny. Stay here ... at Belle Vue. Because Scatcherd won't risk coming to Manchester. There are too many people searching for him. And even he can't hate you enough to take the chance.'

Larkin strode away across the courtyard but Danny didn't watch him go. He was too busy staring at the picture. Carefully, he traced a finger over each fine brushstroke. Across the woman's delicate chin; around the wide eyes, and along the black ink of her hair. And only after a long time did it occur to him to examine the back of the wooden frame.

Five letters were etched across the panel. He was fairly sure what they spelt, but he sounded out each letter just to be certain.

A-n-a-y-a.

An-ay-a.

Anaya.

His heart raced. He didn't know for certain if the woman was his mother. Or if any part of what Larkin had told him was true. There had been so many lies it was difficult to sort out what was real from what was false.

But one day he would find out; one day he would discover the truth about who he was and why he'd been abandoned. Without a voice. Or a home. Or a name.

But not now.

Now he was going to make the most of the life he had.

The life he had at Belle Vue. Because he had very nearly let it slip from his fingers. And he thought that probably would have been the worst mistake of his life.

'Come on, Danny!' Mr Jameson stood in the doorway of Belle Vue House, waving a hand. 'We're all waitin' for you. Supper's on the table. Hurry up!'

And Danny ran across the courtyard to where the front door was wide open for him.

'Coming, Pa!' he shouted. 'Coming!'

The star of *The Great Animal Escapade* is, of course, Maharajah – but the elephant existed beyond these pages. In real life, he was part of a travelling menagerie until he was sold at auction in Edinburgh in 1872.

His new owner was James Jennison, of the Belle Vue Zoological Gardens in Manchester. Jennison hoped to transport his new acquisition to Belle Vue by train but moments after boarding the rail carriage at Edinburgh Station, Maharajah ripped it apart.

So instead, Jennison decided to walk Maharajah to Manchester. The two-hundred-and-twenty mile journey took ten days and attracted huge attention – from newspapers and the public.

That real-life story was the inspiration for my first book, *The Elephant Thief,* but Maharajah's adventures did not stop there.

Over the next decade, he became a much-loved favourite at Belle Vue, giving rides to thousands of visiting children, and taking part in parades through Manchester.

But perhaps his most high-profile role was as the star of the military-themed firework shows staged each year on the island in the middle of Belle Vue's lake. Local men – paid in pies and beer – were enlisted to play soldiers and act out scenes from historic battles.

Huge painted canvases – covering more than 30,000 square feet – formed the backdrop to these dramatic performances, while overhead, rockets and fireworks coloured the sky.

One of the most successful of these spectaculars was 'The Prince of Calcutta' in 1876. Jennison's nephew George was dressed as a young Prince of Wales and rode 'a huge but docile' Maharajah on to centre stage. (The show was attended by the *real* Lord Mayor of Manchester).

But the displays were not without danger. Almost every night, the wooden stage caught fire and on one occasion in 1883, flames broke out on the island destroying half the painted scenery.

Like my fictional Belle Vue, the park boasted a number of attractions – including a menagerie, ornamental maze, dance hall, archery field, several tearooms and Italian gardens. And as it became more self-sufficient, many businesses were set up, employing hundreds of local people. Among them was a firework factory, smithy, coopers, gasworks, ice works, brewery and bakery.

Such was Belle Vue's success, that Jennison launched his own omnibus service to transport visitors to and from the park, and a rail service ran to the nearby Longsight Station every half hour.

But the zoological gardens were not popular with everyone. Local clergy denounced Belle Vue from the pulpit, and wardens at St James' Church in Gorton demanded Jennison stop business during Sunday services. His reply was, 'I'm like you: I make my living on Sundays.' They didn't bother him after that.

During this period, there were a number of animal escapes. In 1874, a lioness jumped through an enclosure window to get free, terrifying a passing nightwatchman. Fortunately, a keeper found her fifty yards away and calmly encouraged her back inside.

I used all these real-life stories as inspiration for *The Great Animal Escapade*, alongside another notable tale told by George Jennison. He remembered Maharajah walking across a bridge over Belle Vue Lake, when one of the planks broke beneath his weight. He fell, splintering a tusk so badly that it had to be sawn off 'with great loss of blood'.

There are many more incredible tales of the Belle Vue menagerie during its Victorian era. But now, with modern eyes, they can be seen in a different light. The zoo animals were not always protected and cared for in the way they would be today. Rather, they were treated as sources of entertainment – often dressed up, made to perform, and act like humans. And there was little thought given to preserving endangered species – the last-ever Tasmanian emu died in captivity in 1873, and the sole surviving quagga (a type of zebra) in 1883. Both have featured in my books.

But views were changing. Charles Darwin had published his work highlighting the common origins between humans and animals. The Royal Society for the Prevention of Cruelty to Animals had been established, closely followed by the Royal College of Veterinary Surgeons. People were starting to understand that in order to keep species alive, they needed to be protected.

I've tried to place my fictional Belle Vue at the forefront of that conservation movement – thanks to William Saddleworth's 'modern ideas' and Danny's instinctive understanding of animals. But in reality, Belle Vue was simply not forward-thinking and innovative enough, and after 140 years as a zoo, it closed in 1977.

As for Maharajah, he lived for ten years at Belle Vue before dying of pneumonia in 1882 at the age of eighteen – relatively young for an elephant. His skeleton is on display at the Manchester Museum where, interestingly, the tips of *both* tusks are broken off.

But he still attracts thousands of visitors. Because, as Jennison once said, 'Of the many elephants, Maharajah was the chief.'

ACKNOWLEDGEMENTS

As always, there are many people to thank for helping to write this story. Firstly, my thanks to my publishers, Chicken House, and in particular to Barry Cunningham who once again took a chance on me.

And thanks also to my fantastic editor Rachel Leyshon (there's always a voice in my head as I write, asking what would Rachel say?); to Laura Myers for her patience with the occasional missed deadline and my red ink scrawl; and to Claire McKenna who smoothed out all the rough edges. To Jazz Bartlett and Laura Smythe for their tireless and creative efforts to publicize a very new author. And to all of the other chickens – Rachel Hickman, Kesia Lupo, Elinor Bagenal, Esther Waller, Sarah Wilson and Lucy Horrocks – for their help and support.

I must also mention the author Brian Keaney and my agent David Smith for getting me to this place. I don't think I would be here without them.

Further thanks to Henry McGhie and the Manchester Museum – where Maharajah's skeleton is still on display. I have been there many times over the past few years, and never tire of it.

And my gratitude to Hannah Williamson and all at the Manchester Art Gallery for allowing me a special viewing of what is probably the only image of Maharajah – Heywood Hardy's 'The Dispute Toll'. The painting had a major impact on how I wrote about Maharajah.

This story would not have been possible without two fantastic books about Belle Vue: *The Elephant Who Walked To Manchester* by David Barnaby, and *The Belle Vue Story* by Robert Nicholls. The affection they both have for the menagerie shines through – and made my research a lot easier.

A special thank you to Emma Martin, Judy Lyons and all at Stanley Grove Primary School and the Bright Futures Educational Trust – for bringing my book characters to life for their 'Bigger Book Bash', as well as during the Manchester Day parade. Seeing Maharajah, Danny and Hetty leap from my pages into real life remains one of my best days as an author.

I must also thank the library services who shortlisted my first book, *The Elephant Thief*, for their children's book awards. After this past year, I have renewed respect for librarians and their committed work to get our children reading. I'm in awe.

Thank you again to all those friends who bought my book out of loyalty and then read it out of enjoyment (at least, that's what they told to me). And special gratitude to all those at BBC Radio Manchester for their enthusiasm, support and spreading the word.

And also special thanks to my family. To my mum, who has to be the world's best cheerleader for my writing. I'm so grateful she's on my side. To my dad and Brenda for their unwavering support and enthusiasm. To my brother, who gave me one of the best compliments of my writing career.

And to all the Kerrs, new and old, for championing the books wherever they go.

And finally, to AJ, Alexandra and Ben – thank you for giving me space, time and cups of tea. I could never have done it without you.